BLOOD TIES

A woman torn between family and freedom. At twenty, trustworthy, dependable Anne was personal secretary to up-and-coming businessman Alex Garnett. Alex asks Anne to marry him and she accepts. It is only after her son James is born that she begins to wonder if she ever really loved his father. Anne's young niece Judy comes to stay the weekend with her aunt in the small coastal town near Manchester where she lives. Judy's work colleague, Ben Davies, gives her a lift and Anne soon begins to fear she is falling for a man young enough to be her own son...

BLOOD TIES

by

Frances Paige

Magna Large Print Books
Long Preston, North Yorkshire,
England.

British Library Cataloguing in Publication Data.

Paige, Frances
    Blood ties.

    A catalogue record for this book is
    available from the British Library

    ISBN 0-7505-1035-8

First published in Great Britain by Severn House Publishers
Ltd., 1995

Published in Large Print 1997 by arrangement with Severn
House Publishing Limited.

Magna Large Print is an imprint of
Library Magna Books Ltd.
Printed and bound in Great Britain by
T.J. International Ltd., Cornwall, PL28 8RW.

Chapter One

'What is the point of doing without a sea view when we live in a coastal town?' Alex, Anne's husband had said. Alex, always definitive. And, as he had pointed out, they could well afford it. This pleasant July morning, therefore, she sat in their dining-room with its wide windows embracing the costly sea view reading a letter she had received from old Aunt Elspeth.

'Dear Anne,
    As you have always been more punctilious about family ties than your sister,' (she had never liked Margaret), 'I thought you should have this. I found it when I was rummaging around...all I seem to do nowadays...'

'Hint, hint,' James used to say about his great-aunt when Anne read out her letters at the breakfast table. 'She wants you to invite her here again.' How honest, and yet cruel, children were nowadays; but he was more than willing to accept the generous cheques she periodically sent him in London.

5

She examined 'this' closely, a faded sepia photograph, she and Margaret standing in front of the wooden porch of the family house, 'yonks ago', as James might have said. The wooden porch had never been right, an addition, not in keeping with the Yorkshire stone, the bay windows, like a wedge between bulbous cheeks. Mother had always wanted to have it taken off, Father had said, no, it served a purpose. Nowadays he would have said it was 'functional', she would have said it was not 'aesthetically pleasing'. They had died as they had lived, hardly agreeing on anything, but bound more closely by their disagreements than their empathy.

The two sisters, standing a few inches apart. She would be about eight, Margaret ten. Thirty-five years ago. There was a head's difference in their height, and a world of difference in their attitudes.

Obedience had been her strong suit, still was, and her whole stance proclaimed this. Her feet were placed neatly together, the left ankle slightly turned outwards, 'your aristocratic twist', Father had said, (he considered himself a cut above Mother because *his* father had been a vet), her hands were at her sides. She was smiling shyly with a downbent head. Her fair hair was pulled back severely by a ribbon bow which looked as if an outsize butterfly had landed on her head. Her early femininity had demanded it, Anne thought now, examining the small-featured face, or as much of it as was possible because of the foreshortening.

Margaret, on the other hand, was standing easily, head up, with 'All right, if you want to photograph me go ahead', body language. Her legs were apart, one knee bent, the hands crossed on her front, she was looking boldly at the camera so that the full oval of her face was seen framed by smooth black hair parted in the centre. Anne remembered her dancing plaits, and how one bow was invariably undone.

They were dressed in identical pleated skirts, white blouses, black strapped shoes, and yet they could not have been more different. We are in our forties now, Anne thought, and we haven't changed.

She examined the photograph again and saw the conch shell on the step with its pink interior. She remembered sitting entranced for hours with it to her ear. Margaret had said it was rubbish, you couldn't hear the sea, but she had, a surging, ebbing sound which had been magical. Perhaps her love of the sea had started then, her wish to live near it, and her happiness when she and Alex had come to High Croft twenty years ago.

And her love of cats. Smoky, she noticed,

was sitting beside her in the photograph, its feet placed neatly together like hers. She had never been able to find one of that exact colour, a dense blue-grey, half-Persian. She could remember the tactile delight of stroking the soft fur, seeing it flatten and rise up again with the passage of her hand. The simple pleasures of childhood, the surging sea in a conch shell, the smooth fur of a cat, its yellow eyes slits of ecstasy at her touch.

And there were her dolls, a constant docile classroom of twins, sailors, Shirley Temples, chubby baby dolls, the result of Margaret's scornful rejection of presents brought by visitors anxious not to be labelled partisan...she smiled at herself. She must stop this daydreaming.

But there was no rush. Alex was away on one of his numerous business trips, James was in mid-term at the London Poly—he was doing a Business Studies Course—and she had put in her stint at the Citizens' Advice Bureau for the week. When she had found herself with time to spare she had toyed with the idea of taking a belated degree in English. Her friend, Jane Skottowe, had completed one in Law recently, travelling down the twenty-five miles of motorway every day. Her picture, wearing gown and mortarboard had been in the local paper, captioned 'Mature

Student's Success.' 'What's the point?' Alex had said. She was obedient.

Shopping, she thought. That was it. She would walk along the promenade to boater-hatted Mr Proctor and buy some fish. There was a certain romance in thinking that it might have been caught by Mr Proctor himself, who discarded his boater nightly for yellow oilskins and went out on the Bay. She had toyed with the idea of asking him if she might accompany him sometime. She knew she wouldn't. Had she been Margaret she might have done.

A fish pie for Alex tonight with a fresh prawn garnish. Some feathery fennel. They had gone off meat lately in line with the current trend. They used skimmed milk which looked like blue water and went bad rather than sour, and ate porridge oats for their cholesterol. She was obedient. Sometimes she longed for real milk which frothed and the rich steamed puddings spiked with fruit she had made when James was at home. But there was a certain satisfaction in the fact that she weighed the same as she had at twenty when she married. She went to get her anorak in the cloakroom, don sensible boots.

The sea was brisk and business-like, short snappy waves which seemed to have no design in them, not like the smooth rollers of that Virgin Island beach where they had spent their holiday early this year. And it was grey, a blue-grey almost like the fur of her long-ago cat, Smoky.

She breathed in deeply, looking around, liking the Edwardian jumble of the houses and hotels lining the front. They were painted in a pleasant mixture of colours, giving them a Mediterranean air. Some had opulent glass-fronted porches tacked on, not at all like the wooden one on their old house...that photograph had brought Margaret into her consciousness. She remembered her saying in her bold way not so long ago, 'Actually, Anne, you have to thank *me* that you and Alex got married.'

'Thank you?' She had pretended surprise. 'What do you mean?'

'That time when I wrote to him... Oh, I know I hadn't any excuse, but I was desperate. We were terribly in debt. I didn't know where to turn. And Mother and Father hadn't a bean. It was a last resort.'

'I don't think of it now,' she had said, falsely.

'Yes, you were very good, and you have never cast aspersions, but it was after that, wasn't it, that you and Alex began to go out together? It must have jogged him into

10

noticing you...' What a typical Margaret remark!

Her mind went back to over twenty years ago. She had been Alex's personal secretary, as neat and well put together as she had been in the photograph at eight, her appearance saying, 'Here I am, the perfect personal secretary, trustworthy, dependable, smartly dressed but not flashy.' She had never had any trouble in getting jobs. She was the epitome of what employers were looking for.

She had gone into Alex's room at the summons of his bell.

'Have you finished the letters I gave you, Miss Warnock?'

'Yes, I've brought them with me.' She laid the plastic folder on his desk, the rows of perfect typewriting showed through, she could even see the small indentations in the paper which the typewriter keys had made.

'Good.' She had her notebook open, her pencil poised. 'No, it isn't more work. I'd like to have a word with you. Sit down, please.' She sat, wondering what it was. He had been generous in his increases. As far as she knew there was nothing at fault with her work. 'I'm sorry,' he said, shuffling papers on his desk, glancing up at her, 'that you seem to talk about me at home.'

'Seem to talk about you!' She was astonished. 'What do you mean?'

'That I'm, er, rich.' He had a habit of turning down one side of his mouth, 'That I run a Bentley, that I'm unmarried...'

'I...' She couldn't find the words, 'I never consciously talk about you, Mr Garrett. I...well you know how it is, the family sometimes ask questions, only in a general way, of course, but I'd never dream of...*divulging* anything.'

'And you haven't ever told them about my...style of living?'

'Your...style of living?' She tried to fight off her unease by lightness, forced a smile. 'Well, everybody knows Garretts. The lorries run all over the town. You see them at building sites...' She felt close to tears at the injustice of being accused of gossiping, 'And, yes, they know you drive a Bentley. Don't you remember you once ran me home and my sister, Margaret, opened the door? I introduced you.'

'I remember,' he said. He was turning his pencil over and over in his fingers, examining it. He looked up at her, youngish, broad-framed, tanned.

She could have told him that Margaret had speculated *why* he wasn't married. 'Do you think he's...?' She had smiled knowingly, pulling in her cheeks. 'I must say he doesn't look it.' Nor was he. She could have told Margaret that in spite of his burliness he was only thirty-one; about booking double rooms in various hotels, of feminine voices on the telephone, seductive, sometimes haughty or supercilious, treating her as a minion. If she had given it any thought at all she would have said he was too ruthless and too busy pushing the firm to bother about marriage.

'A week ago,' he said, 'your sister wrote to me and asked me for a loan of five hundred pounds. She said she was in dire straits and she knew I was in a position to help her.'

The blood left her face, her head swam, as the words sank in. Even worse than the request was the implication that she had put Margaret up to it, said perhaps that he was 'a soft touch'. And then as shame engulfed her and the blood flooded back again, even, it seemed, into her eyes, her senses left her. She gripped the edge of his desk, thought he must hear the heavy beating of her heart in the silence.

'I was waiting for you to explain,' he said. 'I waited a week.'

She fought with faintness, the blood in her arteries seemed to be behaving like the sea, wave succeeding wave. She sweated in her armpits, felt sick.

'Miss Warnock, are you all right?' His

voice came faintly to her. 'It's not the end of the world, you know. Shall I get you a glass of water?'

'Yes,' she said, 'please...'

She sat in dumb misery until he came back with the glass. Her eyes were clear now. The glass was so bright, it hurt. She sipped the water and felt calmer. 'This is the first I knew of it,' she said. 'I assure you...'

'It wasn't like you, I admit. I was disappointed.'

'I'll pay it back, of course.' She didn't know how. She had a Post Office savings account with twenty-five pounds in it. Most of her salary went to keep the house together, the house her mother wouldn't leave although it was far too big. 'I'm...distressed beyond words. It's as if I had betrayed your trust...'

'Tell me about your sister,' he said.

She had to pull herself together. 'She made a bad marriage at twenty.' (She had been pregnant.) 'Well, I think it's only bad in the material sense. Her husband only works spasmodically. They have two children and now her husband's ill, permanently, a liver complaint. They live with us...but if she had only told me she had written to you! Somehow I could have helped. I could have done evening work...'

14

She looked directly at him. 'In any case, I'll pay it back.'

'I don't want it,' he said. 'Your sister seems a deserving case. I wasn't annoyed at *her*...but now that you've explained...let's drop it, shall we?' He had smiled, as if satisfied. Long after she had remembered that smile. Mission accomplished?

Then, she had said, 'I think I should leave.'

'Now why should you do that? It's over and done with. I'm glad that I was able to help, now that I know it wasn't your idea.'

She had shaken her head. 'I don't know how to convince you that it wasn't me, to make you see how sorry I am...'

'Supposing you let me take you out to dinner tonight and you can say it all?'

'No, no. I couldn't do that.'

'Yes, you could. Quite easily.' There was hardly any persuasion in his voice. It was like a command.

Because of delayed shock, she supposed, she had drunk more than she was used to in the expensive restaurant by the river where Alex had taken her, and later, in his parked car, had allowed him to fondle her.

She had stupidly permitted it, because in her confusion and misery she had thought it would *balance* what Margaret had done.

15

It rankled that he might still think it had been a plot they had hatched together. She was hardly aware of him, physically, she was puzzling whether she should tell Margaret that she knew all about the letter, whether the resultant row would upset Ralph. He was easily upset. He cried like a child, not a brother-in-law.

Six months later when Alex proposed she had accepted, telling herself that her acceptance was the final payment. After all, in today's money, she now reminded herself, five hundred pounds was the equivalent of fifteen hundred, and that kind of sum had to be paid back in kind.

It was only after James was born that she was able to admit to herself that she had never really loved her husband.

Chapter Two

'Good-morning, Mrs Garrett.' Mr Proctor was at his counter, boater-hatted, the white straw making his deeply tanned face darker than ever. His eyes were royal blue.

'Nice to see you in the shop, Mr Proctor.'

He grinned. 'Mrs Proctor says I'm as slippery as one of my own fish. Can't get me to the counter for long. Says I'm always off to that old boat of mine. What can I do for you today?'

'It's up to you. What did you catch last night?'

'Mostly flounders. Small, but as sweet as a nut. Lovely eating.' He smacked a glistening heap of them affectionately.

'I'm sure they are, but I want to make a fish pie.'

'Ah, then, hake's your answer. Just look at the milky whiteness of those chaps. Non-oily too. Everybody's watching what they eat nowadays.' He spread one in front of her proudly. 'You can tell by the way a fish looks at you if it's fresh. Just like children. A bright eye. Pink gills. Or the difference between a healthy man and one with a hangover. Well, you wouldn't know anything about that. Mr Garrett's well respected in the town.'

She smiled. 'Did you catch those yourself?'

'No, I'm sorry to say. Bay's not yielding up much of this kind, worse luck. Blame the Government. But I've some lovely fresh prawns.'

'That's just what I want. I'll take a quarter of a pound as garnish for my pie.'

'Just the thing. And don't forget the garlic butter.' He filleted, weighed and wrapped with easy expertise. 'You look at fish with a sympathetic eye, Mrs Garrett. You ought to come with us on one of our fishing trips. You'd enjoy that.'

'I believe I would.' She thought of herself in a fishing boat in the darkness, the spray dashing into her face, her yellow oilskins running with water, the boat rocking underneath her feet, saw the scales which had been ground into the planks gleaming as the moonlight caught them. Yes, she'd like it. She had never been timid, only shy.

Her head was clear of worries when she got back home. The brisk two-mile walk along the promenade had made her feel happy, or at least content with her lot. There had been old people walking along, lashed together, it seemed, by their arms, for support; old men pushing fat old women in invalid chairs, gaggles of white-haired women giggling, probably released from some factory for their annual holiday. There seemed to be a kind of desperation in their gaiety.

The town hadn't kept up with the times. There was nothing to attract the younger people nowadays. They preferred to dash off to their various costas to eat fish and chips, the girls to be seduced by the Spanish waiters or their beer-swallowing compatriots. The boarding houses kept busy by catering for elderly parties, the hotels by business conferences from the neighbouring manufacturing towns. The sea was polluted in any case, no one in their senses would dream of bathing in it. They preferred the Mediterranean brand of soup. There, at least, the sun was hotter.

But there was still the expanse of sea, the visual clout, she thought of it. That was its principal attribute. No one could build on the sea. 'The only view you can buy,' the estate agent had assured them. That had been in the days before the possibility of a monstrous oil rig rising up in front of them.

Alex didn't worry about that. He said it would bring prosperity and they could always move from High Croft. It hadn't taken her long to discover that, like her father, he had no aesthetic appreciation. She had to prevent him from the use of plastic everywhere in the house, particularly in the kitchen and bathroom. It was functional, he said, and he could get it at wholesale rates.

And there were the seagulls. Some people didn't like them, saying they were raucous, greedy birds. But no more than humans, she thought, and what could excel the sight of a seagull beating strongly against the blue of the bay or, in contrast, the tiny dunlins like sea rats, running about in the ebb tide when the setting sun had flooded the mud hollows with rosy pink. She kept her binoculars under the seat of her car so that she could spot the oystercatchers, or the rarer Canada geese.

She was cheerful when she went into the kitchen and began to put away her shopping, always a satisfactory operation. She would make a special fish pie tonight with tomatoes and peppers and capers, and, of course, the prawns. Not for her the ubiquitous egg and breadcrumbed offering.

She had discovered the joys of improvisation in her cooking during the last few years. People praised her dinner parties. There was no secret. Anything she put her mind to she did well. It was part of her nature.

The telephone rang shrilly and she answered it. She heard her sister's voice. 'Margaret!' she said, 'I was just thinking of you today.'

'I hope they were good thoughts. I'm never sure with you quiet ones.' Her voice was brash and insouciant as always.

She ignored the remark, 'Aunt Elspeth sent me a photograph of us when we were children. Taken in front of the old house.'

'Has that old bag not kicked the bucket yet?'

'Far from it. She's coming here for her annual holiday soon.'

'Trust you. I must write to her and butter her up. She should have quite a nice little nest egg. When is she coming, did you say?'

'Next month. At the beginning of August. In a week's time.'

'Oh, good! It's Judy I'm phoning about, Anne. I wondered if you would have her this weekend.'

'Of course. I'd love to see her.'

'The thing is, I have this new man. He's quite a dish, and I don't want her around. I've asked him for this weekend and I'm rather hoping he'll take the plunge, so to speak. He's good in bed and as rich as Croesus. I don't want anything to go wrong.'

'Why don't you want Judy around?'
She knew why. Beautiful daughters were a hazard.

'Well, you know how maddeningly attractive she is, and I'm afraid she'll make me look rather...faded. *You're* all right. You have a son.'

'So have you.'

'Yes, but Richard stays in his pad in London, as you know, and I rarely see him.' Margaret never liked to say in so many words that Richard was homosexual. Only let it be understood.

Margaret had strange areas of reticence. She talked about Ralph, her late husband, in a disparaging way, even about his final illness, as if his failure to make money and get cancer eventually had been done deliberately. She accused Judith of being beautiful rather than showed pleasure in the fact, and yet she didn't like to say that Richard was gay. Anne had long given up trying to understand how her mind worked. The influence of the elder sister was strong. She loved her for her strong darkness, her vigorous quality. She loved her because she was her sister.

'Well, that's fine,' she said. 'Tell Judy any time. I'll pick her up at the station.'

'You're a good sort. Will you keep your fingers crossed for me? I'm getting tired bashing my brains out in that old office.

I wouldn't mind a life of leisure like yours for a change.' She liked to infer that Anne lolled on silk cushions all day.

Alex was quiet. He always was when he came back from one of his trips abroad. Once or twice the thought had crossed her mind that they were cover-ups for an affair, but then he had scotched that idea by occasionally suggesting that she should come with him. 'It's London this time. You could do some shopping, see James.' Or it might be Brussels, or, again, Amsterdam. For the most part she didn't give it much thought. She had her own life, her voluntary work, her friends, and lately she had been attending classes on modern poetry in the local college.

'How was Amsterdam looking?' she said.

'The same. People, canals, teetering houses on it, the American hotel with buttered eggs and smoked salmon for breakfast, and cheese. A peculiar race.' Because they were not British. 'You came once. You went to that museum.'

'The Rijks museum. Yes, that was lovely. *The Night Watch*. When is your next trip?'

'To Amsterdam?'

'Anywhere.'

'Brighton, but you'd hate that.'

'You told me you didn't stay in Brighton.

23

That you'd found a hideaway in a Sussex village.'

'Did I?' He looked vague. 'What did you do today?' He changed the subject.

'CAB in the morning. Shopped.' She didn't say she had worked on her essay on T.S. Eliot, developing the theory that good poetry can communicate before it is understood. This was, in fact, what had drawn her to the class in the first instance. She wanted to analyse her pleasure.

He didn't understand poetry, especially modern stuff. He had said in Margaret's presence that it was only for queers. Her eyes had flashed hate at him for a second and then she had laughed and said, 'Trust you, Alex, to put your foot in it, right up to the balls.'

And yet they were good friends. They related to each other. When Margaret came for a weekend they would sit up till the early hours of the morning talking and drinking together. The relationship was like that of two men, at times. Anne usually gave up about one o'clock when her eyes were popping out of her head with boredom, and went to bed.

These were the nights, or rather, early mornings, when he would waken her by kissing her roughly, climbing on top of her, forcing her mouth open with his whisky-tasting tongue. It wasn't pleasant.

'Judy's coming for the weekend,' she said.

'The little siren? Is she? Has her Mum turned her out?'

'Yes, she has a guest coming. She wants to be alone with him.' She smiled.

'Got someone on the boil again, has she?' His smile was mocking. 'She's getting desperate, that sister of yours. Terrified she'll soon be too old.'

'The mature woman is in.'

'She knows how to enjoy herself all the same. I'll give her that.'

'More fish pie?' Was there a criticism implicit in his remark? She sometimes wished she had Margaret's matiness with men, her bawdiness. It would do me good, she thought, as she dolloped some more fish pie on to his plate, to let myself go occasionally.

Judith arrived the following day, not alone, but with a dark young man of pleasant but uncommanding aspect at first sight. His swarthiness made his smile white. 'This is Ben Davies, Anne.' She had given up saying 'Aunt' on her sixteenth birthday. 'I knew you wouldn't mind. Actually he was visiting his parents on the way up and he offered to come on and dump me.'

'That's all right. You're welcome to stay too, Mr Davies.' She might have remembered Judy usually had a man in tow.

'Ben, please.' He would be a year or two older than Judy, she thought, his extreme youth had gone, his face had settled into a mould which he would keep for a long time unless he put on weight. He was engagingly thin, his smile had charm, Welsh charm, she realized. It was in the lively brown eyes, the broken-backed inflection in his voice.

Alex welcomed him in what Anne thought of as his 'lord of the manor' tone, effusive, slightly patronising. 'Any friend of Judy's is a friend of ours, isn't that so, Judy?'

'I prefer Judith now, Alex, if you don't mind. I'm building a new image, a more mature me.' She raised her chin at him.

'What was wrong with the last one?'

'Too *dégagée*.' She was like Margaret with her smooth, thick black hair, the pale skin, the huge lustrous eyes. But more curvaceous, smaller, and she invariably wore *décolleté* blouses or dresses. There was a promise of riches in the deep cleavage. She was luscious. It was the only word for her. Her lips were slightly moist and went into a pout easily. She was twenty-three and already had been married and divorced.

'What's your line, Ben?' Alex asked.

'Oh, didn't Judith tell you? She works in the same office. Software consultants. We set firms up with computers, the whole works. I killed several birds with one stone on the way up. Called in at my parents then two firms at Ellesmere Port.'

'I'm thinking of updating my stuff. If you're taking Judy, sorry, *Judith,* back, you might like to take a stroll round my outfit, give me the benefit of your advice. You're staying?'

'Well, it's kind of you.' He looked at Anne, clear-eyed, a quirk lifting his mouth. 'Are you sure it isn't too much trouble?'

'Not...'

'Anne's easy.' Alex took him by the arm. 'We've been thinking of...' He led Ben Davies to the window for men's talk.

Anne looked at her niece. She wanted to say, 'Quid pro quo,' but instead said 'Come and have a walk round the garden, *Judith.'* She smiled, 'Yes, it suits you.'

'All right. Just for a breather.' She was wearing trousers, and Anne thought she looked better in a skirt, a small satisfaction. She had experienced an absurd feeling of envy of their youth when she and Ben Davies had arrived, their easy air, of being streetwise. All the young were like that nowadays, even babies in their strollers no longer looked like babies, especially when they were dressed like little adults.

'Is he your young man?' she said as they walked between the carefully tended beds. She would have liked a more informal garden with flowers with romantic names, like windflowers and heliotrope, but their gardener thought in terms of 'bedding out'. He had worked with the Town Council in their parks. At the moment he had taken a shine to what used to be called double daisies, and consequently there were bright lozenge-shaped patches of colour. The grass was still a bright green due to his intensive watering. If he had heard of a water shortage due to the hot summer he had disregarded it. Anne thought of his brain, the working part, as a narrow line running through a stalactite cave of unused brain cells. Alex said he 'knew his job'.

'Ben? God, no! He saved me the train fare from Manchester. Mummy's filthy mean with the car. She won't let me take it.'

'She probably needed it.'

'Well, I suppose everybody needs wheels. She was intent on buying lots of goodies for the latest. She's going to feed him with champagne and smoked salmon and God knows what.'

'Is he nice?'

'Not bad, but dull. He's a doctor. She needn't have worried about me. I wouldn't have touched him with a barge pole. It's just he's done me out of a weekend. I hate my flat then. I share with three others. It's bedlam. We have some good times together, Mummy and I.' This was true enough. They quarrelled wildly at times, but basically they were very close.

'Don't you think the view of the sea from here is very beautiful?' Anne asked. They had stopped beside the wooden fence at the foot of the garden. 'Saturday's race day. I watch it sometimes with binoculars. Last Saturday I saw two men in the water and telephoned the Yacht Club. I thought they might drown.'

'I expect they told you to mind your own business.'

'Something like that, but politely. So Ben isn't your young man?' He was still hovering in her mind.

'Not yet.' Judith turned and smiled at Anne, her lips moist, her blue-white teeth showing. She felt like rearing back because of the impact of her beauty.

'There are three spare bedrooms, two are *en suite*. Choose what you want.'

'You're saying, Aunty dear,' she laughed, 'that you would turn a blind eye?'

'Officially, yes. It's a dying cause. James educates me.'

'How is he?'

'Working and playing in equal proportions, I hope. What job are you doing now?'

'I sit at a computer all day. Deadly boring. My alimony wasn't as good as I'd thought, so I had to get back on the wheel. Ben's a whizz kid in hardware. I do quite a lot of work for him. Actually it was my idea that he combine business and pleasure and bring me here. He jumped at the chance.'

'I bet.' Who could resist her? 'I'm going in to start dinner now.'

'I'll come with you and choose *our* room.' She emphasized the pronoun. Her lips gleamed. How was it done? Anne had often wanted to ask her niece for some cosmetic tips, but had decided against it. Moist, gleaming, blueberry-coloured lips wouldn't look the same on her.

The four of them had a surprisingly pleasant evening together. Alex had said earlier, when he was mixing drinks in the kitchen, that he wished James showed as much respect as this young man did, but Anne had reminded him that James probably behaved beautifully when *he* was a guest. He hadn't looked as if he believed her.

After dinner they sat out on the patio and watched the coloured lights which encircled the bay, the town's only concession to its visitors. But the blackness of the sea beyond was fascinating in its expanse, and where it met the smoke-grey sky it was still faintly tinged with pink, a residue from the setting sun.

'How lucky you are to have a view like this, Mrs Garrett,' Ben Davies said. Judith and Alex had gone inside to watch a late night chat show. 'In my Manchester flat I only look out on dustbins.' He came and sat next to her.

'Anne, please. You make me feel like a hundred.'

'Anne.' He laughed.

'Cities use up the sky. Even London's a snare and a delusion now. Shabby. Its cardboard city under the Festival Hall. Have you seen it? The last time I went to the Hayward Gallery I had no heart for the pictures.'

'You can't trail sweetness and light with you. Nor shut your eyes to squalor,' he replied.

'How lordly you sound.' She felt rebuffed.

'I didn't mean to. I expect you do all kinds of good works here. Small towns. My mother's the same.' Thank you very much. I like being equated with your mother...

'Anyhow,' she tried again, 'your flat can't be as bad as my son's. He's in London. He pins his curtains together with

31

a safety pin to block out the horrible view of dustbins and works by electric light.'

Ben Davies shrugged. Perhaps he'd done the same thing himself. 'What does he work at?'

'Oh, he's only a student.' Did she look *that* old? 'He's at the London Poly. Alex hopes he'll come and work with him but I don't think there's a chance.'

'Your husband is taking me round his place tomorrow.'

'He'll bore you. It's his baby.'

'I'm more or less always bored. Except now.' He turned his dark face towards her and the smile lit it, even to his eyes. He was a true Celt. There was the charming broken-backed voice to prove it.

'Are you really always bored?'

'Maybe that was a bit steep, but how many people are doing the thing they wanted to do? I was pushed into the computer field because I was bright at maths. It's just a knack. Nobody noticed I was just as good at English.'

'You should have told them.'

'It was only when I started doing some freelance reading that I had hindsight.'

'Do you like poetry?' she enquired.

'I buy it, anyhow. I've just acquired Larkin's book. Too gloomy for me. I'm young enough not to want to be reminded of the imminence of death.'

'What age are you?'

'Twenty-four.'

'Since I was rude,' it cost her an effort to say it, 'I'm forty-two.' Eighteen years older... 'Fair exchange is no robbery, as my mother used to say.'

'You don't look it.' He turned and looked at her squarely. 'You have a schoolgirl look in spite of your grown-up manners.' He smiled, 'And your lower lip is full, a sign of a passionate nature.'

'My goodness!' she said, trying not to appear embarrassed. 'Is that what's called Welsh charm?'

'No, I'm sincere. Judith looks older. She'd be one of those schoolgirls who wear perfume at eleven and sneak out to meet boys.'

'I should think boys would sneak out to meet *her*. She's very beautiful.'

'Beauty is in the eye of the beholder. A cockroach can love a cat.'

'Archy and Mehitabel?' She was enchanted. 'Do you know why it's all written in lower case?'

'Because Archy was too small and light to press the shift key. You're smiling as if I'd passed an exam.'

They exchanged smiles. It was as intimate as an embrace.

She didn't go upstairs with them. She

busied herself in the kitchen, and when she got in beside Alex he was asleep. Drink took him in either of two ways, amorousness or oblivion.

There was no sound, no noises from any of the other bedrooms. Were Ben and Judith lying entwined, limbs around limbs, or were they in separate rooms? Did he always travel with his own Gossamer equipment, such a lyrical word for such a prosaic object. The first inventor must have been a poet. She couldn't sleep. The moonlight shone into the room, from the open window she could hear the shushing sound of the sea, a distant train.

Someone in the town had once said to her, an insomniac, that he had counted twelve trains during the night, 'Trucks of nuclear waste. Sneaking it away when we're all in bed and then denying the whole thing.'

At four o'clock, exasperated with herself, she got up, went down to the kitchen and made herself a cup of tea. Wrapped in her dressing gown, she opened the windows and went out on the patio, her hands round the cup to keep them warm. She heard a noise, lost a heart beat before she turned to see Ben Davies behind her. He too was in a dressing gown, and pyjamas, presumably, although she couldn't see any collar, only an expanse of shadowed chest. She had always told herself that she didn't like hairy men, and had been pleased when she had discovered that Alex was smooth-skinned.

He came and sat down beside her. 'You too? I couldn't sleep either. No aspersions cast at that wonderful meal you gave us. I get runs of insomnia. I generally work out computer problems...and other things.'

'I try poetry. Trouble is, it makes you wide-awake and then I have to get up.'

'Have I put you off your train of thought?'

'No, I hadn't one tonight. I just felt restless. Sometimes I walk round the garden. I've always wanted to walk along the promenade, but I never dared on my own.'

'I'm your man,' he said, his voice quickening. 'Let's be bold, what do you say?'

'If you knew me,' she smiled, 'that's the last thing I could ever be. Judy's mother was, is, the bold one.'

'Well, here's your chance. You may never get another one.' The lilting Welshness of his voice charmed her.

'We'd have to dress. We might be run in.'

'Wouldn't take a minute.'

'Done!' She felt the years slip away from her as she stood up.

Even in the dusk she was aware of his smile when she rejoined him in the garden. There was a rapport certainly. Did he feel it? Alex had been impersonal for years, except in bed, and then he was personal enough but it was directed towards himself and his own pleasure. Habit ordered so many marriages. She didn't feel theirs was an exception. 'Ready for the muggers?' she said, returning Ben's smile.

The promenade pavement was bone-white against the black of the sea, except for the banal silver path on it from the moon. She used the words deliberately to play down the romance of the situation. And she had to smother the wish to rest her head on this strange young man's shoulder as they walked, the desire to feel his arm round her waist. There was a soft wind and an occasional whooshing from the sea, otherwise silence. The first shelter they passed had a huddled figure in it, motionless.

'There's your mugger,' Ben whispered.

'I think it's a woman,' she said softly. 'Do you get lady muggers?'

'Why not, if they're feminists.'

They walked briskly, she setting the pace, pretending the walk had been embarked on for its health-giving properties. She didn't want to stroll, like lovers. There were lovers sitting in the next shelter, or rather, lying. She could see the back of the man's head, his pale raincoat.

'Probably homeless, poor sods,' Ben said. She didn't tell him what she had thought.

He liked the uneven skyline of the roofs, saying he would not have minded seeing the place sixty years ago when everybody came to the seaside, an Alan Bennett kind of seaside with characters, charwomen on holiday. No one said 'charwomen' now, did they? Even his mother said, 'the girl who helps me...'

'I have a character who works for me,' she said. 'I just call her Nan. She's seventy now, but walks a mile along here to our house winter and summer, unless I pick her up. She changes from her outdoor shoes into furry slippers when she arrives and keeps on her woolly cap. I think she's bald.'

'I imagine you're easy to live with?'

'I don't know.' She shrugged. 'I'm meticulous, but only with myself. Nan can't see cobwebs now, so I have a going-over when she leaves. I think I must have a rigid personality.' She smiled at him. They could see each other now. 'I don't even like going away on holiday.'

'A psychiatrist would say you suffer from a sense of insecurity.'

'Would he? If I do...' She didn't say it was because she had a domineering sister. It was no excuse for a woman of forty-two, eighteen years older than her companion.

A Panda car passed very slowly, crept alongside the kerb beside them, but they must have satisfied the two officers inside that there was nothing suspicious about them.

'They probably thought I was having an early walk with my son,' she said. Was she harping on about the age difference?

'Does it feel like that to you?' he said. She knew it. She had struck a wrong note.

'Gosh!' she said—that was schoolgirlish enough—'it's getting quite light. I really must get back and...'

'Go to bed?' He was teasing her.

'Well, Alex might raise the alarm if he found me gone.'

'True. Pity, though. We were just getting into the swing of things.' She didn't know what that meant.

The house was warm and silent. They walked through the hall and up the stairs together. At the top he whispered, 'Good-morning', and the timbre of his voice, the latent Welshness, made her shiver inwardly. She would be glad when he went tomorrow. She didn't think she would sleep while he was here.

She was trembling when she crept into bed, and Alex, half asleep, gathered her to him with one arm and slid the other between her legs. Marriage was a free-for-all. She ought to know that by this time.

Chapter Three

When Margaret had classed Aunt Elspeth as an old bag, Anne could have said, 'You mean a bean bag?' The phrase occurred to her as she saw Miss Craig slowly lolloping along the railway platform towards her, and thought that since she had begun to study poetry and even to try and write some, she had become more perceptive and more precise in her selection of words.

But Aunt Elspeth *was* like a bean bag. *Everything* lolloped inside her flowered, white-collared summer dress. You had the feeling that had it not been made of some stout cotton material, some of her might have escaped. When she clasped Anne to her bosom it was like sinking into a feather duvet of tog value 13.5 minimum, 'the higher the tog,' the shop assistant had said, 'the warmer the duvet.'

'How lovely to see you, Aunt,' she said, taking the heavy leather suitcase in one hand, and with the other under her aunt's elbow, guiding her up the stairs. 'The car's just outside.'

'You're a dear good girl.' She was puffing lightly. 'Are you sure I'm not incommoding you by coming for my little break.' She never said 'a few days', always 'a little break'.

'Of course you aren't. I like to hear all your news.'

This was perfectly true. Miss Craig was a member of an elderly coterie whom she referred to as 'the girls', and who each at seventy-odd seemed to be remarkably enterprising, sallying forth from their base at St Albans on far-flung jaunts.

When Anne had once compared her reluctance to leave home with her aunt's intrepidity, Aunt Elspeth had said, 'Ah, well, you see, at my age you have nothing to lose. I never worry on a plane. Even if it crashed I would call it a good way to go. Short and snappy. All that we girls worry about is being a "burden". Your family don't like it when you become a "burden".'

'You're never that, Aunt,' she had said, which was perfectly true.

She seemed to have an iron digestion, fell in with any suggestion to amuse her, disappeared for an hour or two in the afternoon, if there was nothing planned, to write to 'the girls'. The only concession she made to old age was to ask for a 'facility for nights'. That had been before Anne had had their guest bedrooms made *en suite*. 'It's not that I can't "go", but

41

one of the girls, Doris Hardwick, fell in her niece's house when *she* "went" in the middle of the night and they were saddled with her for weeks! Such a burden! She never forgave herself.'

Unfortunately the weather was inclement while her aunt was in residence, but they passed the week quite happily together. She sewed or read while Anne was at the Citizens' Advice Bureau, and she went to bed soon after dinner, 'to give you two good people time to be on your own. I know what it's like when hubby comes home in the evening. There are things to discuss.'

How she knew this, not having been married, was difficult to understand, and in any case, Anne and Alex rarely 'discussed things'. He was out a good deal at various committees and societies, Lions, Rotary, and the like, 'Someone in my position in the town has to create a good impression', and on the other evenings he was a devotee of various programmes on television, mostly crime, which were generally so noisy with the sound of sawn-off shotguns, and cars screeching round corners on two wheels, that it was better to get away from the scene of battle and sit in the conservatory facing the sea. The fact that they had a guest staying with them made no difference to his usual practice.

That was Anne's affair.

Alex telephoned late one wet and windy afternoon when she and her aunt were having a cosy tea together. 'I'm at the Depot. I had the garage run me here while they were servicing the Merc. They've just phoned to say they won't have it ready until tomorrow. Could you pick me up?'

'Of course. It will be an outing for Aunt Elspeth. She's been in all day. What time?'

'Make it seven. I've a lot to do here. I want to surprise the men coming on the evening shift. Does them good occasionally.'

'I'll be there.'

'It's part of the town you've never seen,' she explained to her aunt when they were getting ready. 'You've seen what James calls the "posh end", where they've done a bit of developing, but it tends to dwindle into anonymity when you get further down the river.'

'Towards the sea?' Aunt Elspeth liked to get her facts right. 'It's *up* to the source, isn't it?'

'That's right. It degenerates into a marshy, dismal-looking area with some small holdings on it and derelict cottages. Sometimes there are one or two gypsy caravans. The town council likes to keep them out of sight. The police always look there first if any crime has been committed.'

'The deprived are always blamed,' Miss Craig said, pushing the pin of a cameo brooch firmly into her large bosom. She seemed to have an uncanny knack of knowing when to stop. 'I might take a few photographs to show the girls. We've joined a photographic club and the entries are due in at the beginning of September.'

'I'll fetch your camera,' Anne said, secretly amused.

They drove through the 'posh end' where certainly an effort had been made to create the illusion of a French port with black-painted railings, old lampposts and the natural aid of some poplars which must have been planted a long time ago. They passed a restaurant called The Blue Dolphin with some cars outside. It was there Alex had taken her for dinner after he had told her about sending Margaret the money she had asked for.

How incredibly naïve I was then, she thought. That wasn't sensitivity or shyness. It was pure stupidity. No one should feel that responsible for anyone else's behaviour. Perhaps it had taught her a degree of sophistication. It had also landed her in a loveless marriage. She was surprised at the bitterness of the thought after so many years.

I've never known lightness with him, she thought, a lifting of the spirit, we've never been carefree together, we don't laugh at the same things. She saw quite clearly for a second, Ben Davies' dark face and how it lightened when he smiled, she felt again the pleasant sensation when he bent a direct look on her, as if she mattered to him. I wonder if I'll ever see him again...

'There are a lot of disused buildings,' Aunt Elspeth said. 'Perhaps you could stop and I'd take a picture of them. Just when it's suitable, of course. I shall call it "Derelict Warehouse". Mr Cholmondley-Brooks says it's important to have a title. We are not Minimalists.' Anne controlled her face. 'I'd like those railway arches in the foreground to give it perspective.' She held up her hands to make a frame.

'Right.' She went into second gear, the car bumped along over the cobbles. 'They've talked about repaving this, but the Civic Society was up in arms.'

'You need cobbles for atmosphere,' Aunt Elspeth explained, 'but you have to watch your ankles. One of the girls turned hers when we were visiting Edinburgh Castle and she's never been the same since. Walks with a limp. Has to use a stick. We all fight against having to use a stick, except Daisy Butterfield who needs a white one, poor soul. But she won't miss one of our jaunts. Says she makes up pictures in her head by what we say. This would do, Anne. The curve of the road will lend interest to the composition.' Anne stopped, obedient as always. It was second nature.

She saw the vista through her aunt's eyes, a dull early evening vista with a wind blowing off the river making the cluster of tall spars by the wall sway above the parapet. The fishermen kept their boats here. The deserted warehouses rose gaunt and gloomy against the stormy sky, she saw the rocking sign of a shabby pub, the darkness under the railway arches, a solitary car disappearing under it.

'Don't be "misled",' James was in the habit of saying—he had pronounced the word to rhyme with 'tousled'—'The Eagle and Child keeps the best prawn sandwiches for miles around. Gets them straight off the boats. It's a fishermen's howff.' She looked at the bobbing spars. They would be waiting for the evening tide.

Aunt Elspeth climbed back in. 'Got it!' she said with satisfaction. ' "Atmosphere", Mr Cholmondley-Brooks says. "Go all out for atmosphere, ladies." '

'It's got it here,' Anne said, starting up. Her spirits had sunk unaccountably. 'I can feel it. It's sinister, somehow, a different world, out of step with normality.'

They had left the warehouses behind now. There was a stretch of shaggy grass, then an incongruous modern pair of semi-detached houses, neglected, paint falling off, grass-grown. They had an uncanny air in their emptiness. Had the occupiers had the same uneasy feeling and left for the cosiness of a council estate on the hill?

'The road's unmade now. Sorry, Aunt.' They bounced up and down. 'It's been torn to pieces by Alex's lorries, but the Council refuse to repair it. They say it's his responsibility. But you know Alex.' She regretted saying that. 'Now you can see the marshes stretching to the sea. Lonely-looking, isn't it?'

'There are certainly vibrations coming from it. "Vibes" the young call it.'

I love you, you old bean bag, Anne thought. 'Further down there's an old port which fell into disuse around the eighteenth century because the river silted up. The trade was mostly with the West Indies.'

A flock of seagulls were hovering low over them as if scavenging. Could it be for rabbits? It would be a change from mussels. On the skyline against the lowering sky there was a rusty derrick surrounded by two or three corrugated sheds. She noticed how the coarse grass

47

was flattened by the tearing wind, as if by a giant hand.

'Not a nice place to be at night,' Aunt Elspeth said. 'You could imagine all sorts of things. Still, I hope I caught the atmosphere.' She pointed. 'Is that Alex's place of business?'

'Yes.' 'Place of business'. She smiled at that. 'The road ends there. And behind the Depot, nothingness. His place must occupy acres, but then he needs acres. He bought the land dirt cheap years ago. He was... clever.' Or, rather, 'shrewd', 'on the make', 'knew a good thing when he saw it.'

'This, then, is the heart of the operation,' her aunt said, nodding sagely and looking around with interest. 'I've only been in that nice office in town where his secretary always gives us tea. It must be quite a change for Alex to come here.'

'He likes it in a strange kind of way. It has a fascination for him. He's more...at home here than sitting in his office dictating. He's a tradesman at heart.'

'Perhaps it gives him a feeling of power.' She was surprised at her aunt's astuteness. 'Perhaps it does.'

The man at the box stopped them. She had never liked Spiers. He had a skull-like face and suspicious eyes. They never stayed still. She supposed he had to be like that to keep an eye on things, or rather she

48

knew that was what Alex thought. He had said it was absolutely necessary to have someone on the ball because of the amount of pilfering and vandalism that went on. 'He was inside once,' he had told her, 'and that taught him a lesson. I said I would give him this chance, and I've never regretted it. It takes a thief to catch a thief...'

'We're going to see my husband, Mr Spiers,' she said. 'He's in his office.'

'Don't think so.' He was offhand. 'His car never passed through here.'

'I know it didn't. The garage ran him up.'

'Did it?' Was he insolent, or merely thick? She knew Aunt Elspeth was thinking along the same lines, felt her move beside her.

'Supposing you ring through and see? That should settle it.'

'I know the Mercedes never went through here.' He was aggrieved. 'Marks them all down in this book, see...'

'Just telephone, will you, please?' she said. His face was surly as he lifted the receiver. She exchanged a quick glance with Aunt Elspeth, saw her slight nod of approval.

'Yes, Mr Garrett,' Spiers was saying, and then hung up the receiver. 'You've to go right through. He's waiting for you.'

'Thanks.' She thought of saying, 'Don't you owe me an apology?' but knew it would be useless. Her dislike of the man would surface and she would say something she regretted. Besides, with people of his type she always came off worst. She wasn't 'streetwise'. The word occurred to her. It was fitting. She was polite and obedient. She could never understand people who weren't.

'I always suspect insolence,' Aunt Elspeth said as they drove through the open gates. 'There's usually something to hide.'

'Sheer cussedness. I've told Alex about him before.' She wouldn't go on about it, nor mention it to Alex before her aunt. He would make her feel small by dismissing her complaint as 'sheer imagination', his favourite remark. She waved her hand, deliberately clearing her mind of the incident. 'It's all spread out for Alex here, his empire. He likes it kept tidy and properly marked. See that path? It leads to the Glass Department. There's the notice board. And we're coming to another one on the other side. Here we are. The Tile Department. Those two are under cover. Then you have to steer your way carefully through the outdoor sections. Here we are. Divided by concrete paths. Flags, Paving Stones, Roofing Tiles, Cement, goodness knows

50

what. Sundries for building. Sometimes he comes here and stays quite late. Monarch of all he surveys.' She laughed. 'Alex is the modern equivalent of those eighteenth century smugglers and brigands who used to be down on the Point, and these are his spoils!'

'I hope he doesn't ask you to drive down here late at night. It's eerie.'

'Oh, no, this is quite unusual. His Merc breaking down! He could have telephoned for a taxi, but Alex...' she pulled a face, 'he has some odd foibles.'

'Most men have foibles,' Aunt Elspeth said, 'You have to put up with them.' Anne, smiling to herself, thought there was no reason why she should presume, because her aunt was unmarried, that she should have led a blameless celibate life. She glanced fondly at her and saw that her face seemed to have a greyish tint.

'Are you all right, Aunt Elspeth? Maybe you would rather have stayed at home?'

'No, no, you have to keep your mind open for new ideas, sensations, experiences. But there's something... I don't know what it is. As if it's lying waiting, *has* been over the centuries. You could believe anything could happen here.'

'Yes, you could... I believe there was a particularly grisly murder once...' She stopped herself, remembering that the girl's

51

torso had been found on the marshes, and her head had been caught in a fisherman's net. 'Fisherman's Gruesome Find...' James had shown her the caption in the local paper, revelling in its gruesomeness. 'Then we've caught it at an in-between time, at the tail end of the day. The men will have gone home, and the fishermen won't have arrived yet to take their boats out on the bay. It gets quite lively then, I believe.'

'I'm sure...' She felt her aunt shudder, like a large jelly quivering against her shoulder. But she was right. This was not a happy place.

'Alex will be waiting,' she said cheerfully. 'We'll soon be home and then we'll have a nice glass of sherry before dinner.'

'You're a kind girl, sensitive.' She felt her aunt's hand briefly on her knee. 'I've always got on with you, but never with Margaret. I haven't ever said that to you before...it must be this place.'

Chapter Four

Alex didn't object to her decision to drive Aunt Elspeth home and then go on to London. Margaret had telephoned her again and said she was going there for a day or two's shopping and suggested they might meet. She would look in and see Richard. Anne would no doubt want to see James.

'All the young migrate to London,' Margaret had said. 'Manchester isn't good enough for them. They like the anonymity.'

'James got in at the Central Polytechnic. That was his reason.'

'Richard's is his work.' Anne had never been sure what exactly that was. He was 'a kind of art dealer', she had been led to believe by Margaret. 'Makes a bomb on one picture then has to starve the next month.'

She left Aunt Elspeth at her neat Georgian house in St Albans, waving aside her protestations of gratitude.

'You find as you grow older, Anne, that not many younger people can be bothered with you. You make me feel so welcome.

And to run me to my own door all that way! Wait till I tell the girls.'

'It was no trouble. I'm killing two birds with one stone, three actually, if I can see James as well as Margaret. She'll be pleased to hear you're still hale and hearty.'

Miss Craig looked dubious. 'Maybe so. Anyhow I have a splendid record of my little break with those photographs... What a strange place that is where Alex has established his place of business! It made quite an impression on me. I hope I captured its ambiance.'

Fortunately James was free the evening she arrived in London, and she took him out to dinner, at his suggestion to a Greek restaurant near Baker Street where he said it would be easier to park.

He was full of his own doings, as usual. James was an organizer, she thought, listening to him, admiring his bright face, his assured air. His sandy colouring and brown eyes were Alex's, but he didn't have his essential 'northerness', nor her essential shyness. He had the casual air which she had always longed to possess, and which Alex certainly didn't have. *He* was taciturn and hearty by turns. There was no easy in-between stage.

'You look smashing, Annie,' he said. This was his new title for her. He thought

'Mother' was quaint, and 'Anne' belonged to Alex or her friends. 'Annie' had the casualness he sought. 'I saw that Greek waiter eyeing you when he brought the *taramasalata.*'

'Oh, rubbish!' She was pleased.

'They usually have a knees-up when they've served the food. I think they're all out-of-work actors.'

It certainly became lively as time went on. The clientele was mostly young, there were gales of laughter from the other tables, music from a man who played the bouzouki, a great deal of hand-clapping, and eventually, possibly in response to many demands, their waiter, with a Greek skirt over his jeans, did a solo dance. He was tall, very thin, with wavy hair and a long questing nose.

As if impelled by the rhythm, everyone rose from their tables at the end of it, James, too, sprang to his feet and dragged Anne, protesting, to join a large ring of people who were dancing straight-backed round the waiter in a jerky, formalized kind of way which she supposed must be Greek.

She saw that they all had their eyes on the man in the centre and were closely following his movements, and she too quickly got the hang of it, indeed beginning to enjoy herself, her hands held high on either side by James and a strange young man.

Her eye caught that of the dancing waiter, and he, to her horror, came towards her and drew her into the centre of the ring beside him. With one hand on her waist, the other held high, he whirled her round while the others clapped and shouted.

'What have I let myself in for?' she mimed by expressive shrugs as James passed her. She saw the amused surprise on his face. Because she was adroit and light-footed she acquitted herself very reasonably, and when, flushed with pride, she was delivered back to him, the look on his face as they went back to their table was distinctly unfilial.

'Well, well, Annie,' he said, filling her glass. 'Hidden talents, eh?'

'When in Rome,' she said, trying to be cool, and assured.

'You looked really young. I never thought of it before. Dad to me is just an old codger, he's too heavy for one thing, but you're...'

'Just Mum?'

'Far from it. What age are you, really?'

'Going on for forty-three, *really*. Now stop discussing me for goodness sake and tell me about your courses and what stage you're at. Your father is bound to want to know.'

'You wouldn't understand.' He was still looking at her, 'You should have a toy boy. That's it. I'll try and fix you up with one at the Poly.' She immediately thought of Ben Davies.

'Judy, Judith, she prefers now, brought a young man for the weekend. Not that I'm thinking of him in *that* capacity,' she added, too quickly.

'Your eyes are shining.'

'That's with the exercise. No, I was just thinking he would be useful to you. He's a Business Analyst, or whatever they call it, computers, in Manchester. That's the sort of thing that would interest you, isn't it?'

'Yes, it would.'

'I think your father wants you to go into the business with him.'

'Oh, I'd like a run for my money first. What was this chap called?'

'Ben Davies.'

'I wouldn't mind meeting him. Is Judy likely to bring him again?'

'I doubt it. I gather he was more a chauffeur than anything else.' She hoped so. 'She works in the same firm. But if you'd really like it I could always ask him when you come home next time.' She was surprised at her effrontery, her coolness.

'There's the late summer holiday soon. Could you give him a ring?' Was he too cool? And were her eyes really shining?

'I think he gave Alex his card. He took him round the whole bit, town office and depot, to see if he could come up with some new ideas for him.'

'On the cheap? Trust Dad never to miss a trick. Right, you do that, Annie. Have a little house party.'

'I thought of asking your Aunt Margaret and Judith. And your aunt's latest.' That sounded casual enough. 'They might enjoy being out of the city.'

'Aunt Margaret gives me the pip. She can't keep her hands off me. Judy amuses me.'

'How nice for her!' She tried to be scathing, and then something made her say, 'I took your great-aunt Elspeth along by the river to pick up Dad. It was a miserable day. She thought it was full of atmosphere down by the Depot, but spooky.'

'The old bod's right. Downright spooky. I used to be terrified when you drove me there as a schoolboy.'

'You never said.'

'I think it was because of that murdered girl. I read about her and I had nightmares for ages. The head... I never wanted to fish after that.'

'Why didn't you say? I never knew.' She was appalled even at this late date, to think of him suffering like that.

58

'I wasn't encouraged to run for comfort with Dad around.' He looked at her and his face was like that schoolboy's. 'He once gave me a belting for having a crying match at a party. You were ill and he came for me. He *bossed* me around.'

She remembered. She had had 'flu and Alex had gone to fetch James. She had dozed off, and because she was fevered had lost track of the time. She was wakened by Alex's voice. He was shouting angrily and in between she could hear short high yelps like that of a dog which had been run over. It was James. She had staggered to the door and opened it, just in time to see Alex pushing him into his bedroom. Alex's face when he turned and saw her was a boiling red colour.

'What are you doing out of bed?' he said. Words wouldn't come because of the sickness rising in her throat. 'Don't look like that. The little devil led me a fine song and dance at Carol's...'

'He'd be over-tired...'

'We're not having temper tantrums...'

'There was no need...' She swayed and must have fainted because when she wakened again the house was quiet and dark. It must be late. It had been June, those long summer nights, which she loved, when the sea lay calm in the bay. And then she saw that Alex was standing at the window, his broad frame filling it.

'Alex...' The memory came flooding back of James being pushed into his room like a whipped dog. 'Did I dream all that... James?' He didn't answer. She struggled to sit up.

He turned, his face now calm, a rock-like calmness. 'Dream what?'

'I saw you...heard him crying. You said you had only...' The words strangled in her throat. It hadn't been ordinary crying, it had been like an animal's yelp, a mixture of pain and fear.

'It was nothing. You look better. Less flushed. I'll go down and make you a cup of tea.' When he moved away the room became suffused with the summer evening light.

When he had gone she got up, and not stopping to put on her slippers or dressing gown, she crossed the landing, opened James' door and went in. He was curled up on his bed reading a comic. The face he turned on her was sullen. 'Get back to bed, Mummy. Daddy says I've not to bother you.'

'James,' she said, touching his arm, 'I'm sorry I couldn't come to Mrs Musgrove's for you. But Daddies often go for their little boys...' He shook himself free, his face closed and mature for a five-year-old. 'They don't shout. And belt.'

She looked down at him, saw his likeness to Alex, and turned away, defeated. At the door she stopped and said, 'We'll all be good friends in the morning, you'll see.' She should have cuddled and kissed him, but her head was swimming.

When Alex brought up her tea she turned her face away, disgusted at herself because she was afraid she would weep if she spoke to him. She heard him going heavily downstairs. Tomorrow they would talk about it, or perhaps they wouldn't. Alex's temper was like summer lightning. So was his son's. I rushed into this marriage, she thought. I have only myself to blame. We're incompatible.

The doctor said he couldn't understand why she took so long to recover. It must have been a bad bout.

Margaret liked the Piccadilly Hotel. There was always a lot to watch, she said. It was handy for the shops and a good meeting-place. Despite the latter, Anne had been waiting for half an hour before she turned up. She watched her coming towards her, tall, dark, boldly made-up, dark hair to her shoulders, a long red jacket, short black skirt, high-heeled shoes. She walked like a model, sway-backed, looking from side to side, inviting admiration, supremely assured.

'Hello, little sister.' She dropped a brief kiss on Anne's cheek before she sat down. 'Been waiting long?'

'Only half an hour. I've been pro-positioned twice.' Margaret gave her a wary look.

'That's not like you, Anne. Come to think of it, you do look different, somehow, younger...'

'I *am* young. Forty-two's no age nowadays.'

'I agree but I'm not taking any chances. This man I was telling you about... I asked his advice about hormone therapy when the time comes and he's all for it.'

'How's that going?'

'It isn't.' She shrugged. 'It was a forlorn chance, but I'm not too worried. He was dull beyond words, and I don't think I should have made a good doctor's wife. From what he told me, his last one spent most of the day on the telephone. Who wants to be an answering machine? Besides, I've other irons in the fire.' She looked away, a slight smile curving her mouth. Anne remembered the same expression when they had both been children, how sometimes she had rained fists on her to make her talk, to no avail. Margaret had always been bigger, and stronger.

I'll never get to the bottom of her, she thought now. Long ago it had been simply to tease, now it was impossible to know whether she made herself out as a *femme fatale* for effect or whether she led a rich sexually-fulfilled life elsewhere. She remembered, strangely enough, the photograph, the bold stance which perhaps covered up her secret fears. No one could be that impervious.

'How did your shopping go?' she asked.

'Oh, wait till I tell you!' She turned on Anne a face filled with excitement. Margaret went into a shopping expedition as if into battle. It was a challenge. She compared prices in various shops. She confronted one shop with the indisputable fact that the same article could be had cheaper in another one. She scored points. She wore down assistants and even store managers. She always managed to come away with 'bargains' which she rarely used or wore, as if the successful completion of her sorties was reward enough.

'How's Richard?' Anne asked.

'Same as usual. Why?' She looked belligerent. She couldn't understand that Anne liked him without reservations. 'How's James?'

'Fine. We had a good talk. Usually he's so full of himself and his doings that I feel a non person. This time we were talking about when he was a little boy...and Alex.'

'Alex? What's wrong with Alex?' She had lit a cigarette and now blew a cloud of smoke in Anne's direction. I'm a passive victim. I don't want to get cancer at second remove. She didn't say it.

'Nothing, nothing.' Everything is wrong with Alex as far as I'm concerned. We don't fit. 'James was recalling some of his childhood memories.'

'Men never get on with their sons. Ralph was the same with Richard. I had to take his side all the time. He said I made him a mother's boy, petting him and so on. I did it to annoy Ralph. He was easily annoyed...' Anne remembered Margaret's husband, a thin man with elegant hands and feet, crimped hair and a long chin. He had been no match for Margaret. 'It's the Oedipus complex. You know, the mother and the son having it off together. I must admit, when Richard used to come crying and snuggling up to me in bed, I thought it could easily happen...'

'Margaret!'

'Why shouldn't we say what we think? You've always been a purse mouth. I don't know what you're thinking all the time. It could be quite fun to bamboozle you.' She laughed, her white, bold teeth showing. 'I'm talking nonsense. What about tea? Have you ordered?'

One of Margaret's more admirable traits

was her capacity to command the attention of a waiter almost immediately. It must be a question of concentration, Anne thought, as she watched the man bowing deferentially over her.

'Toast, Anne?' Margaret asked.

'Yes, thanks. No cakes for me.'

'Come on, indulge yourself. Let yourself go. And cream cakes,' she said to the man, 'real cream, not your synthetic stuff.' The smile she gave the waiter was seductive. It broke through his veneer. He was an ordinary little man for a moment, servile about cream cakes, assuredly with real cream.

'Right away. Toast and a selection of cream cakes, *real* cream, for two. I'll see you all right, Madam.' They exchanged glances.

'Are you doing anything on the Bank Holiday?' Anne asked her when the waiter had gone away.

'Not a thing. Holidays are the end. No one is ever available. You get a left-over feeling, especially in Manchester.'

'Come up to us. Bring Judith and Richard, and Con if they'd like it. James is coming.'

'I can't answer for them but I'll pass the message on. Judith is broody these days. She's looking for a man to give her a baby.' She threw her glance to the ceiling. 'Wants to know what it's like.'

'She brought a nice young man with her last time. Ben Davies.' She would be bold, like Margaret.

'Oh, yes, the bright one? She told me of him, and that he quizzed her about you all the way home.'

'He's years younger than me.'

'Are you considering him as a substitute for Alex?' She was quick, too quick.

'Don't be silly. I was telling James about him and he says he would like to meet him to pick his brains about computers.'

'So?' Margaret stubbed out her second cigarette as the laden tray arrived. She gave the waiter a brilliant smile but didn't thank him. He had served his purpose.

'Why are you looking at me like that, Margaret?' She was flustered. 'I've promised James I'll ask him to come up at the weekend too, give them a chance to talk.'

'Oh, yes?' Margaret said, passing Anne's cup. 'It's as good an excuse as any.'

She smiled. It was ridiculous that at her age she should be discomfited by her own sister. 'Why do you judge everyone by yourself?' She took the cup but refused a cream cake. 'I haven't a sweet tooth. You know that. You can gorge away yourself. I'll have a piece of toast, please.'

'I like to see you rattled, Sis.' Margaret

bit into a chocolate éclair. Anne saw there were traces of cream on either side of her mouth, making her look...she searched for the word, abandoned. Why was it that everything Margaret did seemed unconfined by rules? If I feel that, Anne thought, what kind of effect must she have on men?

Chapter Five

She decided to write a short note to Ben Davies rather than telephone him. She had rung Judith who had said she had another engagement. Richard, when she telephoned him, told her he was going with Con to Dieppe for the weekend. 'We like the French sailors,' he said. She imagined his teasing smile.

'So do I,' she said, refusing to rise to the bait. 'And the fish market. Have a good time, and any time you and Con want a break in the far-flung North, we'll be pleased to see you.'

'Okay. Thanks a lot. We'll come sometime when Mama isn't there.' That's sad, she thought, hanging up, very sad.

Her letter to Ben Davies was circumspect:

'Dear Ben,
My son, James, who is doing a business course in London and wants to set the Thames on fire, was interested when I told him about your job.
He's coming home for the Bank Holiday and Alex and I wondered if

you would like to join us? You would be very welcome.

Anne Garrett.'

He telephoned in a couple of days. 'What a good idea. I'd love to come. When would you like me?'

'Drive up any time you like on Saturday. We'll be around. Judith's mother is coming. Not Judith, I'm afraid. Dinner at eight.'

'Dinner at eight,' he echoed. She heard the broken-backed inflection and shuddered, then told herself how ridiculous that was.

'Thank you very much.' He rang off.

Alex liked guests in the house. It suited his expansive temperament. Anne did, for a different reason. Had there been a close rapport between them, nothing would have pleased her better than to be together alone when they had time, to make expeditions to places she loved, the Yorkshire Dales, particularly Swaledale, the Lakes, particularly Newlands in a fold of hills near Keswick, to picnic and talk together, but she had long since taken it for granted. Even after twenty years of marriage, they had nothing to say to each other.

She had grown used to his look of puzzlement when she expressed an opinion or followed a train of thought, as if she spoke a different language. His Philistine attitude to art or literature she could accept. What was more difficult was his choice of friends.

'I don't understand you,' he would say, 'the Harrisons are grand people. Always game for a laugh.'

There was no doubt about that. They laughed uproariously at things she didn't find amusing. Her jaw would be stiff, when they had gone, in her efforts to be polite and laugh too. And she found it screamingly tedious Jean Harrison's lengthy descriptions of the searches she made in her favourite stamping ground, Kendal Milne's, for bathroom tiles and fittings, Italian and gold-plated, naturally.

Her husband's chief topic of conversation was the restaurants he frequented in a radius of fifty miles, their menus, their wine list, the smart people one saw there, the cost. Once when she had said to Alex that Egon Ronay better look out he had given her a cold stare of disapproval.

She had come across in her reading a saying of Camus to the effect that human beings do not do well without a purpose or meaning to life. The Harrisons certainly proved this, even although they were concerned only with the minutia. And perhaps, she chided herself, tolerance was as important.

Ben Davies had arrived at six o'clock on the Saturday evening, and after being pleasant all round, had gravitated towards James. They were hitting it off, Anne thought, when she went into the kitchen, drink in hand, to put the finishing touches to the meal. Occasionally she heard gales of laughter from the conservatory where Alex was no doubt being lavish with drinks.

She noticed the slight tremor in her hands as she garnished the salmon bought from Mr Proctor...'a little dinner party, is it, Mrs Garrett? Well, we'll have to do you proud.' What, she asked herself, are you up to? Are you really chasing a young man almost young enough to be your son, certainly young enough to be a friend of your son's rather than your own?

'Chasing?' she queried, taking a sip from the glass and placing radish roses between crimped cucumber slices. 'Surely not? You invited him for James's benefit, and because you like him the way you would like any of your son's friends. But did *they* make your hands tremble?' She went to the cooker to stir the Bernaise sauce in the double boiler. There was nothing like that...like what? It's non-sexual, you crave affection, particularly from a kindred spirit...but how do you know he is? There were people in the poetry group who might well be kindred spirits. She poured the sauce into a white Leeds pottery jug and took it into the dining-room.

'Dinner's ready,' she announced, going from there to the conservatory. 'Alex, would you mind carrying in the salmon?' That was the husband's job, along with mending fuses and turning off the water and gas when they went on holiday. This stout, slightly grizzled man in the cushioned cane chair, in a light grey summer suit and pale blue shirt, was her husband. She occasionally had doubts. *Her husband.* He even wore a heavy gold signet ring on his left hand to prove it.

'Just in time, Anne,' Margaret said, looking round, dark eyes sparkling, heavy dark hair looped over one ear to show a dangling green earring to match her emerald green silk shirt. She saw James and Ben exchange glances, exchange smiles.

After dinner, when she was clearing up in the kitchen, Ben Davies appeared, smiling, at ease. The wine had flowed, his face was flushed.

'I've come to help the magician with the washing-up. Rule Number One in the "How to Become a Popular Guest" Book.'

'No need, thanks.' He was standing too near her and she had to move away because of the effect he had on her. She was afraid to look at him. 'I have a dish-washer. I'm just stacking it and then I'll join you. How do you get on with James?'

'Oh, fine! He plies me with questions. I've suggested he drives back with me to Manchester and see our office if he can fit it in.'

'He's going on holiday.'

'Yes, he told me. Rock climbing in Greece. Lucky chap.' He hesitated. 'You must be tired after all that effort. Such attention to...detail.' Had she been fussy?

'Is that Rule Two in the book? Be kind to the hostess?' She was under control now. She smiled at him for the joy of looking at him. 'I like cooking when there's an audience. Especially the fiddly bits. Alex likes good plain wholesome fare as his mother used to make. It's a change.'

'Would you be up to another early morning walk?' She was taken aback by his directness.

'Fancy you remembering! No, that was a one-off thing.' She changed the subject. 'How do you like my sister, Margaret?'

'You're very different.'

'Judith's more like her.'

'Yes.'

73

Something made her say, 'How's that romance going?'

'Oh, nothing doing there, thank you very much.' He was leaning against the refrigerator in an easy manner, hands in pockets. 'She seems to have designs on all men at the moment. It must be something to do with her marriage. Was it unhappy?'

'It fell apart. She could tell you herself if she wanted to.'

'Well, I'm definitely not her man.' Something in his stance and the remark displeased her. Was it the blatant chauvinism, or simply that she was a generation removed from that kind of talk?

'Could you get out of my way and I'll get on?' She spoke lightly. 'Go and see what James is up to.'

'Dismissed by teacher,' he said. She had to drag her eyes away from his smile. Oh, stupid, stupid woman, she told herself when she was alone. Stop now before you make a fool of yourself...

They had been praising Mr Proctor's prawns at dinner, and Alex had said that they tasted much better in the pub near his depot, washed down by some good local ale. 'Tomorrow,' he had said, pouring out the Pouilly Fusée, 'we'll all go there for a pub lunch. What do you say, Margaret?'

'You know me,' she had said, 'always ready for a new experience.'

So, here they were, Anne driving James and Ben, Margaret with Alex in the Mercedes, going to the shabby-looking pub which she remembered pointing out to Aunt Elspeth.

'Strange sort of place this,' Ben said, looking round at the dilapidated warehouses, the railway arches, the mud on which the boats were beached—there were no bobbing spars today—'It definitely has an atmosphere.'

'That's what Aunt Elspeth said when I brought her, James.'

'Had a fiver from her in the post the other day.' She saw him in the mirror put a hand to his mouth. 'Meant to write and thank her. She said she'd had a super time with you, or words to that effect.'

Alex was familiar with the owner when they all went in. 'Decided to do a bit of slumming today, Ron.'

'Didn't expect to see *you* at the weekend, Mr Garrett.'

'I've been singing your praises, or rather, praises to your prawn sandwiches. Have you enough to feed us all?'

'Sure, sure! Albert Proctor keeps me well supplied. Come this way.' He led them to a corner where there was a wooden settle which looked like a church pew, and a few stools around a ring-marked table. At least it's not plasticated, Anne thought.

'Not exactly the Ritz,' Margaret said when they had sat down.

Alex laughed. 'Oh, we can't come up to your Manchester standards. Ron's not a great one for decoration. I've been at him often to get cracking and get up-market, but he says his customers like it as it is.'

'He'd spoil it if he changed it,' Ben said. 'It looks like what it is. Plastic blots out all the character. It looks like a fishermen's howff. Can you see *them* on nylon cushions?'

'Or surrounded by painted mirrors with lilies on them?' James laughed.

Alex turned to Margaret. 'What's your poison?'

'I'll have the local brew, thanks.'

'It will grow hair on your chest.'

'As long as that's the only place.' She looked at him and they both burst into laughter. 'This husband of yours brings out the worst in me, Anne.'

She was pointing out the flood level mark on the wall to Ben and she pretended not to hear. 'I think it's still the same furniture...'

'Little Sis doesn't like Big Sis being rude.' Everyone laughed and she tried to join in, discomfited.

While they gave their orders she thought

of the photograph again, Margaret's bold stance, her own downbent head. Had she avoided what only *she* considered unpleasant, distasteful, all her life? She saw in her mind's eye that foreshortened face of hers with the high cheekbones. Now there were shadows underneath them. She lost weight easier than she gained it. What was it Ben had said on their first meeting? 'A schoolgirl look in spite of your grown-up manners.'

Something like that. Why don't you plunge into life for a change, let yourself go? 'Purse mouth', Margaret had called her.

The prawn sandwiches, so full that they oozed out in their mayonnaise coating between the thick slices, were declared excellent, the ale of the right darkness, bitterness and potency. Alex was abstemious, as befitted a pillar of society, but although they had only a pint each, they became merry, possibly because of the rough local voices and laughter around them.

The place was now full of fishermen and local tradesmen, some of whom Anne recognized. When Alex joined them at the door after paying the bill, he said Margaret wanted to see the depot since they were so near. 'Any takers?' He looked around.

'Not me,' James said. 'I cut my teeth on

those cement blocks of yours. Too mean to give me wooden ones.' He laughed at Ben.

'What about you?' Alex said.

'Well...' Ben was being diplomatic. 'I had a good look round with you the last time, thanks. I'm working out a system for you at the office. You'll have it soon.'

'Good. The sooner the better.'

'Sure. What intrigues me is the hinterland beyond your place. All that unused land. Could we get through to it?'

'Not very easily. What do you want to see that for? Coney Land, it's called. Only the poachers go there. And people up to no good,' Alex replied.

'At the end of it there's the Point.' James became interested. 'How's this for an idea, Annie? We could cross the bridge, join the other road and get to it that way. I've just remembered I told Anthony...' he said to Ben, '...my flatmate, that if we were near I'd look in on his old aunt.'

'Miss Hardwick?' Alex said. 'I thought she had crumbled long ago.' He laughed.

James laughed dutifully. 'They live for ever, that lot.'

'There's the tide to consider.' Anne looked doubtful, and to Ben, 'The Point's cut off for part of each day.'

'We can find that out when we get to

78

the ford. Don't fuss.' James had the bit between his teeth.

'Are there houses on it?' Ben looked interested.

'Oh, yes, a few old families, and fishermen. People living in the town used to have their summer houses on the Point. Fantastic. That was in the time of the coach and horse when seven miles seemed like seventy. Anthony's aunt won't budge. She's getting on for ninety and she waits for the fishermen bringing in their catch every day. They fill a newspaper with small flounders for her cats.'

'My God!' Margaret said. 'Are you sure it isn't her ghost? She can't *still* be alive.' She shuddered. 'That place gives me the creeps.'

'You don't have to worry about a bit of old crumble,' Alex said, laughing again. 'Come on, then. Let that lot get on with what they want. You and I are going to have an edifying afternoon seeing where the money's made.' Anne wondered what on earth Margaret would find to interest her *there*. She gave up.

She drove James and Ben because last year James had run her car into a ditch, and Alex had insured her new Fiesta for her own use only. There were times when she wished she was independent enough to have bought her own car. James had accepted the ban with good grace. He wasn't home very often.

She heard him chatting away in the back. 'Yes, at the mouth of the river. It had its heyday in Regency times. They came out for the sea bathing! Some even had summer houses there. Who said second homes were a new thing?'

'At least they wouldn't be set on fire.'

'You're Welsh. I'd forgotten. Crazy. And, of course, the river was busy then with traffic. Even smugglers!'

'What on earth did they smuggle? Crack?'

'Tobacco, fishermen liked their baccy, silk, rum, brandy. And tea, the great opiate of the time. That's good, eh? The great opiate of the time...'

Anne listened happily as she drove. This must be one of my happiest days, she thought, James home and Ben here. She heard his laughter, that charming voice which broke on the syllables. She had never imagined she could fall in love with a voice...

Fall in love...the words stayed with her as she negotiated the narrow road running between scattered cottages. 'Do Not Proceed If The Water Is Beyond The Level Of This Post'. She heard Ben read it out. Fall in love...with a voice. Was she going out of her mind?

'We're quite safe,' James sang out. 'Heaps of time to get there and back before the tide. This is the ford now, Ben.'

She drove between the mud flats, seeing the busy oystercatchers poking with their long orange bills for shells, the bright bar of colour which might be a sheldrake. Years ago, when she had been acutely unhappy, she had taken to bird-watching here to give her some kind of solace. The vastness of the mud flats, of the sky, made her own problems seem puny. You had to come to terms eventually with everything, even being married to a man you couldn't love. James had been the deciding factor. She couldn't bring herself to disrupt his life at the tender age of five. Besides it was her own fault. She had gone into the marriage deliberately. Everyone had to pay...

'Here we are,' she said, running on to the shelving stony beach. 'We can't take the car any further.'

'I've never *seen* so much sky,' Ben said. He got out and opened her door, smiling at her.

'And mud!' She laughed. 'Often they are the same colour, but who's caring?' And still laughing because she was so happy, 'Now you two, don't run about too much. You might fall and skin your knees.'

'For God's sake, Annie,' James said, looking disgusted. As well he might.

Chapter Six

'I remember the bleakness at the riverside when we had lunch at that pub,' Ben said, 'the "forgotten" feeling, but this is different. Then there was that scrubby half mud, half marram grass edge to the river...two children were playing there, and they seemed unreal looking down on them, their movements, their lips moving, but their voices blown away. And there was the unrelieved *flatness*, but this,' he looked around, breathing deeply, 'this is different, racy, and there's a feeling of continuity with those houses and the boats and the birds, of habitation...' He broke off, 'I can't believe it, is that a man standing waist deep in the water just for the fun of it?'

'Goes on a bit, doesn't he?' James laughed at Anne. 'For your information, that man is fishing by half-net. It's an old Pointy custom. He's standing facing the current so that the net he's holding on a wooden frame flows out behind him. If a salmon swims in it's had its chips, so to speak. Chips with everything here, you know. There's a place near here which serves, wait for it, champagne, oysters and chips!'

'I don't know what's worse, chips with everything, or standing up to your waist in water.' Ben laughed.

'Business consultants and computers seem a long way from that fisherman, I should think.' Anne smiled at him.

'He may well have the right way of things. No angst.'

They were walking slowly along the unmade road flanked by a higgledy-piggledy row of houses of various styles.

'Which is Anthony's aunt's?' Anne asked. 'Is it that one with the bow windows?'

'No, it's up the lane here.' They turned into a narrow cobbled lane made dark by the gable end of one house, and the high wall, presumably surrounding the garden, of another. 'This is it. And here's the garden door. It's the only way in as a matter of fact. The front door is built up because of flooding. Everyone uses this one.'

'Are you really going to visit her?' Anne enquired.

'Yes, I think I should. She's devoted to Anthony. I think he's her heir. He says he's got to keep her sweet. He'll stand me a Chinese takeaway if I go.'

'What a mercenary lot you all are! Shall we wait for you?'

'No, don't. She'll insist on giving me tea. She has an old servant about the same age as herself. It takes for ever but I quite like it, that dark front room with the green daylight and the smell of damp. There's always a fire, even on the hottest day. And lace mats on everything. And she has a super telescope. I can make out Garretts on the opposite side. Can even read the name on the gate.'

'See what Dad's up to,' she said, laughing.

'That might be dangerous. Right, then, see you back at the car in an hour or so. Remember the tide. We forgot to ask.'

What did he mean, she thought as she and Ben walked on. Not about the tide—she would watch that—but that it might be 'dangerous' to spy? Margaret? Alex? She dismissed her uneasiness. 'Do you like it here?' she said. 'It's quaint, isn't it?'

'Yes, a time warp in spite of those racing clouds. Where does this lane go to?'

'It peters out into fields and if we cross them and the marshy ground beyond that—there are paths made by the farmer's tractors—we come out on the other side. You get a grand view then of the Bay. It will be racy all right.'

'Let's go, then.' He looked as young as James, and yet he wasn't, he was almost twenty-five, attractive, he wouldn't be an innocent at that age. She knew very little about him, or his background. He didn't talk about his parents. And why should a young man of his age want to visit a middle-aged couple?

But there had been reasons, she reminded herself. The first time he had ferried Judith, and this time it was to meet James. Perhaps he'd had nothing better to do on a Bank Holiday... 'Is it having an effect on you too?' Ben said.

'What?'

'The place. You're deep in thought.'

'I'm like that, I'm afraid. Not a great talker. I tend to forget when I'm with someone that I *should* talk. It doesn't come naturally. As a matter of fact,' be bold, 'I was wondering about you, if you had any friends, no,' she saw his smile, 'I mean lots of friends, why you weren't with them, or your parents, no, that's not right, I mean...'

'Why I jumped at your invitation?'

'I didn't say that.'

'You implied it. You wouldn't believe me if I told you the real reason.' He looked directly at her. 'Yes, I have friends, mostly business ones. I'm quite normal, I think.' She turned away from the directness of his look. 'I'm at a crossroads in my life. Mind your ankle in those rabbit holes...'

'I'm an old Pointer...a crossroads at your age?'

'Yes, possibly the normal age. At James' age one is playing the field like mad. Then one by one those friends drop off as they start living with a girl or getting married. I did the same for two years.'

'Got married?'

'No, shacked up with someone. It didn't work out. I found sleeping with her wasn't reason enough to get married. She didn't agree. There was some bitterness. Now,' he said, turning to her as they walked, 'if she had been like you...'

'Middle-aged?'

'You're terribly conscious of your age, aren't you? No, I mean, if she had looked like you, if she'd had your...delicate sensibilities...yes, I'm going to say it, your true refinement...'

'Oh, for Heaven's sake!'

'I know it creases you, doesn't it? And your...innocence...' He stopped, keeping his eyes on her. Behind his head there was an immensity of opal grey sky. His hair was being blown into his eyes by gusts of wind and he combed it back impatiently with his fingers. 'I haven't finished. And yet at the same time your way of looking through people—you're doing it just now. You listen and you watch, don't you?'

'I told you I'm not a great talker.'

'You're a people watcher?'

'So what if I am? Let's walk on. I'm not a butterfly on a pin. I want to show you the opposite shore and then we must get back before we're marooned.'

'We could stay with Miss Hardwick and her companion and have a party.'

She laughed. 'It wouldn't be necessary. One of the fishermen would row us across, but it would be in the local paper next week and my name would be mud. "Well-known business man's wife in escapade with two young men".'

'Okay. Let's hurry on,' and when they were walking, 'I didn't just come because of James, you know.'

'Didn't you?'

'No, no.' He shook his head. 'When you phoned me I ran up and down the stairs all day. Our office is on the fifth floor. I had to work off my energy somehow, my...joy,' *Joy,* her mind echoed. Was it joy *she* had felt, that unnameable sensation when she had heard his voice? She hadn't dare call it joy. 'I was afraid I'd smile all over my face if I took the lift and people would think I was a nutter...'

'James said you went on a bit. Here you go again.' Her joy made her speak lightly, cruelly.

'You don't like me saying "joy". It's an un-Larkin-like word.' She didn't answer.

They had to battle against the wind now. The rough grass was flattened as it tore at its roots. They had to hold on to each other to defeat it.

'It's worth it, don't you think?' she said when they saw the broad expanse of water. 'Like the other side of the world.'

'I feel like Columbus!' He had his face lifted up to the sky. 'My God, this wind! You can't even stand up in it. Let's lie on our stomachs and contemplate the view for a second. Look, here's my anorak.'

'Then we must go back. The tide...' They lay in a slight hollow about fifty yards from the stony shore. In front of them, as close as ten yards, a rabbit sat washing its paws. Ben nudged her.

'Yes, I see.' She whispered. 'Coney Land. Isn't it sweet? It reminds me of my cat. She did the same.'

'Coney watcher,' he breathed in her ear, but his slight movement made the rabbit stop its ablutions. Its ears went up and then its white scut flashed for a moment as it disappeared down its burrow.

'Now you see me, now you don't,' Ben said, 'like death. My fault. Where is your cat? I didn't see one about the house.'

'It died.' Her throat, her voice filled with tears. Five years ago and she could still be a fool about it.

'What happened?' His eyes were on the

grass in front of them, coney watching.

'Its back got broken.'

'In an accident?'

'Alex said it was.' She heard the ugliness in her voice. 'It was sleeping with me. Under my chin. He came in late one night—he had been at a Rotary Dinner—and threw it out of the bed. It slithered on the rug. We have parquet floors and I prefer rugs. It broke its back against the corner of the wardrobe...' Her voice rose in a wail and she turned away from him, disgusted at herself. She wept. The tears were as fresh as they had been when she had picked up the cat, gone downstairs and rang for the vet.

She had wept for days and Alex had abased himself. 'I didn't mean to hurt it. You know that. But I get fed up always finding it there. Maybe I was a bit well-oiled. I'm sorry, Anne, so sorry,' and then in a small burst of self-justification, 'you know I always wanted wall-to-wall instead of those damned rugs...'

Ben had gathered her to him. He was stroking her back, as if *it* had been broken, long, smooth strokes. He didn't speak. He waited until she had stopped weeping, had pushed him away and sat up.

'What a thing to do! I'm ashamed of myself. And ashamed I didn't give Alex the benefit of the doubt. You see, it didn't die right away. The vet said if it lived it would be paraplegic and I didn't want that. I had to decide. Alex was miserable. I see now the extent of his misery. I was distraught. Afterwards I packed up and went off to Paris. Can you believe it? I know it well because I have a friend who lives there but I didn't go near her. I stayed in a little hotel in Place St Sulpice, and, oh, I was fair, I phoned Alex and told him where I was.

'All I remember of the days there was walking in the Luxembourg Gardens watching people exercising—you don't think of the French doing that, do you? But they jog, and do stretching and posing, Japanese style. They're intense individualists. And when I grew tired of that I would hurtle back and forwards on the Porte D'Orleans-Clignacourt line. It diverted me to work out the *Correspondances*. I'd get off at Odeon, Chatelet —it's worse than Piccadilly—Réaumur, and walk about.

'Other times I'd sit quietly in the St Sulpice church. It was when I was sitting in on a funeral service that I came to my senses. I found I was noticing how the priest's robes toned with the marble and gold of the church in a truly French way. Black and white would have been too harsh. So I went back home...you must

90

think I'm a nutter talking like this.'

'No, I don't. It was very...moving. Diff-er-ent.' It was his voice which was broken-backed now, the syllables standing on their own feet. 'For the first time with any wo-man, I wanted to be inside her mind instead of inside her body.' He looked at her. 'Oh, you!' he said. 'Come on, let me give you a good hug.' His arms and his closeness were pure joy, but after a second or two she sprang away from him like the rabbit going down its burrow and stood up.

'I'm crazy. James will be champing at the bit. We'll have to hurry...'

James was indeed champing at the bit. He was walking up and down outside the car on the shelving beach, kicking at stones with the side of his foot. 'For God's sake, Mother!' He came towards them. 'Annie' was forgotten. 'What were you thinking of? You know all about the tide. It's over the road now.'

She felt stupid, and the feeling made her tone sharp.

'Don't fuss, little boy. It's not over the whole road. It only takes five minutes to drive the length of it.'

'Is it safe?' Ben asked. 'I've heard of people being stranded.'

'Yes, bodies found later, bloated, staring eyes, hair like seaweed. What a pair you

91

are! Go on, get in instead of wasting time fussing.'

James had calmed down. 'It's your car. Are you on?'

'Of course I'm on. Get in.' They all tumbled in and she started up and drove slowly over the stones.

'We could always have gone back and stayed with Anthony's aunt,' James said. 'Joke.'

'Really, you're the limit.' She drove carefully onto the tide road. *Don't rush it.* It was scarcely wet, but she felt its sponginess through the wheels. 'I thought you went to London to make you independent. It's not done much for you.'

He laughed. 'Expect I've been urbanized. You don't see tides rushing over Baker Street every day.'

'It isn't rushing.'

She drove carefully but confidently. It was only a mile after all. She was pleased with her boldness, like Margaret, like that long-ago photograph, the bold stance. Gets you anywhere. The front wheels dipped and she accelerated, the car responded and rose up easily, although the engine didn't sound as strong as before. How bleak it looked, the reeds rising through the water, the parallel lines of posts half-covered, the only vertical things in the landscape.

One had a gull sitting on it like an

inspector. Inspector of what? Fools? Bleakness. Utter bleakness. Edward Hopper's pictures... With poetry had come an avid interest in art, especially modern art. How did Ben feel about art? 'Just a small hollow,' she said.

'A great big hole, if you ask me,' James said.

'You're unduly silent, Ben.' He was sitting beside her.

'Am I?' When she glanced at him she thought his face looked strained. 'I'm navigating. Look out!'

She swerved to avoid a lake in the middle of the road, a little lake, really, with little waves made by the wind. The car engine puttered and stopped. She was still bold.

'Well,' she said, smacking the wheel, 'you'll have to swim now.'

'Don't be a damn fool, Mother!' Where was the delectable 'Annie'? 'Don't just *sit* there. Start the car! Rev the engine! Here, I'll come over!'

'Don't be stupid! Do you want Ben to get out?' It was she who felt stupid, all the boldness gone. And her heart was beating, hammering. Ben would notice.

'Start the car, Mother!' James shouted at her.

'No, not right away. I have to be sure... This isn't new to me.' What was she doing, play-acting like this, risking people's lives? She'd never been in this situation before. She was far too cautious. Generally. People had been drowned. Not every day of the week but there had been accidents. A drunk returning from the pub on the Point had sat happily in his marooned car and drowned, just as happily, she hoped.

Automatically she was seeing that the choke was full out, turning on the ignition, trying to catch the engine at the right time with her foot. She was a good driver, even Alex said so. She listened to a car the way she listened to people. If only her heart would stop hammering...

'Now, now!' James banged the back of the seat.

'Shut up! I'm listening.' She strained her ears, caught the sound she wanted, intensified it into a steady roar with the ball of her foot. The engine was running smoothly now, she let out the clutch and drove smoothly and confidently forward and out of the lake, the wheels gripping the damp sand at its edge...the engine puttered and died.

'Would you like me to try?' Ben said.

She turned on him. 'Another expert?'

He reared back. 'No, it's just that sometimes another driver...'

'Oh, I see what this is. A conspiracy against women drivers! Well, you both

94

choose a fine time, I must say, to voice your prejudices! Well, there's nothing else for it. We'll have to walk the rest, or swim for it. I had hoped to keep my feet dry. Now it seems I have to abandon my car as well.'

Ben didn't answer. James said theatrically, 'Women!'

'If you say that just once more, James, I'm warning you, I'll throw the key through the window. It's come to a pretty pass...' She rambled on while she went through the procedure again. Choke out, hand on gear, foot on accelerator. She was calm now. She would apologize later for losing her temper if they apologized first.

The engine roared, she slid smoothly into first gear and gunned the accelerator. The car shuddered like an offended virgin and seemed to leap over the rim of the lake. She could feel harder ground underneath. They were away.

'Well done,' James said, mollified. 'Still, you must admit you cut it rather fine, Annie.'

'All adds to the excitement. I have to show you townies what we have to contend with in the outback.' She didn't feel bold at all now. And it wasn't natural for her to show off like a high wire trapeze artist dicing with death. 'All right, Ben?' she said. She ran off the ford through puddles and onto the road through the village. 'You're rather quiet?'

'Well, you see I can't swim.'

'You can't...?' She choked with laughter, James beat the back of the seat with his hands.

'He can't swim!'

'How on earth can anyone get to your age and not swim?' She was wiping her eyes. 'Oh, I'm sorry...'

'Terrible, isn't it? But I have a good excuse. I had asthma as a child and I suppose I wasn't allowed. I never learned, then I never had time to learn, then I was ashamed, and so the years rolled by with me hiding my guilty secret.'

'Well, you nearly had your first lesson.' James was still laughing.

'Shut up. I'm taking lessons. I want my pilot's licence.'

Anne drove on, listening to them ribbing each other, chatting about swimming, flying. Her boldness had gone, but the joy had come back.

Margaret and Alex were sitting watching cricket on television when they got back. They had drinks in their hands.

'We were just beginning to wonder what had happened to cook,' Margaret said. Her eyes were brilliant. She looked beautiful. Anne's heart overflowed with sisterly pride.

'She was trying to drown us on the tide road to the Point.' James was at the drinks table.

'Making it three less for dinner,' Ben said. Alex guffawed.

'What would you like after that ordeal?' James asked Ben.

'Whatever's handiest.'

'We have the lot,' Alex said.

'White wine, if I may.'

'Annie?'

'Sherry.'

'Did you really get stuck?' Alex looked interested, not alarmed.

'Only for a second. I only did it to amuse.' The phrase sounded familiar to her.

'Anne's a good driver,' Alex told Margaret, as if he were glad to find something to praise. 'Damned good. Trust her anywhere.' He was too fervent. He had probably knocked back a few. She caught Ben's eye, and he put a pleading, lost dog look on his face. *Forgive me...*

'You wouldn't have thought so half an hour ago,' James said, still holding on to his prejudices.

'But she is, she is!' Margaret was also too fervent. 'Not like poor stupid me.'

'But you have other attributes,' James replied.

Now that Anne looked at Alex, his eyes

were brilliant too, well, not brilliant—they were too deepset for that—but different. Had they been knocking back the gin while they waited?

'I'll take this into the kitchen,' she said, lifting her glass, 'and get started. Don't anyone come to help me.'

'Anne's a darned good cook,' Alex said, excelling himself.

'Is there any end to my virtues?' Yes, there was a distinct aura, an atmosphere, or was it that *she* felt different, because of the joy?

Chapter Seven

She attempted to get back to what she called normal living the following week. She did an extra morning session at the Citizens' Advice Bureau because a colleague was on holiday, and she buried herself in the problems of the people who consulted her.

It gave her, she told herself, a sense of proportion when she listened to distraught couples who had started off so well and were now hopelessly in debt. It was unfair to categorize them as being foolish spenders, or of trying to get a quart out of a pint pot. Indirectly it was people like herself, living in easy luxury in houses which were fully paid up, cars which were bought outright, who set false standards.

And why even criticize in her own mind the young girl living with her common law husband and pregnant to another man? Didn't *she* have lustful thoughts about Ben while she lay in bed beside Alex? She could tell herself it was only a tenderness she felt for him, the attraction of youth for middle-age, the feeling she had for James transferred to a non-blood relation, then she would remind herself of the tug of disappointment she had felt when Ben had said, 'You're the first woman whose mind I have wanted to get into instead of her body.'

She entertained the Harrisons, excelled herself in the kitchen with her Beef Wellington and spinach pancakes, listened politely but with insufferable boredom to Jean Harrison, when they were upstairs in her bedroom after the meal, to let the men have a little 'get-together' over their brandy.

She parried Jean's questions about her own sex life while listening with polite amazement to her revelations about what went on in the Harrison's nuptial bed.

'Of course, I wouldn't tell anyone but you, Anne, but we're old friends and you keep your mouth shut, not like some, but the things he asks me to do! It's only in the last few years. Male menopause, Barbara Jenkins calls it. As if he'd become fed up with the usual stuff, which at least didn't take so long. I sometimes ask myself if those men, when they're away on their business trips, don't learn a few tricks from "the ladies",' heavy emphasis, 'they meet, probably in bars. Or who are laid on. Some firms lay them on now, you know. I've never pretended Frank doesn't have his fling, they all do, so will Alex, I bet. He's the aggressive type they like, has all the charm of a...'

'Charging bull?'

Jean looked at her in half-tipsy surprise. 'You say the funniest things, Anne. Goodness knows what goes on in that mind of yours!'

'Goodness knows indeed.' She was standing at the wide window looking out on the rippled black of the sea, the twinkling lights on the opposite coastline. Shangri-la. Ben...

The only person whom Jean Harrison didn't talk about was their mentally-retarded son who had been 'put away for his own good' when he was eight. It wasn't lack of feeling, she was sure. People didn't talk about what hurt them most.

'Let's go down and have some coffee,' Anne said, putting her arm round the woman as they went out of the room together. The tenderness in her spilled out. She remembered the bitter tears, the hand-wringing and the anguished telephone calls when the little boy had been put in a home. 'It's only for his own good, isn't it, Anne?'

So why couldn't she feel tenderness for her sister, Margaret? But then, she thought, giving Jean a reassuring pat and sending her in to join the men, she needed me, came to me for help. Margaret never does.

Ben rang her towards the end of the week. 'I ought to have telephoned earlier to thank you for that super weekend, but I've been in London.'

'There was no need.' But it was no good. His voice had her by the throat again, making her speak huskily. There was a bright river of sensation running through her.

'Oh, but there was. I enjoyed it so much, especially that walk to the other shore on that strange, shaggy piece of land, a broken biscuit piece of land.' The poetry must come from his Welshness.

'It was the rabbit you enjoyed.' She knew her voice had taken on a new tone.

'And you.'

'Don't go over the top,' she said, laughing coquettishly and disgusting herself.

'Oh, I'm not. It's the truth. And I enjoyed the trauma on the ford. Your coolness against my fear. I'm an arrant coward, really.' *Cow-ard, re-ally.* 'Are you coming to Manchester soon?'

'As a matter of fact I am.' She didn't even pretend to be doubtful. 'I have to shop. I have to choose new wallpaper for a bedroom and there's no choice here to speak of.' The necessity had just arisen.

'Could you stay up and I'll give you dinner?'

'Oh, no, that's impossible.' She immediately regretted her refusal. 'I have to be back for Alex.' That made her sound like a serf, an acolyte, a nothing.

'Don't you ever stay overnight with your sister?'

'Sometimes.' Hardly ever. 'But I'm doing extra duty at the Citizens' Advice Bureau because of holidays and I have to be there in the mornings.'

'What a busy person you are.' *Bus-y.* The broken-backed inflection made her dizzy. She shook her head to clear it.

'No, no, it's a matter of organization to make me *think* of myself as a busy person. And so that other people will.'

'Do you still go to your poetry class?'

'Yes. That's not organization. That's pure pleasure.'

'I have a present for you. A thank-you present.'

'How nice. Well, perhaps I could meet you for a coffee. It would save you postage.' The tinkling laugh was quite unlike her. She knew, of course, what the present would be. But *whose* poems?

'No, I insist on lunch.'

'Well, all right, a quickie.' Where did she get those words? She never said a 'quickie'.

'You like Chinese food, don't you?'

'How do you know?'

'I've watched you. You're a picky eater. We'll pick at the contents of a few bowls together.' He named a restaurant near the car park in Mosley Street, and she said that would be fine but it would have to be...this time she didn't say a quickie, no longer than an hour.

He met her in the darkened foyer of the restaurant and his dark suit merged into the background, highlighted his white shirt. His hair was sleekly brushed, he looked like a rising young executive, all his weekend casualness gone. She fell in love with him at sight, straight in, like a high, clean dive. It had the same knife-like, clean-cut sensation.

'You look very sophisticated today,' he said, when they were seated. 'It makes you look even more feminine, by contrast.' She was glad of the round-necked, buttoned jacket whose simple severity had cost a lot of money and had demanded the purchase of a plain black skirt in Marks and Spencers to counter the extravagance.

'So do you,' she said, unfolding her napkin to show she was in a hurry. 'Now I know two of you.'

'Which do you like better?' His grin was mischievous, almost whiter than the shirt.

'I'll tell you at the end of the lunch.'

'Perhaps it depends on that.' He put a largish envelope on the table. It was the book of poems, of course. 'Open it while we're waiting.'

She did, and saw the title, *Archy's Life of Mehitabel*. She looked at him, knowing her eyes were shining in a childish fashion, not at all in keeping with the sophisticated jacket.

'Look at the inscription.'

She opened the slim book. He had written, 'In memory of a cat she loved.'

She closed her eyes and held herself rigid for a moment, suffering deeply, then reopened them, blinking. 'Don't make me cry in a Chinese restaurant. They wouldn't like it.'

'I've never admired impassivity. That's what makes you so childlike. You haven't acquired a mask yet.'

'And I try *so* hard.' The waiter had presented her with a menu. She had to stretch out her arms to hold it. She raised it to cover her face. When it was in place again, her mouth pulled into a middle-aged shape, her eyes cool, she said, 'You order and we'll share, but nothing crispy fried. Duck skin is loaded with fat, did you know?'

'Yes, but forbidden sweets are sweeter.' His white grin was naughty, like James's.

Over the small portion he helped himself to, the plain noodles, the prawns, the snow peas, he said, 'I told you about me the last time we met. Now you have to tell me about you.'

'Here I am,' she said smiling at him, 'this is me. You said you could read my face like a book or something like that, that's me, not quite sure of me, waiting to grow into myself.'

'Waiting to grow into yourself?' His smile was tender, not naughty. 'How did you get on with your sister when you were a little girl?'

'Ah,' she said, 'I wonder what made you ask. I admired her, and tried to copy her. I'm trying to come to terms with the fact that I'm better to be me. I have a photograph of us together, eight and ten. An old aunt gave it to me. Some day I may show it to you. It says everything. It's not only our minds which are formed when we're young. It's our bodies, *by* our minds, I expect, the way we hold our heads, put our feet, our arms, how we stand. She was always bigger than me, not fatter, just made on a bigger scale. So is everything she does. Grander, more spectacular. I've had to grow out of feeling wimpish beside her.'

'I'd never call you wimpish, rather, feminine. I won't call you "sweet" because that word has been debased beyond speaking about. A secret... Did you know your son admires you greatly?' She was overwhelmingly pleased, as if she had received an accolade.

'Oh, James and I have the hang of each other. I let him go quicker than Alex did. That's where I scored.'

'Well, of course, you and your husband are very different.'

'Yes,' she said, and speared a prawn on a chopstick.

'Have I put my foot in it?' He wasn't subtle enough. Her age gave her the advantage.

'No, but you might. It sounded as if you were fishing.' She twirled the prawn on her chopstick.

'He wouldn't mind you having lunch with me, would he?'

'If I said I had met one of James's friends, no, he wouldn't mind, but if he thought it was a pre-arranged thing...' She raised her eyes to him and found that he was looking at her intently, found that she couldn't take her eyes away. Caught in a net, she thought, of my own choosing. Hazel eyes, she noticed, thickly lashed, already a few wrinkles. *Good.* Men aged quicker than women.

'I love you,' he said lightly. His lightness broke the spell.

'And I love you,' she said as lightly. 'I love all James's friends.'

'But you knew me before I knew James.'

'Now you're being too clever. Naughty!' Her mouth turned down in a smile.

'Don't be motherly. You're not at all motherly, Anne. You've put it behind you, almost with relief. You have a lot of living to do now.'

'Have I? Tell me, so that I can go out and begin.'

'Get to know me better for a start. Is your husband going away soon?'

'Yes,' she said calmly, looking at him. 'He's always going away. Or coming back.'

'Is he going away soon?'

'Yes.'

'Like when?'

'Next Wednesday. To Huddersfield first, I think.'

'You won't go with him?'

'Not to Huddersfield.' She shrugged. 'Too woolly.'

'When will he come home?'

'In a week's time, probably.'

'Will he be away over the weekend?'

'Most likely. Why all the questions?'

'Would you show me the Lakes that Sunday? I'd promise to drive straight back again. I get the hots for the Lakes.'

The hots? She accepted the hots. 'Why not?' She was amazed at her calmness, her boldness. It was as if she had jumped into Margaret's skin. 'A week on Sunday? Shall we go in separate cars?'

'Why not?' He was imitating her. 'If it pleases your suburban conscience. Do you know that bridge at Levens Hall on the A6?'

'Who doesn't?'

'Right. Eleven a.m, pub lunch somewhere and then you can be my guide. We could stash your car in Windermere. Will you lay on a fine day as well?'

'Why not?' she said, and they were both laughing at each other, chopsticks poised, when they heard a female voice above them.

'Ben! So *this* is where you hang out! Who'd have thought it?'

He looked up, then jumped up. 'Jenny! We share the same tastes, or is someone standing you lunch? No, I can't believe it!'

'Strange as it may seem. He's gone to get the car.' She looked pointedly at Anne.

'Anne Garrett,' he said. 'An old family friend.'

'Hello,' Anne said.

'Jennifer Adamson. Don't expect any of the civilities from Ben! Oh, there's my man waiting at the door. Must run.'

'Don't keep him waiting,' Ben said. *'Ciao.'* He raised his eyebrows at Anne as he sat down again.

'Short and sweet,' Anne remarked. She

109

had been pretty, and confident. Could she have been the girl he had told her about, the one he'd been shacked up with?

'She works with Judith in the Design Department. A nice kid.'

She nodded, her pleasure gone. The easiness and rapport between Ben and the girl was that of youth. In spite of her sophisticated jacket she felt dowdy and out of place. And she had made a dreadful mistake in agreeing to see him again. Boldness didn't suit her. 'I'll have to skip coffee.' She looked at her watch.

'It was tea.' He indicated the teapot on the table which had been placed there although they were drinking wine.

'Whatever. I must get on with my shopping.' She lifted the book in its envelope from the table and confidence flowed back to her at the feel of its hard cover. 'Thank you for this. And the lunch.'

'Thank you for agreeing to come. And thank you for promising to show me the Lakes.'

'That was a joke, really.'

'It wasn't to me.'

'Well, if nothing else crops up...for either of us.'

'Of course,' he said, smiling at her. 'It won't, at least not for me.'

Chapter Eight

Alex went off on a tour around the Yorkshire stone quarries in the middle of the next week, as she had said to Ben. He didn't suggest she should accompany him. 'I suppose you're busy with all your stuff...' This was how he generally referred to her voluntary work. 'And you don't seem to feel lonely in the house.'

'No,' she said, 'I'm never lonely.' She felt kindly disposed towards him. A marriage of over twenty years had to stand for something, she told herself, at the same time noticing, as she stood in the hall with him, how he filled his suit to the last inch.

She felt a wave of affection for him. He had never ill-treated her, (only Melissa, her cat, and that had been an accident, he said), and he had been a good provider. Everyone said how lucky she was to have such a handsome, successful man for a husband. She flicked a speck of dust from the collar of his well-cut, well-filled blue suit.

'Aren't you ever afraid in the house?' He'd been reading the local rag about snoopers, thieves, muggers, rapists—they could do as well up here as in London, it inferred.

'No,' she said, 'there's the sea.'

He looked at her with the puzzled, slightly pitying expression which he had begun to assume recently for her.

'What good would the sea do you for God's sake, if you were burgled? Or raped?'

'Oh, Alex, there's the security system.' He had gone to a great deal of expense to have it connected to the police station. She was included with his depot as a tax reduction.

'I know. It's the very latest. Maybe we should have a dog?'

'No animals,' she said firmly, remembering the feel of her cat's broken back in her arms, a fur bag of broken bones, remembering the questioning, pitiful face it had raised to her as its eyes glazed.

'I'll finish up in Manchester,' he said. 'Maybe I'll look in and see that young man, Davies. He's working out a scheme for me for the office.'

'Are you going to give him the contract?'

'If the price suits me I will. He's bright, but they say, never trust a Welshman.'

'Taffy was a Welshman...' That was the colour of his eyes. 'So you won't be back until after the weekend?'

'No. Let's see.' He took out a diary. 'This is Wednesday. There's Graingers, then Dale Yorkshire Stone... I'll spend the weekend with them, Ted Smethurst's an old pal, then I'll get to Manchester at the beginning of the week. Back a week from today.' He took her in his arms and she felt his solidity against her. And there was a woody scent from him. 'Pour l'Homme'. She had given it to him for Christmas. It was like being clasped by an oak tree.

'You're a cool customer, Anne,' he said, 'give me a kiss.' She held up her face and one of his hands slid down her back and pressed against her buttocks, then gave them a smart little slap. It was a familiar action.

'Have a good time,' she said, 'but not too good.' That felt like a habitual remark.

'Same goes for you.' He looked at her when he released her as if he was still puzzled.

She passed the remainder of the week being 'bus-*y*', as Ben had said. Most of Saturday she spent at the newly-opened health farm nearby, having a massage, sauna, being coiffured and manicured. She had her hair cut above her ears and invested in large gold earrings. 'A change is as good as a holiday,' the girl assistant

113

said. She wasn't sure.

It made her look different, but then it was a different woman who was going to spend a day with Ben Davies, eighteen years her junior. The Anne of a year ago wouldn't have recognized her.

He was sitting in his car at the lay-by near the bridge, and when she drew up in front of him he got out, walked towards her, put his face in the open window and kissed her. She drew back. The kiss landed on her nose. 'Good-morning,' he said, 'You ordered a good day.'

'Yes, the right kind of Lakeland day,' she was breezy, like the day, 'plenty of clouds, occasional sunshine. If it's too hot the haze kills the view.' She knew she was blushing slightly from the kiss, and that the blush would show more because of her shorter hair. 'Do you like my hair?' she said, to cover her confusion.

He considered, head on one side. 'It's different, but thank God your face is the same.'

'That's that, then.' She stretched herself away from the wheel to ease her back. 'I'll lead on to Bowness and we'll park one of the cars there. Right?' It didn't seem right. It felt like an assignation.

She drove up the Lyth Valley, hoping he would notice its gentle beauty, then over the hill road which dropped down

114

to the Lake. She saw him flashing her, and drew in. He came up to her car. 'That's a decent-looking pub we passed, with a car park. Supposing we eat early and leave your car there?'

'Okay.' She made it sound businesslike. 'Bowness is a disaster area just now.'

It was all right once they were sitting across from each other at the oak bench with their lagers and their beef sandwiches. The pattern had been set at the Chinese restaurant in Manchester.

He was back in his casual wear, a light blouson and unbuttoned shirt, and when the owner had gone he took her hands. 'This is smashing. I've been thinking of it for days. Have you?'

'No, I've been too bus-*y*.' She mocked him, and he laughed.

'And at the last moment I had a telephone call. My aunt's housekeeper rang to tell me she was worried about her. I nearly put you off and went to see her.'

'So now I've made you feel guilty?'

'No, I'm just telling you. The housekeeper is fussy, but Aunt Elspeth isn't. It's just that she's getting old.'

'Aren't we all?'

She couldn't resist it. 'You're just a young thing.'

'That's because I want to keep level with

you. Sometimes when you open your eyes wide and listen in that intent way you have, I feel like Old Father Time.'

'Don't go on about ages,' Anne replied.

'You're one to talk. I just want you to know I don't feel younger, *or* older. However long or short a time it's taken us, we're at the same stage now.'

'Except that I have a grown-up son.'

'You're untouched by it.'

She shook her head. Now he was younger. 'The father of that son is coming to see you at the beginning of the week. Will you tell him you met me?'

'Will you?'

'No. I know Alex.'

'I'll benefit from your experience then. We'll just talk business. Now, eat up your beef sandwich and let's pretend this is a desert island and there are only the two of us...'

Her eyes were on him again as he was speaking. He caught her at it and she lowered them, opened the sandwich and examined it, scraped at the streaky fat with her fork. Alex preferred his beef rimmed with fat, and pink. He didn't like what he called sandwiches of cardboard.

She was the navigator when they got into his car afterwards. She directed him across the ferry to the west shore and then on to Near Sawrey and Hill Top Farm

116

because he wanted to remind himself of his childhood and Beatrix Potter's cottage.

'Did you really like it?' she asked. 'Arthur Ransome, yes, but, bunnies?'

'Loved it. There's a feminine streak in me, I think. Perhaps my mother wanted a little girl. I *drooled* over their tea parties, and the baby bunnies in their cradle. I'm a real Mrs Tiggy Winkle.'

'I thought you would have been a Johnny Town Mouse, at least. James couldn't bear it. He called it twee. He couldn't get away fast enough.'

'I'm a miniaturist. When I make enough money I'm going to collect things. I haven't decided what yet. I prowl about junk shops when I have time.'

'I'm not acquisitive. I'm in the stand-and-stare category. This countryside here...' She swept her arm around. She couldn't begin to convey to him what it meant to her. 'Let's leave the car and walk.'

It seemed that they strolled rather than walked for hours, not following any plan, but footpaths which led across fields and through copses as they presented themselves. They disturbed sheep resting against stone walls, they sat at becks on mossy boulders, they passed isolated farms, and all the time while they talked she was absorbing the landscape, the sky with its high sailing clouds, the far gleam of the

117

lake when they stopped to rest at a wooden gate. All the time she felt joy surging in her so strongly that she thought she would die of it. The Lakes always lifted her spirit, but this was more, a completeness, a conviction that she would look back on this day as the happiest in her life.

They talked. She had never met anyone in her life with whom she talked so easily. Perhaps as he had said it was the feminine streak in him. They talked of themselves chiefly, there was nothing intellectual, or political, or even topical, it was an exploration of each other's psyches, a therapeutic experience.

'Only children always want to talk about themselves,' she said. 'I've noticed that in James, an innocent kind of arrogance.'

'And you always talk of yourself in relation to your sister. It's as if you didn't have a personality of your own when you were young.'

'That's almost true. I expect if you have lots of brothers and sisters you have the corners rubbed off, but if there's only one brother or sister, one or the other will be the dominant.'

They walked with his arm loosely round her waist. Sometimes when they laughed together he hugged her close to his side as if he felt the joy too, this steady river of delight.

118

About six o'clock, he said, 'Let's find a hotel where we can have a drink and something to eat.'

She shook her head, smiling. She had kept this surprise to herself. 'I baked a salmon quiche and I've fruit and cheese and wine and two chairs. We could sit at the shore at Esthwaite and have a picnic.'

'You're wonderful,' he said. 'I couldn't resist your quiche.'

'Wait till you taste it.'

She was light-footed when they parked and scrambled down to the shore of the lake, she carrying the picnic basket, he the two chairs. He set them up a yard from the water while she spread out the picnic on a flat boulder. She gave him the bottle and a corkscrew and sat down in a chair. 'I've cooked the meal,' she said, 'now you can wait on me.'

The wind had gone now, and the little lake was calmly beautiful, the only ripple on its surface being made by the coot and moorhens lazily swimming about. The water weeds in the shallows were still, except when disturbed by a passing wildfowl. She remembered reading, with her capacity for gathering unusual pieces of information, that there was a rare variety of waterweed at Esthwaite. She could even remember its Latin name, *Eloden nuttallii*.

119

She kept quiet about it now. Nothing was more 'ancient', as James would say, than imparting information.

Far away, near the reeds on the opposite bank she could see a couple of mute swans. One was swimming about purposefully, almost aggressively, as if it resented their coming, infringing on their territorial rights. The other one was placid, a typical married couple.

'Perfect, isn't it?' Ben said, 'Look at those white houses nestling among the fields on the opposite bank. I'd like to live there with you, run down in the early morning sun to bathe...'

' "...gilds gloriously the bare feet that run to bathe..." You wouldn't be very popular with the National Trust,' Anne remarked.

'Who was the poet?'

'Rupert Brook. He's not very popular either. It's a crime to be too sweet nowadays. There should be bitterness.'

He dismissed that, raising his shoulders comically. 'This quiche is absolutely smashing! Could I have another slice please?'

'Help yourself.' Bitterness she didn't approve of either. Poignancy—that was a different cup of tea. There was poignancy in sitting here in this evening calmness, this evening pinkness, the trees and houses on the other shore swam in the pinkness, the two swans were startingly white in it. She noticed that one had left its partner and was in the middle of the lake.

'Do you like the wine?' she said. It was well down. She should have brought two bottles.

'Delicious. Everything's delicious. This is a time warp. Where has everyone gone?'

'Eating in hotels and restaurants, I expect. We seem to be the only picnickers.' Now she didn't want to talk. They had talked themselves dry. As well as the poignancy, there was a sadness. Life was passing for her. Ben would pass out of it too. This was simply a dalliance for him, a transient wish to see how a relationship such as theirs would work, an experiment. Or did he feel the poignancy as well?

She looked at him. His profile was contemplative. Where were his thoughts? Were they with some girl in Manchester, or his computers, or was he a hedonist who simply enjoyed the present? He had said it was a time warp. Did he include her in it?

'The pinkness has gone,' he said. 'Look how the little ducks are black against the paleness of the lake.' She didn't correct him and say they were moorhens. 'The only white thing is that swan. I say, it's coming towards us at a hell of a lick!'

He was right. The huge bird seemed to

have materialized only a few yards away from them. They were both delighted, laughing at each other, saying, 'Imagine it coming over to see us, imagine...!'

The bird stood up in the shallow water, flapping its great wings, and waddled to the shore, all its gracefulness gone, belligerence in its place. It opened its yellow beak and reared its head on its sinewy neck. It had become malevolent, its little black eyes gleamed wickedly.

'What's wrong with it?' Ben said. He stopped eating, put his glass down.

'It resents us being here. Or maybe it's the salmon in the quiche—a change from perch or roach. Look, there's a piece left. Throw it to it.'

He got up quickly from his chair, and taking the slice of quiche from the cardboard tray, threw it in the swan's direction. Anne got up too. The swan's wings looked powerful from close-up. It could upset her chair with her sitting in it quite easily.

The quiche disappeared in a few quick snaps, but instead of going back into the water, appeased, it advanced on Ben, wings flapping ferociously, beak open, little eyes seemingly black with hate. The beautiful neck was humped like a snake about to strike.

'Let's get out of this,' Ben said. He

looked agitated. His voice shook. He retreated a few paces, stumbling in his haste, then turning on his heels, scrambled up the small bank into the coppice between them and the road. She watched, saw the bare band of skin between his T-shirt and the top of his jeans, the beginning of the anal fold, and had to smother her laughter.

Some errant knight, leaving her to face the music! Memories came back to her of James, a small boy, having to be protected from barking dogs in farms, or cows which grazed too near him. The swan wasn't interested in her. It stood hissing after Ben's retreating back, then turning, as if in disgust, waddled slowly into the water, leaving its ugliness behind like a discarded snakeskin, and sailed gracefully away.

Ben came back, red-faced. 'My God, that was frightening! I didn't give you a thought!' He laughed. 'It was every man for himself. Weren't *you* frightened?'

'No, it wasn't after me. You were the purveyor of the goodies. I think it was greedy rather than ferocious.'

'You were as cool as cucumber.' He was sheepish. She wanted to hug him.

'It's strange, I'm shy, but not timid.' She looked at him, still smiling, and something in her eyes, perhaps, made him come towards her and take her in his arms. 'Some protector, me!'

'Oh, I can run very fast when it's necessary.' She looked up at him, and his mouth came down on hers, not a light kiss this time. His voice was thick when he released her. 'Let's pack up and go somewhere...'

'I should be going home.'

'Forget about that.' He was brusque. He folded the chairs and stowed away the remains of the picnic. They had emptied the bottle. He shook it and put it in the picnic basket as well. 'Come on.' His voice was rough, urgent.

'What are you talking about?' Her voice was as rough as his, 'Go somewhere...'

'A hotel, a bloody B & B, anywhere I can have you. You know you want it. You kissed me, wanting it.'

He wants to show me what a brave boy he is in spite of the swan, she thought, surprised at how her heart raced. Of course she wanted it. She wanted to kiss and kiss and go on from kissing to something really good, something she hadn't experienced with Alex for years. Had she ever experienced it?

She said. 'I'm not staying away all night. Besides, my car is at that pub. Had you forgotten?'

'I want you, Anne. That bloody bird made me realize it.' Was she to be his

Leda? 'We'll talk about it on the way.' He was helping her solicitously up the slope, almost too solicitously. She wasn't his *mother,* for God's sake.

He drove swiftly. It was dark now. They didn't cross the ferry this time, but took the lakeside road to Newby Bridge and then backtracked to the hill road, and the pub. He didn't speak, but occasionally his hand stroked her knee and thigh to keep her on the boil, she thought. Half of her was on fire, the other half didn't believe in the situation. It concerned two other people.

Her car was still there. She looked at her watch. Nine o'clock now. In spite of having said they would talk on the way, they hadn't, and she in any case had nothing to say. All she knew was that at some point she had to announce she was driving home. She wasn't staying out all night with him. Things had gone far enough. Maybe it *had* been that bloody bird.

'You could have a drink at least,' he said, as if he were reading her thoughts. 'We owe it to the publican.'

'All right.' If you don't at least talk, she thought, you'll regret it until the end of your life. Her brows were knitted in concentration. And you can't take him home. It's Alex's house. There's a limit...

The bar was snug, as bars should be,

there was even a token fire in spite of the fine day it had been. 'I know what you need after that fracas,' Ben said, 'a brandy.' How Jamesian, she thought, her brows clearing, how brave after the event.

'What fracas?' she said sweetly.

'You know, that great big bloody bird frightening us.

'Frightening us,' she agreed, loving him to death. 'All right, a brandy would be very nice, thank you.'

It dulled her senses, and her agitation, but not her thoughts. Would she spoil something if she *did* spend the night with him? She loved him as it was, his sweetness, his croaky voice, his boyishness, loved him even more for the timidity he had shown. If they made love, became adult together, perhaps they would lose something. She looked around. There were three couples altogether, all of them immersed in each other, one youthful one, one middle-aged one, and their own piebald one. When she met his eyes they were hot. He had the 'hots' for her—the horrible phrase came back. But, then, hadn't she for him? The brandy flamed inside her.

'Anne,' he said, 'Anne...'

She shook her head, waving him away, swallowing because her throat hurt.

'You don't want me?'

'Oh, I *want* you,' she said, 'that's the easy part.'

When the owner came to the table, Ben said casually, 'Have you a room left?'

'Just a back room, sir.' He was amiable, but rushed. If he had looked at her meaningly she would have got up and left. 'It's a busy time.'

'I'll take it.'

She said, not coyly, 'Do you mean you're staying here, even if I don't.'

'Yes.' His face was grim. 'I can't be bothered driving back to Manchester tonight. You'd be all right.'

'What do you mean?'

'Getting yourself home. Your car's outside.'

'Oh, yes, I know the way backwards. Every twist and turn.' Her mood lightened because she suddenly knew she was going to stay. A cowardly drive back alone, full of regrets? The brandy made it easy to decide. 'Whitbarrow Scar. We used to go there for the wild flowers. It's limestone, you know. You get orchids. I once thought of going every season and writing some sort of Nature diary, taking photographs. There are wood anemones and violets and primroses, and then loosestrife and orchids—I said orchids, didn't I...?' She thought of the high places on the Scar, the feeling of being above the world, not even part of it.

'You'd make a good diarist,' he said. 'Pepys.' He was humouring her. She shook her head.

'Or the Edwardian Lady? No, I've never been confessional. Nor bold.'

'Now's the time.'

'My boldness is in my mind. Margaret's is there for all to see. She lives in the high places, when it suits her. Boldly.'

'Your sister again.'

'I'll stay,' she said. She saw his chest rise as he took a deep breath.

It was a twin-bedded room and they undressed and lay down singly. She saw his one-sided smile as he meekly got under his duvet. It was ridiculous. She wasn't even sleepy, nor even desirous, now that they were here. She stretched, tried to get rid of Alex and James, even old Aunt Elspeth. She felt his weight on her bed, and then the naked length of him beside her.

'Luckily we're both thin.'

'Yes, Alex could never have done this. He needs a king-size.'

'For God'sake, don't mention him at a time like this.' He buried his head on her shoulder, laughing, she put her arm under him and it felt natural. He turned and they lay face to face. His eyes were filled with laughter.

'What's the joke?'

He shook his head, his eyes full.

'I'm...fixed up, but if you're afraid or anything you know what to do.'

She saw him draw in his breath, his eyes widen. 'My God, Anne, you're badly in need of this. You're so direct.'

'I'm sorry. Alex doesn't go in for a lot of foreplay. I'm out of the habit.'

His touch brought a shutter down on her mind. All she wanted was him, the way she had never wanted Alex, even when they were first married. She was shivering like a dog, like a bitch, with desire. 'I'm afraid...but I trust you.'

'You should never trust anyone.' He seemed to melt into her. How could one think straight in a situation like this with Ben making ardent, selfish love on top of her? She waited for him like an old-fashioned bride, then grew impatient. Her own boldness surprised her. Was this how Margaret felt all the time, letting herself go, no holds barred? She forgot the quiet, unassuming Anne, ditched her public persona, revelled in the private one.

It was stupendous, it lasted, it repeated itself, she was delighted with herself and incidentally with him. Such great surges of feeling, like the Bay on a stormy night. But when the passion went, the poignancy and the sweetness were there, the little fishing boats returned to the harbour... She was twee, as James would say...she was shy, hiding her face. 'Ridiculous to be shy at my age,' she said.

'Shy but not timid.' He stroked her back. He let out a long sigh. 'What a day, God, what a day-ay-ay!'

'Except for the swan.'

He got rid of the swan. 'What swan? Oh, Anne...'

He had no love language, she noticed. Perhaps that only happened in books. She could hardly know. Alex only grunted, sometimes farted. In her new boldness she could think that, could have said it except that Alex, or the mention of him had been debarred.

'This is where we'll meet,' Ben said next morning when she was sitting in her car. 'I like this pub, rustic, and the grub's good.'

'It wasn't a one-off thing, then?' she joked. Young people didn't sigh and swoon about love nowadays. Just talked about the grub. Both were part of their normal life.

'You know it wasn't.' Now he was the one who sighed and swooned. 'It was special for me. I thought it was for you.'

He grinned, 'Did the earth move?'

'That's Hemingway's copyright. Yes, it was, and it did.' She felt the blood pulsing through her veins at the thought of last night, knew that her eyes and skin were clear and young-looking, as good as a tonic, love. Internal lavage. 'But I hadn't thought...'

'I can't do without you now. Let's meet here again soon. If you can stay over, so much the better, but we must make plans...'

'I can't. Alex's movements are uncertain. And there's my aunt. I'm worried about her, simply because she's so uncomplaining as a rule.' It was the first time since she had left home that she had given her a moment's thought.

'You're making obstacles.'

'No, truly I'm not.' She put her hand on his which was gripping the edge of the window. 'I feel like Lazarus, Lady Lazarus...you raised me from the dead.' She saw his unease. 'I'll phone you as soon as I can. I have your number. It was on your letter.'

'Right, but don't make it too long.' He bent and kissed her through the open window, and she felt the faint scraping on her chin from his beard. Young men's beards grew quicker. 'I shan't be able to wait.' He said 'shan't' with a deep vowel, reminding her of his Welshness.

She drove home up and down the switchback road, past Whitbarrow Scar, (and thought she must take him there some day), to the main road and into the traffic, where she weaved skilfully—and boldly—through it.

Chapter Nine

The house looked different. She could hardly bear the light in the kitchen which was gleaming white as a protest against all the folksy pine kitchens her friends had.

She went out to the garden and picked an armful of roses, her lovely 'Dapple Dawn' because she liked single blooms. She regretted she hadn't a herbaceous border which would have supplied some delphiniums to mix with them, but it was too windswept on their high ground. She took pleasure in arranging the roses in several vases. A house was like a blind man until it had flowers in it.

There was a postcard lying in the hall which had come from Alex, from Wensley, which he must have passed through. It looked a pretty village, typically Yorkshire, with its green and old stone houses. Instead of guilt when she thought of him she experienced an unholy glee. I've done it, she thought, I've got away from him. I've done my own thing, I'm alive again, really alive.

With her coat on she made some tea in the still hurtful white kitchen and sat down at the table. When she finished this she knew what she was going to do. She couldn't bear the thought of sleeping with Alex after Ben. Not immediately. She would telephone Aunt Elspeth and say she was coming to see her. Poor Aunt Elspeth. She had never known love. She would take her to the Planetarium—she was an amateur astronomer and admired Patrick Moore. That had been before the photography classes, and now Don McCullen had taken his place. Aunt Elspeth had explained that Mr Cholmondley-Brooks admired the truthfulness of Don McCullen, so different from the Society photographers.

She would take her up to town to have tea at Fortnum and Masons, to Whipsnade to see the animals. She would get lots of photographs there, and animals in captivity were just bearable at Whipsnade. Immediately she had drunk her tea she would telephone the Citizens' Advice Bureau to say she could not come this week. She was going to nurse a sick aunt. The telephone rang.

It will be Alex, she thought, getting up quickly. He'll want to check up on me. Or, her heart beat faster, perhaps Ben had arrived in Manchester already and was telephoning from his flat. What was it like. A city mews flat, surrounded by buildings, not much sunlight nor air. You had to forego all that if you lived in cities.

The voice had a rough edge to it, although female, it was Mrs Crosswaite, Aunt Elspeth's housekeeper. Now there was guilt. She should have telephoned before she went to meet Ben. 'Yes, Mrs Crosswaite,' she said. 'What is it?'

'I have tried and tried to get you, Mrs Garrett.' There was a faint reproach in the tone. 'The doctor's just left. Your aunt has died, quite suddenly. It was her heart. Oh, she did want to see you!'

'Oh, no! I can't believe it! I'm so sorry. I had to be away. I was just going to ring you.'

'One minute she was there, and the next she was gone. I can't believe it either. The doctor said she didn't suffer, but she wanted to see you, oh, yes, she did. "Get Anne," she said when she was poorly, before...she must have known she was going to go.'

'Have you telephoned any of her friends?' The guilt was making it difficult to speak, and with it a real sorrow for that aunt with all her hobbies, her photography, her astronomy, her girls. Snuffed out.

'Yes, I've let them know, but they're all old. They don't want to come to the house. But they'll turn out for the funeral. They dress up for them...'

'I'll come right away. You need someone with you. I was planning to come in any case.'

'I saw my own husband dying, Mrs Garrett. It isn't the first time for me. But I'm older now, can't stand up to it so well.'

'I'll drive down right away. I haven't even my coat off. My husband isn't at home but I'll leave a note.'

'Well, it's good of you. I hate to put you out. If only you had seen her earlier, but it wasn't to be...' The rough voice broke.

'Go and have a little rest. I'll be with you sometime in the afternoon.' A bit late to be purposeful, she told herself, all the joy gone out of her.

She wrote a brief note for Alex. 'Aunt Elspeth has died suddenly. Have gone down to arrange the funeral. Will telephone you. Love, Anne,' and propped it up on the mantelpiece. Would it give him a fright when he saw the envelope, wonder for a brief moment if she had left him? No, not Alex, she decided. He had no imagination.

She did the journey in four hours, not stopping. She enjoyed motorways. She was bold on the road but not careless. Here the masculinity in her temperament surfaced, whereas Ben admitted to having a feminine streak. They complemented each other, she thought.

She nibbled at some chocolate she had put in the car and kept the radio on all the time as a background to her thoughts. I knew right away there was something special between us... Her mind was suddenly full of him, ardent, no subterfuge, his needs coming first, not gentle—who wanted a young man to be gentle—arms like steel but remembering her halfway through and saying quaintly, 'Is it all right for you, Anne?' Politely. 'Is this how you like it, Anne?' Alex never asked that. She could take it or leave it, she was his property, wasn't she, bought and paid for, so to speak, the wife, there to be wifely when he needed her.

She reproached herself for having a mind filled with Ben at this time. Aunt Elspeth was dead and wasn't able to appreciate her fine gesture. It should have been made when she was still alive. She didn't like herself very much.

When she drove through St Albans she was struck as always by its cosiness, its quaintness, its smugness, its southerness. Its brick houses with their pargeted fronts were self-consciously beautiful as if flaunting their heritage and you are being grudging, she told herself. But the streets on the whole were narrower and hillier than at home, as if space was at a premium, although in fairness that could not be said about the serene precincts of the Abbey where Aunt Elspeth had so loved to walk. Never again...

The chief difference, she told herself, driving towards Fishpool Street is that St Albans is a composite entity bounded on four sides, whereas my bay is open-ended. From Aunt Elspeth's sitting-room above the cobbled pavement *her* vision had been bounded by the houses opposite. But I can breathe at home, she thought, I can stretch my eyes as far as they can see, there is a vastness, a huge dome of sky, I can see what's happening in it, read the weather from the clouds, see the use the birds make of it, I can stretch out my arms and know they won't touch anything on either side.

Mrs Crosswaite had tea ready for her, the old Crown Derby tea set, the crocheted teacloth, the Queen Anne teapot. She wondered if she would like to see her aunt first. She evidently expected it, and Anne, concurring, got up and walked fearfully through the door which she held open for her.

At almost forty-three she had never seen a dead person before. In the Hospice many were hovering on the edge of it and death was in their eyes, but helpers were kept away discreetly at the end. She found it poignant, the sudden, sleight-of-hand disappearance of a patient she had grown fond of, the bed smoothed, such a well-ordered departure. She likened it in her mind to the parting and closing of the Red Sea by Moses.

Aunt Elspeth lay on her back, her large nose pointing to the ceiling, her mouth relaxed, so different from its primness when she had been alive. She looked content and not at all reproachful. She had never been one to bear a grudge, had always been grateful for her 'little breaks'.

Give her a kiss, the other Anne inside her said, the bossy one, you're full of love. She bent down. The lips were cold, but when she straightened, the mouth was still relaxed, almost smiling, a generous mouth, the true mouth of Aunt Elspeth, released at last from its everyday primness.

'So sudden,' she said, looking down on her like a friend as well as a niece. The quick and the dead. The words came to her. Here in this quiet room she could relive the liveliness of Ben's lovemaking, like a playful puppy, biting and licking and liking to be bitten and licked. She had such a rush of feeling standing in the silent room that it seemed sacrilege to remain there with its already faint smell of decay.

This was it, then, the quick which was Ben, the dead which was this woman with the relaxed, even beautiful mouth which gave away her secret. She went out and closed the door quietly behind her.

Hold fast to that which is good, she thought in the next day or two as she helped Mrs Crosswaite with the necessary arrangements to have Aunt Elspeth cremated. There was a funeral service first of all in the church. The vicar had called and said that Miss Craig had been a generous giver although not a regular attender. 'Quirky', was how he put it, but with a good heart. She was always touched by any mention of children in need.

She telephoned 'the girls', she saw that the necessary announcements were made, she telephoned home and got Alex, newly returned from his trip that evening, Wednesday, as he had said.

Yes, he had netted a few orders and had had a pleasant weekend in the Yorkshire Dales, found a grand little pub. Cheerful landlord, kept good beer.

'I thought you intended to stay with Ted Smethurst.' She heard the slight hesitation.

'No, that fell through. He was abroad,' and then, rushing on, 'but I saw Davies, that computer chap, at his office. I told you I was coming back via Manchester.'

'You didn't see Margaret by any chance?'

'What gave you that idea?' A shade defensively. She wondered why, wondered again why she thought he was being defensive, but was more concerned to appear casual about Ben.

'Are you sure you can't manage to get to Aunt Elspeth's funeral?'

'No, it's impossible.' He often said he was no good at funerals. 'There are a hundred things waiting for me to attend to and I could scarcely get down and back to St Albans in a day. Do you mind?'

'Well, it would have looked nice. I'll come back...a day or two later. I have to see the solicitor, see that Mrs Crosswaite is fixed up all right. I might arrange to meet James since I'm so near London. I'll be back by the weekend.'

'You should have gone by train. It would have been easier for you.'

'No, the car's been invaluable with all the running about to be done, and I hate being dependent on British Rail. Will you eat out?'

'Yes, probably at the canteen in the Depot. Gives any workers who have a grudge a chance to talk to me.' His voice softened. 'But I'll miss your home cooking.' That was as near as he was going to get to an endearment.

She hung up and dialled Margaret's

office number in Manchester. Her voice came loudly, brashly, to her over the ether. 'What is it, Anne? Hope there's nothing wrong.' She rarely telephoned her office.

'It's Aunt Elspeth. She died suddenly. I'm at her house now.'

'Oh, God, the poor old stick. What was it?'

'Heart failure, the best way to go. The funeral is fixed for Thursday. Will you be able to come?'

'Oh, no, I don't think so. I'm a working girl and I've just taken a long weekend off. I can't do as I like, like you.'

'It's not always as I like, Margaret, it's when it's necessary. Alex can't come either. He's been away too.'

'Has he? I hope you're not inferring anything?'

'I just said...'

'Okay. I'm joking. Keep your hair on.' Her voice changed. 'Alex hates funerals. I know. Can't say I blame him. Will you tell the boys?'

'I'll phone James, but would you phone Richard? He might like funerals.'

'What made you say that?'

'I don't know. Why have I to explain everything? I just thought... What about Judith?'

'Oh, she's the last person! Her mind's

full of *anything* but funerals.' Anne hung up.

But as she supervised the removal of Aunt Elspeth's body to a Chapel of Rest which the Funeral Directors had thought appropriate, she was astonished that in this house of death she was filled with a glowing sense of the richness of life and the necessity for her to partake of it.

'Miss Craig wouldn't have liked to be moved until you had said goodbye to her,' Mrs Crosswaite said over a well-earned cup of tea. The rough voice had softened a little, 'But I'm sorry your husband won't be able to come to the funeral. Men give it the right look, black coat and hat. There won't be many there, if any.'

'A man rang up when you were out shopping. He said he ran the Photography Class. I invited him.'

'That would be Mr Cholmondley-Brooks. She thought the world of him. Though I doubt if he could rise to a black coat. More the Bohemian type.'

'He said she was invaluable to the class with her sense of humour.'

'Yes, she always put up a good front, did Miss Craig. "No point in letting life get you down," she said to me often.'

'I've been worrying about your future, Mrs Crosswaite. Have you any plans?'

'Oh, you needn't worry about me. She

always said she would see me all right.' Her mouth folded smugly. 'Then I have a younger brother, he's only sixty, but his wife died last year. "Grace," he's said often, "My home is yours", although he always agreed I should never leave Miss Craig in the lurch.'

Anne telephoned James that evening and told him of his great-aunt's death. 'Could you possibly come up to the funeral?' she asked him. 'Dad can't come.'

'Not possible,' he said, 'I'm in the middle of exams. But Les Girls will be there, won't they? That'll swell the congregation.'

'It was men I was after. A black overcoat here and there.'

'I don't possess one, Annie, so I'm out in any case.'

'And you wouldn't like a visit from me if you're in the middle of exams?'

'Not really. I'd love to see you, but I've got my head wrapped in a towel.'

'Far be it from me to disturb you. Good luck, then.' Children didn't want you, or need you, only when it suited them.

That evening, before Mrs Crosswaite went to visit her brother, she gave Anne a bunch of keys. 'She wanted you to have them. She always said, "Only Anne is to see the contents of my desk." ' Grief was brought to her for the first time, unadulterated grief, untainted with the thoughts of Ben or anyone else. She trusted me, she thought. I'll be gentle with her things.

She sat in the pale-walled sitting-room amongst the gleaming mahogany furniture, the precise ornaments on the mantelpiece, china figurines and silver candlesticks topped by rose pink shades. In one pile on the desk she had gathered the official documents which the solicitor required, in another the ribbon-tied bundles of letters. He would be another black-coated man at the funeral which would please Mrs Crosswaite.

She untied the first bundle reluctantly, and yet prodded by her curiosity. The first letter she took from its envelope was in her own handwriting, and skimming through its contents, she took a shred of comfort that at least she had carried on a correspondence with her aunt. She had always enjoyed writing letters, and Aunt Elspeth had been a woman who treated telephones as stop-gaps only.

'James was confirmed today.' (Strange to be reading one's own words.) 'He didn't want to have it done, said he was a non-believer, but I said it would save him trouble when he wanted a passport.

But that was a joke, really. I wanted to say to him that there's such a thing as the certainty of doubt, but I knew he would have given me an old-fashioned look. Besides there are the everyday benefits if nothing else, a place to sit and be quiet, the singing, and it's an identity card when you die. There, *I*'m being frivolous after accusing James...'

At least I wrote more than 'thank yous', she thought.

She took a letter from the top of another bundle, having noticed the thick masculine handwriting on the envelope. She felt uneasy. They weren't for her eyes. They should be handed over to the solicitor. But Mrs Crosswaite had said that her aunt had said...her eyes were being drawn to the contents while castigating herself.

'Darling, dearest Elspeth,
How can I ever thank you for last night? Joy unconfined. You said immorality was in the air, but I don't regard it as that, adultery on my part certainly, but surely love like ours is never wrong. Those snatched meetings of ours are precious beyond words. I need you beside me more and more.
I shall try to find a suitable time to speak to Constance about us. It isn't easy. My little daughter is at such a

tender age. But surely Constance will understand if I break it gently...'

She put down the letter as if it were a living thing, thinking of that relaxed mouth in death. A loving woman imprisoned in conformity. She remembered her aunt's intense interest in James, in what he said and did as a child, the child perhaps she never had.

She took up another letter, not so reluctantly this time.

'...Constance has been ill. She has some kind of nervous complaint, the doctor says, and she musn't be upset in any way. That's the reason why I haven't been in touch with you. But we all do our best, even Rebecca, my little girl, who wears a white apron with a Red Cross on it which she was given at Christmas.

My little helper...'

Anne opened another letter quickly, grimacing, hoping it would allay the suspicions which were forming in her mind about this fearful lover...who didn't sign his letters. Fearful and careful.

'Yes, I shouldn't have misled you. It was a miscarriage. We so wanted a boy.

Poor Constance, she looked so frail lying there...'

'Oh, no,' Anne muttered, riffling through the letters, careless now, 'I don't like you at all...' None of them were signed. Nor was there an address. Perhaps he had been a solicitor. They were always careful. It couldn't be Aunt Elspeth's own solicitor, could it? The thought was like a firecracker in her head. 'Don't let your imagination run riot...'

'This is a difficult letter to write. The most difficult letter I've ever had to write in my whole life. I have decided to end our relationship. It has been four years now, and during that time you have given me much joy. Dear Elspeth. But I find it impossible to break up my marriage. I know I led you to believe that I would, but it wasn't Constance at first which stopped me but the thought of hurting my dear little Rebecca, and now that there is a new brother it makes it more difficult than ever.

Constance is softer now, easier to live with. I don't know what has brought about the change. Perhaps she sensed there was something wrong with our relationship and tried to make amends.

She had always wanted to give me a son.

As you know, I have an important place in the community. I have a family who will look up to me, I hope, and it's necessary to make myself worthy of their regard. Does this sound cruel? But sometimes one has to be cruel to be kind.

You are a lovely woman, and I console myself with the thought that when we fell in love you were thirty-six, not like a young girl who had been led astray by an older man. I hope you will find happiness with someone else. It would please me if you would accept the enclosed. It is meant in friendship, not as bribery, which I know you will understand. Please don't tear it up.

I hope we can still be friends at least, but you will realize I can never ask you to my home. I thank you from the bottom of my heart for your generosity in everything, and if I can ever do anything for you, please do not hesitate to ask me.

Think of me kindly.'

There was no signature, but written in Aunt Elspeth's hand underneath there were a few lines of poetry by Emily Dickinson. Reading them, Anne thought she too had known the impermanence of joy.

'Nor try to tie the Butterfly,
Nor climb the Bars of Ecstasy,
In insecurity to lie
Is Joy's insuring quality.'
'FINIS'

Should *she* remember them too?

There was something in the bottom of the envelope as she attempted to restore the letter. She poked about with two fingers and brought out a few pieces of paper, a torn cheque. If she pieced them together she might find out who had signed it. She decided against it. At least the relaxed mouth had been explained. Let's hope you got something out of it, Aunt, in your great Dark Room in the Sky...

The funeral guests were lost in the large church. 'The girls' were a bright splash of colour, more suited to a wedding, but there were only two black-coated men, the solicitor and the vicar. Mr Cholmondley-Brooks towered above them, a rangy man with a Jacques Tati look, his hair resting on the collar of his brown velvet jacket. He had a piercing glance. Anne would not have been surprised if he had made the same framing gesture with his hands as Aunt Elspeth.

The last time she had been so closely scrutinized had been by Ben on that first night they had spent together. She had found him leaning on one elbow in the morning looking down at her. 'Anne recumbent with love-bite,' he had said. She had felt the bruise on her lip with her tongue.

The surprise guests were Richard and his friend, Con, not in black overcoats, certainly, but wearing sober leather jackets and jeans. Richard was short and dark, with Margaret's fine eyes, Con tall and fair. She had never been able to decide who was the dominant member of the partnership. It must be a very happy one.

'It's good of you to come, Richard,' she said. 'More than James did. And Con. Hello.'

'I liked the old bird,' Richard said. 'And Con's never been to a funeral. He wants to get into films and they're always having scenes in cemeteries. Surrealistic. He's into Death in a big way, getting people used to the idea.'

'He's come to the right place.' The undertakers' men had arrived in the vestibule and were standing respectfully flanking the coffin.

She would have preferred to attend the service only, but she was acting as chauffeur to Richard and Con—they didn't possess a car—and Con wanted the whole bit, as he put it. She wept when the coffin slid away as the curtains closed, was somehow ashamed of the state of civilization that accepted such a travesty, a coffin on a dumb waiter, canned music, the faint whirr of machinery. But at least she was left with the image of Aunt Elspeth, a revised image, not a spinster, but the lover of some man who hadn't had the courage to sign his name.

She advised Con not to ask if he could see the furnace. 'When you do your film you could have a shot of the tall chimney with its trail of smoke. Symbolism.' He agreed that might be better.

Instead she took them for a drink at The Fighting Cocks before she went back to Aunt Elspeth's house to supervise the tea which Mrs Crosswaite in black gloves would be presiding over. She had felt her own hands very bare beside their blackness as they sat together in the pew.

But it wasn't the only image of Aunt Elspeth she was left with as she found out the following day when Mr Doldren read out the Will to her in his oak-lined casquet of an office... She had become familiar with funereal terminology.

There were legacies to Mrs Crosswaite —Aunt Elspeth had 'seen her all right'

—to James, Margaret, Richard, Judith and herself, and a fair-sized one to the Royal Society for the Prevention of Cruelty to Children.

'That takes care of all her capital,' Mr Doldren said, 'once the funeral expenses and my own are paid.' He looked closely at Anne, perhaps to see if she was registering any disappointment. One of the small rewards of practising law must be to observe the reactions of the mourners when the Will was read out.

'But, of course, there is her house, a very desirable property and its contents. Some fine furniture. It has been left to you, Mrs Garrett.' He paused.

She wished she could have gasped, or even fainted. She had somehow thought of it being included in Aunt Elspeth's capital. She had never seemed to be a wealthy woman, and although a generous giver, had practised small economies constantly. 'That was very generous,' she said.

'If you should think of selling it, which you might well do, we should be happy to act on your behalf.' He was quite a young man, she thought, looking at him, probably in his early thirties. Could his father have been Aunt Elspeth's nameless lover?

'Thank you,' she said. 'I'll have to think about it.' All she could think of at the moment was that Margaret was going to be livid.

'Did you know Miss Craig well?' she asked him.

'Hardly at all. She was my father's client.'

'He would be sorry to hear of her death.'

'I'm afraid he predeceased her.'

'How sad. Is your mother still alive?'

'Yes, but she isn't alone. My unmarried sister lives with her.' *Is her name Rebecca?*

'That will be a comfort to her.' She said her goodbyes and thanks.

She rang Alex that evening to tell him she would be home by the weekend. 'Aunt Elspeth has left the house and contents to me,' she said. She didn't mention the legacy. 'I must stop off on the way back and tell Margaret.'

'My God!' He sounded envious. 'You're in the money! That will fetch a pretty packet down there. Two hundred grand at least.'

'It would make me independent,' she said.

'Is that a threat?' She thought he sounded unsure.

'I'm only joking. Margaret only got a legacy. Two thousand. I know she'll think it's unfair.'

'Yes,' he was still hesitant. 'She *is* your sister. And you get all the furniture as well?'

'House and contents.'

'Some of it may be family stuff.'

'No, it's all hers.'

'Well, just don't do anything at the moment. We'll have a talk about it when you come home. Now, take care coming off the M1 at Manchester. That road is becoming a deathtrap. I know you drive well, but keep your eyes skinned.' He was more caring than usual. Was it because she was now an heiress?

Chapter Ten

Of course, she admitted it to herself, she was deviating to Manchester, not only to see Margaret and tell her about Aunt Elspeth and the Will, but because she might see Ben. When she stopped at the Service Area just before entering the M62, she telephoned both of them. First, Margaret.

'Margaret, I'm on my way home from St Albans. I can stop off and see you. Could you meet me for lunch?'

'How did the funeral go?'

'Fine. I thought you might like to hear about it, and my visit to the solicitor.'

'Oh!' Her voice changed. 'Oh! Yes, I could nip out. What time?' Typically she didn't ask about the Will. She liked drama.

'Twelve-thirty?'

'Right. Meet me in the foyer of the Piccadilly Hotel. I only want a drink and a sandwich. I can park there more easily.'

'Suits me.'

'See you, then. Don't be late.' Margaret hung up.

There had been excitement in her voice,

Anne thought. *I* didn't provoke it, did I? As yet she hadn't made any decision whether she would tell her about Aunt Elspeth's house or not. There would be all kinds of legal formalities to go through, and if it was put on the market, it might take ages to sell. There could be hidden expenses. She didn't know if their aunt had spent much on maintenance. All these considerations made it easier not to be definitive at this point, so she rationalized.

Her heart was beating lightly and quickly when she rang Ben's office number. She cautioned herself. She would have to be circumspect in what she said. Judith worked there. The quickened beat made her feel breathless when she heard his voice, the inflection of which she remembered with such pleasure.

'Ben, it's Anne. I'm in Manchester on my way home. My aunt died. I've been in St Albans.'

'Oh, that's it! I'm sorry about your aunt. I rang you. I knew it was all right, that your husband was still away, but there was no reply.' He made two syllables of 'no' making her even more breathless.

'I had to drive down to arrange the funeral and so on.

Only Margaret's son turned up. Now I'm here to tell her about it.'

'Tell her about it?' He repeated. 'Still, lucky for me. Could I take you out for lunch?'

'No, I'm meeting her.'

'Dinner?'

'I think... I'll be on my way home.' She waited, longing to be persuaded.

'Tea, then.' He laughed. 'Manchester's the place for high teas. Five o'clock? I know just the place.'

'I ought not to wait on...' It was a delicious pleasure, 'and I never eat high tea.'

'It's never too late to start. Don't quibble. I can't get out earlier and I have to see you. You know the Art Galleries?'

'At Princess Street?'

'Yes. Meet me at the Café Gallery there. I can't possibly pass up the chance of seeing you...especially as you've let me know you're here.' His voice was wicked.

'So you're glad I rang?' She was forgetting about Judith, and the other girl.

'What do *you* think?' He was terse. 'Five o'clock, then, Café Gallery.' He hung up.

She had been too coy at the end, overdone it. She remembered the look Judith's friend had given her when they'd met in the Chinese restaurant, 'Who's this old bag he's with?' She was deflated, but had no regrets. She would have had if

158

she'd left Manchester without seeing him.

Margaret came forward to the table where she was sitting, all guns firing, talking as she sat down, a wind-up toy, throwing off her pink linen jacket, scattering parcels on the other two chairs. 'That will stop other people.'

'*You've* been busy.' Considering Margaret only had an hour for lunch, she must have used up a good part of it. Was she spending her legacy already? 'Didn't think you had time for shopping.'

'Oh, I make time. Good journey?' She was lively, as always, beautiful, her vitality was infectious. Anne smiled at her. My sister...she felt like looking around and taking a bow on her behalf.

'Yes, lorry drivers were kind to me. I don't know why they are so maligned, but I do wish they wouldn't drive at eighty. I hate to see sudden death hurtling past me.'

'Speaking of sudden death, what about Aunt Elspeth? A beef sandwich for me.' A waiter had materialized as if he had been drawn, willy-nilly, into Margaret's orbit by her vivacity. 'Anne?'

'The same. And two glasses of white wine. Is that all right?'

She made a dismissive gesture at the waiter with her hand, nodding at the same time. 'Fancy surprising us like that.'

'It must have been more of a surprise for her, poor soul. She had all kinds of plans for her life. Photography was her latest. I have her camera in my bag. I thought I might get the film of it developed.'

'What a strange idea! Spooky. Still, it was the best way to go. Hope I do the same.' She was lugubrious, then apologetic. 'I'm sorry I didn't get to the funeral, Anne, but I'm a working girl...'

'Yes, you've told me. Neither did Alex. But Richard and Con came.'

'*They* came!' Her voice expressed disbelief and displeasure in equal measure. 'What on earth for?'

'For the usual reason, I expect, respect for the dead. Richard said he had always been fond of her. I know she was very generous to both him and James. Anyhow, it was more than James did. He said he was busy with exams.'

'Well, it's a good enough reason, isn't it? Why don't you believe James when you're so ready to support Richard?' They were at their usual niggling again. 'It would have been better if he'd had a good excuse instead of gallivanting about to funerals.'

'Oh, Margaret!' She had to laugh. 'Gallivanting about to funerals! That's what Mrs Crosswaite thinks of Aunt Elspeth's "girls", that they regard them as an outing.'

'Anything that gets you off work is an outing, if you have any work to *get* off, but swanning about, from this to that, the way Richard and that Conrad do...'

'Con's interested in films. He thought it would be an experience.' You do it to annoy...

'Oh, him!' She brushed that aside. 'Ridiculous name, Con. Conrad's worse, like that Twenties film star. Maybe that's why he's interested in them. Did you see that haircut? You'd think he had alopecia.'

'Wait till he's a famous film director and then you won't scoff at him.' Their sandwiches and drinks arrived.

'About time,' Margaret said. She smiled at Anne, then bit into her beef sandwich with her strong white teeth.

'So come on, spill the beans. What did Aunt Elspeth leave us?'

'We all get legacies, including the children. I get the house.' She took a slurp of wine.

Margaret stopped chewing, spoke with her mouth full. 'What size of legacy?' The bombshell was to be ignored...to begin with.

'I don't think I should say. The solicitor will be writing...'

'Bollocks. You're my sister. How much?'

'The same as the children, two thous-and.' She didn't dare add, 'the same as Mrs Crosswaite.'

'And you get the house.' Her look was direct, accusing. 'It must be worth at least two hundred grand!' That was what Alex had said.

'I wouldn't put too much stress on it at this stage, honestly.' She wished she could inject more confidence into her voice. 'We don't know what state the place is in. It might cost the earth to put into a reasonable selling stage.'

'Fiddlesticks. It always looked all right to me.'

'There are hidden liabilities, so the solicitor hinted...' She couldn't remember if he had said that. 'Ours has cost a bomb as you well know.'

'Alex has the money.' She was pushing the crusts of her sandwich about on her plate, her brows furrowed. Her mother's voice came to Anne from the past, the joking voice she had used to chivvy Margaret out of her bad temper, 'Don't be glum, come to Mum...'

'There's the contents of the house if I sold it...' She tried to mollify her, 'the furniture...I wouldn't make any claims there except for Aunt Elspeth's desk. There's some good period stuff. You could have what you liked, or Judith, or Richard...and, of course, James. They'll all want to set up homes sooner or later.' There was no ring of confidence in what she said, she recognized.

'Yes, I suppose so.' Margaret was still pushing the crusts about. '*If* you sold it... I was hoping someone would set *me* up in a house. It hasn't materialized. And Judith's fed up working.'

'She's too young to be fed up working, surely?'

'You don't know what you're talking about. You were able to give it all up at twenty-one when you married Alex. It's all very well for *you* to talk.' She stabbed with one of the crusts at her plate.

'I had no intention of marrying Alex! It was forced on me.'

'And just what do you mean by that, may I ask?' She had got the fight she wanted. 'I don't like your tone of voice at all. How you hold your little grudges in your dark little soul!'

'I didn't mean I was *forced*, exactly.'

'What did you mean, then? If anyone was forced it was me! Because I got pregnant, and our precious mother and father thought I should get married!'

'I definitely remember mother saying you weren't to marry Ralph unless you loved him. I admit father was different...but you *did* love him. You were potty about him. You used to talk about nothing else in our bedroom at nights...' She remembered those evenings when Margaret would come in after seeing Ralph Lang, her cheeks flushed, how she would kick off her shoes and throw herself on her bed in their twin-bedded room. 'Oh, if you only knew...!' Anne had noticed once or twice her faultily buttoned blouse.

Anne shook her head now, annoyed, blaming herself as usual. She tried to smile 'What is it about us? We still squabble, after all those years...' She looked at this sister of hers, the head raised now, the glimmer of a smile in her eyes which had now left the plate, and love surged into her because of Ben. He was there in her thoughts as if he were sitting beside them. 'But I love you truly, truly, dear...' She joked, as her mother had done. Was it because there was an element of fear in their joking?

'It's all very well for you to talk, sitting now with a nice house to sell if you wanted to, near London. I could love the whole world if I were in your position.'

Give it to her, or say you'll sell it and split the money...she stopped herself. You might need it... 'Don't bother about the house meantime. I'll see you all right.' That was what Aunt Elspeth had said to

Mrs Crosswaite. 'Would you like another glass of wine?'

'Not likely. I have to drive! They're down on Minis in Manchester, the Police. They hate them more than they hate bikes.' She looked at her watch, 'God, is that the time? I must go. Since you're so wealthy, you settle the bill.' She gathered up her plastic bags, with expensive names on them, Anne noticed, shops in St Anne's Square...pecked Anne on the cheek. 'Must kiss the heiress.'

That was what Alex had called her.

She was left with a few hours to kill, and she wandered aimlessly about, realizing that she could easily have been home long before five. She was being incredibly foolish, a married woman of over twenty years' standing, skulking about waiting for a younger man.

She knew that her temperament went with a degree of obsessiveness, and that she was in the grip of it now. Ben filled her thoughts. She hadn't even properly grieved for Aunt Elspeth, that valiant old lady who had been such a friend and never a bother, had even despatched herself quickly and efficiently to avoid being a 'burden'.

She saw she was outside St Anne's Church, and rather self-consciously she turned into it, finding the contrast between the bright streets outside and its dark interior depressing. But as her eyes grew accustomed to the gloom she began to pick out its fine proportions, saw the purpose of the stained glass windows, hope in dark places.

She bent her head obediently. She had never felt close to God as a person, just as a presence, but you could scarcely start with 'Dear "Whoever you Are"... Bless Aunt Elspeth's life here with us. Help me to remember her brave spirit, and to profit by it. And help me not to make a bigger fool of myself over Ben than I need to.' She saw it clearly as a finite relationship, that it was bound to end sooner rather than later. She must be prepared for that end. 'Help me...' No more words were coming. She lifted her head, looking around. She was the only person in the church. Not many people needed help, or thought they could get it here. It was sad.

When she came out again she cut through the arcade into Deansgate and drifted with the crowds again. When she grew tired of window-shopping she went into a busy café, but the noise of chatter and the crash and bang of crockery sent her out again, leaving her tea half-drunk.

She looked at her watch. Half-past three. Why hadn't she thought of it before? She could go to the Art Galleries. It would be more productive than this aimless wandering. But with the thought came another hard on its heels. Aunt Elspeth's camera was in her bag in the car. She could have the film developed while she was waiting. That was even more constructive than the Art Galleries, and processing films here would be speedier than at home. Hurrying to the car park with now a sense of purpose, she saw a large branch of Boots, which confirmed her opinion.

'One hour,' the assistant said when she handed it in. It would be ready just before she was due to meet Ben. She trailed about the shop, up and down aisles, buying useless cosmetics, trying perfumes, sitting for a time on the seats provided for those collecting medicine, until the hour was up. Whether she would remember this afternoon as a purgatory or a time for reflection, she would decide later.

Ben rose to greet her when she arrived in the café, his face glowing. He looked as if he would like to kiss her. She was overcome by happiness, by sheer joy. 'I was getting worried. You're seven minutes late and I know you're a punctual soul. I thought you must be under a bus.'

'What a grisly thought!' She sat down on the chair he held out for her. 'Good thing I'm wearing my best underwear. I always do when I'm travelling.' She was babbling. 'No, sorry to disappoint you. I was collecting some film I was having developed. It came from Aunt Elspeth's camera. I had to wait.'

'What was the rush?'

'You mean for the film? I don't know. It suddenly seemed important, or perhaps a good way of filling in time.'

'Did you see your sister?'

'Yes, I had lunch with her. I had to tell her the sad news, that my aunt's house has been left to me and she's only got a legacy.'

His eyebrows went up and he burst out laughing. 'Was she dev-as-tated?' Her heart moved with pleasure listening to him.

'Utterly. She sulked, the way she always does. When we were young I used to give her *anything* to get her out of it, generally something I treasured. I told her I'd see her all right, but I don't really know what I meant by that.'

'You're mad,' he said. 'People like that will take everything, suck you dry. You have to learn to be tough.'

'You wouldn't like me to be tough, would you?'

'No,' his smile was engaging, 'I can get plenty of tough women. You're...tender.'

'Oh,' she said, lifting the menu so that

168

she could take her eyes away from him, 'What are we having?'

'It's not the good old fish and chips here. Rarefied. Quiche, or spaghetti? I bet you had nothing for lunch.'

'A sandwich.'

'High tea's a jolly good idea. It leaves you time for dalliance.'

'What kind of dalliance?' She was afraid to meet his eyes. She knew love was spilling out of hers.

'Like coming back to my flat. We can have coffee and a drink.' She heard his whisper. 'Or...'

'Or...' Her throat was hurting. 'Could I have a pot of tea now? I'm thirsty.'

'By all means. What do you say, Anne?'

'I'll have quiche.'

'You know what I mean.'

'I'm due back.'

'You could drive up later. It's quieter at night, or go up in the morning, depending...' Depend-*ing*.

'You'll be the death of me,' she said, unable to look at him for long because of the love.

They sat up in bed, naked, while she spread out the photographs on the bedcover. 'Let's see if Aunt Elspeth had the makings of a good photographer... Oh, Ben,' she said, 'poor Aunt Elspeth, no longer here, and here *I* am, in a strange

169

flat, making love, so soon after...'

'Hardly cold in the grave she is. How terrible.' He put his arm round her and his hand came under her right breast. 'See, we fit everywhere.'

She had to swallow, renewed desire mounting in her. 'We don't know yet. We only know each other through our bodies. We haven't done the important bit yet.'

'You don't call being in bed important?'

'It's marvellous, but only important in relation to other things, as an indication of temperament.'

'Isn't it a quicker way than ploughing through endless meetings?' he asked.

'They're fun too. It's the correlation, finding that one's mind and how it works is indicative of how one's body works.'

'Show me a man running for a bus and I'll tell you how he makes love.' He grinned at her, 'Go on, you guess.'

'Premature ejaculation.'

'You're smart.' He laughed. 'What kind of man am I?'

'You arrive on time at the station,' she said. He held her, not kissing her, as if the closeness was enough.

After a time he said quietly, 'Let's look at the photographs now.'

The film was only partly used, six photographs in all. Two were of Aunt

Elspeth's garden with its weeping willow, two of 'the girls'. There was Daisy Butterfield with her white stick, smiling bravely with that straightforward look of the blind, the other three friends arranged round her in a pleasing harmony of positions.

'I think they'll miss Aunt Elspeth,' she said. 'Mr Cholmondley-Brooks, their photographic tutor, told me she was the life and soul of the class.'

'Those are good.' He was examining them. 'See how she hasn't stuck that tree right in the centre. She had a good idea of composition. The women are arranged like flowers in a vase.'

'She was a good flower arranger.'

'Same thing.' He picked up the last two. 'Oh, I recognize those! Isn't it the road leading to your husband's Depot?'

'Yes, good for you.'

'Both the same subject, slightly different angle,' he said.

Anne looked at them, leaning close to him, smelling his sweat, possibly her own.

'She called that one "Derelict Warehouses". She smiled, remembering her aunt's concentration that day.

'It's a composition all right. This one's slightly better than the other. See how the railway arches stand out more clearly because the light's right, and that curve of the road leading you into the picture is natural. Those are boat spars, are they?'

'Yes, the fishermen keep their boats there. They sail out with the tide to get shrimps. They supply them to the pub there, The Eagle and Child. Remember we went to it, with Margaret and James and Alex?'

'Yes.' He peered. 'I can just about make out the emblem, the child being carried off.'

'Is it biblical?' she asked.

'God knows, and He didn't tell me.'

'Look how that little white car stands out under the arches. That's clever. I can read the letters, ABA, I think, but not the number, it's in shadow.'

'We need a magnifying glass. There's one on my desk. Hop out and get it. I want to see you bare.'

'You're depraved,' she said, but skipped out of bed, remembering to hold her bottom in. She hoped it didn't have an elephant droop from the back. She skipped back quickly, holding the magnifying glass.

'Nice firm little bum. Let's see. Yes, it's ABA all right. That's Manchester. But I can't make out the figures. The light slashes them in half.'

'There must be thousands of little white cars in Manchester.' She shivered suddenly.

'I'm cold, Ben.' She turned towards him for warmth.

'Poor little thing. Have you made up your mind? It's nine o'clock. Are you staying?'

'Do you want me to go?'

'I don't.' His mouth was on her cheek. 'I'd like to sleep with you, I mean, sleep, and that's a rare compliment, Mrs Garrett.' He released her to sit up and lean over her. His hair had fallen over his brow, his chin looked blue. He looked unusually serious. 'Have I told you that you're very dear to me? That there's something over and above your desirability, something very appealing? I want to explore you in every way, inside and outside, take my time, for ever, if need be.'

'Don't, you'll make me cry.' She saw the flicker of embarrassment in his eyes. 'I'm not being jokey. That's the effect you have on me. So much emotion. I'm unused to it. Normally I'm very calm. My feelings never get in the way. That's why I do what I have to do, capably. But, since I met you, tears rush into my eyes, for no reason...' She hid her face against his shoulder, ashamed. 'This must be boring you out of your mind.'

'No, it isn't.' He stroked her back. 'I feel...very humble. God, that sounds wet, but it's true.'

'I'll stay,' she said, drawing back from him, smiling. 'Let's get up and have a cup of coffee or something. I'm ravenous with all this.'

'Are you? Rav-enous, is it? Well, you go and have a shower and I'll put the kettle on and root out some biscuits and cheese or something, or would you like some eggs?'

'No, you never know where they've been.'

'Fool! Okay, no eggs, then I'll join you in the shower and we'll rub each other dry...'

'It sounds blissful,' she said. She had never been so happy.

Sitting later wearing his dressing gown, her hands round her cup, she said, 'The last time I saw Aunt Elspeth was when she came recently "for a little break". That's how she put it. She was so appreciative. One day we were forced to stay in because of the weather. I usually tried to take her for little jaunts when I could...'

'Right.'

'So when Alex phoned and said his car was out of order, and would I pick him up, I was quite glad. It was an outing for Aunt Elspeth. If you have an elderly relative staying you are glad of any diversion for them.'

'I wouldn't know.' She felt the gap in their ages, painfully, for a second.

'That's when she took the photographs. She was fascinated by the atmosphere.'

'Yes? I got it too. Not the kind of place to walk about at night, all the same. Not like our early morning walk along the promenade.'

'Yes, that was nice.' And then she remembered he had come with Judith, lovely, youthful Judith. 'So Ben isn't your young man?' 'Not yet.' Lips moist, blue-white teeth showing. 'How is Judith?' Anne asked.

'Why do you ask that?'

'I suppose I remembered she brought you with her that weekend, when we had the walk.'

'So she did.' He yawned, 'I don't know about you, but I'm knackered.' Was he trying to avoid any discussion about Judith? They could well be seeing each other without her knowing anything about it. They worked in the same office. She was available, her niece, her beautiful niece, so good at getting her own way...like her mother. 'Who's worried about Judith?' he said. 'Let's get off to bed, shall we?'

His arm was round her shoulders, her head on his chest. Almost the nicest part. 'Comfortable?' he asked.

'Mmmh. You'll get cramp.'

175

'Maybe. Go to sleep, you've had a busy day.' *Bus-y...*

'All right. "Now I lay me down to sleep..." Your turn.'

' "Sleep that knits up...?"'

' "...the ravelled sleeve of care..." ' she finished for him.

' "To sleep, perchance to dream." Do you dream much?'

'Yes. Sometimes I don't sleep either.'

'What do you do then?'

'Read poetry. Sometimes try to write it. Thank you for the book.'

'I'm glad you liked it. Sleep, my darling...' It was the first time he had said that. She forgot about Judith.

Chapter Eleven

It seemed that autumn, as if Ben and the sea were the two things which mattered in her life. Often she sat at the window looking out on to the calm, milky blueness which was a feature of that part of the year, a hiatus between full summer and the dark days of winter, a resting time. The hills on the other side of the bay would be blurred by a soft mist. Life seemed beautiful to her, a plenitude. If it's done nothing else for me, loving Ben, she thought, I'm more sensitive, life has acquired a richness.

The people she saw in her work benefited from this. She listened more patiently, felt more keenly, her energy was boundless. She remembered an American guest whom Alex had brought home who had told her a quaint expression. 'Enjoy,' he said, not 'enjoy yourself.' I enjoy. I am in a state of joy.

Why is it, she would ask herself, that sunsets have been described millions of times and yet they remain so indescribable? So bloody marvellous? She noticed her speech had become freer as her behaviour with Ben became more relaxed. The bold

Anne had emerged, she would think, the Margaret in the Anne, lying in his car with him high above the Lake. It was like a regression to adolescence, the fumbling, the tumbling, the wanting. She needed the tranquility of the sunsets to cool her blood after those hectic meetings.

He was vigorous, demanding, but then so was she. Sometimes she felt she was the younger, at least she was younger in experience. He was too attractive not to have known many women. She thought of the girl he had been 'shacked up with', and there was Judith. She didn't want to think of Judith, and he wouldn't be drawn when she mentioned her name.

The less florid sunsets were even more satisfying when she tried to analyse their subtler colours, the smoke greys and violets, the pale china-blue streaks which faded into the softness of a pigeon's breast, or the beech and sand colours deepening to indigo. She had no wish to capture them either by photography or paint, the attempted poems were banal, over-worked. It was enough to 'enjoy'.

There was no difficulty in deceiving Alex. Her affair with Ben made her realize how much she had been leading her own life before she met him. Alex was away as much as ever. He spent a lot of time in the office in the evenings making up for his absences, he played golf on Saturdays and Sundays.

Once, when her handbag was lying beside her, she took out and examined the photograph of Margaret and herself as children. Was it her imagination that she looked more like her sister, that she looked less self-effacing? That blood tie, she would think, meeting Margaret's eyes looking boldly at her, as deep and dark as an underground river. Had she borrowed some of Margaret's boldness in her affair with Ben, a part of her character which had been lying dormant for so long? And would Margaret sometimes show *her* self-effacement or essential acceptance of life? If they both lived for a long time would they become indistinguishable from each other? Would they finish up close together, even living together, supporting each other until death?

Her new boldness asserted itself one evening when she and Alex were at dinner. 'Have you still got that man Spiers at the gate of the Depot?'

He looked up, surprised. 'Yes. Why?'

'He's rude, that's why. He must put your customers off.'

'What grounds have you for saying that?' He was dipping his fried bread, (he insisted on fried bread) in his egg. He insisted on the egg being runny, and dismissed the egg scare.

'Oh, someone I know mentioned him to me.' She waved her hand airily.

'Who?' He stopped eating. She thought his eyes were watchful.

'I can't remember. Didn't you say he had a prison record? Surely it wasn't wise to hire a man like that?'

'I'm surprised at hearing a remark like that from you!' He was triumphant. 'You with all your good works.'

She was stung. 'It's not his prison record I'm worried about, it's the fact that he's such a bad front man for your business, putting people off. I remember when...' She stopped herself in time.

'Don't you realize, you silly girl, that it's his prison record which gives me the hold on him? He would do anything I asked him, Jack would, anything at all. He knows which side his bread is buttered on. One word from me and he'd be back in the nick.'

'Why would he?'

'Because I have some information about him which would be very useful to the Police, that's why.'

'What kind of information?'

He looked at her, frowning. 'What's come over you? It's not like you to be persistent.' She wanted to tell him that there was egg on his chin, but the dominant Anne was in retreat. 'Never mind what. It's not your department. You stick to your good works. You're better at that.' *If you knew about my bad works, you wouldn't be so cocky...like Ben Davies.*

'*Who's Ben Davies?*'

'*You know. You asked him to work out a scheme for you.*'

'*Oh, the computer chap! I turned that down. Too fanciful by half, all that security system, television screens all over the place, laser beams, God knows what. Better with good old Jack Spiers in the box to look after my interests...*'

'By the way,' he said, 'remember that young chap, friend of Judy's who was giving me an estimate for a Security Scheme?'

'Yes,' she said, holding her breath.

'I turned it down. Too expensive.'

'Too fanciful by half?'

'Yes, my very words.' He looked at her, surprised.

Winter hung back, perhaps because of a wonderful summer, and people seemed to be reluctant to pull the curtains and retire indoors in spite of the shortening days. Flowers had a second blooming, Alex's golf improved, and each Saturday he seemed to be involved in some kind of competition.

Ben raced up the motorway and they

would drive separately towards the Lakes. They walked in the Winster Valley, so gently pastoral with its occasional flicker of gold and red in the elms adding to its beauty. Those were talking times, times which she craved for as much as the loving, a relationship which she had always missed with Alex who talked at her rather than with her. She discovered Ben was reticent about his childhood whereas she had a fixation about her own vis-à-vis Margaret. He seemed to have sloughed his off like a snakeskin.

'I had, have, two sisters. They're both married with children of their own, and they're desperate to get me married off too. Have you noticed that with all women? "Come on in, the water's fine." They forget I can't swim.'

'I think you swim very well,' she replied. He was not reticent in his lovemaking. He could still surprise her. 'Look at that, Ben, the sun shining along the valley and skimming the top of Whitbarrow. Is there anything more beautiful in the whole world?'

'I'd like a house here with you, a tree-hidden little house with a view at the back. We could make love all day instead of all this walking and talking...'

'You'd soon grow tired of that.'

'Have you ever seen any signs?' He

preened, a twenty-four-old, at the height of his sexual powers.

'No, I have to admit I haven't.' Was he thinking, by any chance, of asking her to give up Alex to live with him? Even in her most optimistic moments she didn't allow herself to think that. Their affair would come to an end. He would grow tired of her, the excitement would fade. But, meantime, she was charmed, right down to the core of her. She allowed herself to think he might, just might.

They took a sail on the Lake steamer, the last trip of the season, and stood in the bow with other tourists, oblivious of them. It was one of what Anne called her 'loving to death' days, when everything he did, said or how he looked had a sweetness which screwed up her heart. She wouldn't be able to keep up with his youthful ardour, Alex would find out...that worried her least, strangely. One part of her longed for a confrontation, an end to the shallow life they led together.

The lake was choppy, the yachts moored by the shore sailless and stripped of their glory, moved heavily as the waves smacked their sides. Seagulls wheeled, screeching above, and the tourists out-screeched them, shielding their children, laughing.

'A mistake,' Ben said. They stood facing each other, her hands in his anorak pockets to keep them warm. She couldn't be near enough him.

'No, not a mistake.' She wanted to wipe her nose, had to take one of her hands from his pocket. 'It's only sad because it's the last time...my nose always runs in the cold, excuse me. Endings of anything are sad. You can feel them slip away from you. That's why even a photograph is better than nothing. You have the image and you can build on that.' He still looked morose. 'Eliot has a lot to say about ends. You can go on from an end to a new beginning.' He was right. The day was a mistake. He had to rush back to Manchester. He didn't say why.

'What would you do if we stopped seeing each other?' he said the following Saturday, 'if it came to an end.' Late autumn had backtracked to summer again. The sun was warm on their backs as they looked across the valley. Sheep were scattered in a painterly fashion in the fields, cottages nestled in folds, like sheep. It was Herdwick country.

It was a continuation from their conversation on the steamer. 'I'd go on,' she said. Her heart seemed to have swollen painfully. She could hardly breathe. If this was a shadow of how she would feel, the reality would be insupportable. 'What else is there? I might decide to change my life in some way.' Like leave Alex... 'It could be the trigger. It might make me be me.'

'So it would be doing you a good turn?'

'You could say that. Don't tease, Ben. I'm too happy—'

'I wish you weren't.'

'Why, is it dangerous?'

'I don't deserve it.'

'Oh, fiddlesticks,' she said, 'we don't deserve each other.'

It was, nevertheless, a very happy day, as if he were trying to make it so. Their minds ran on parallel tracks, they were delighted again and again at this discovery, and that they laughed at the same things. They were harmonious. And later, when he stopped the car at the side of a wood and they climbed over the fence, they made violent and bumpy love in the bracken. Fierce love. They couldn't get enough of each other. She had not the slightest pang of guilt. Alex had once said to friends who commented on his frequent sorties from home, 'Anne is perfectly capable of doing her own thing.' Ben, crushing her into the bracken so that it scratched and tickled her bare flesh, asked her why she laughed.

They stopped for a drink at their pub, as they called it. Anne had parked her car there. The sun had set, and with it, like a child's tantrum, had come a chill, wintry wind which tore at her hair and whitened the tips of her fingers. Soon, she thought, the dry spell would go. Those meetings would lose part of their glamour in the unremitting Lakeland rain. Her sense of freedom would disappear when they were forced to meet indoors.

'I've done something rather forward,' she said, when they were seated in the cosy bar. 'Remember we talked about that film, *Death in Venice?* I've booked seats for the opera in Manchester, for us.'

'When?'

'A week on Saturday. Maybe it's foolish. Would you go with me? Alex will be golfing, and after that he's going to a stag party. I planned it all, cunningly.'

'I'd like to, very much, but isn't there a chance of seeing your sister there?'

'Nothing would make Margaret go to the opera.' Was it Margaret he was worrying about, or Judith? 'She's into Lloyd Webber now. Her current rave is *The Phantom of the Opera.*'

'Let me pay for them. I do nothing for you.'

'No, it's my treat.' They had cost a lot of money. 'I'm so glad you can come.'

'I'll look forward to it. I shan't be able to see you this coming Saturday, as it happens. Something has come up.' What? She had no right to ask.

'I'll have a sherry, Ben, if I may. I feel cold.'

'Of course. I wish we could slip upstairs to our bedroom. I would warm you.'

'I could arrange to stay in Manchester that night. I'll think up a good excuse, say I'm staying with Margaret.'

'No, don't do that,' he said quickly. 'She's the last one.'

'You're prejudiced. You've always been prejudiced against her.'

'No, I'm not. It's just...I suppose I'm... caring.'

'Or careful?' She looked at him. 'You don't understand about my sister. I may not like her at times, but I *love* her. She's family, the blood tie thing. Surely you feel that with *your* sisters?'

'I don't. We're miles apart. Sometimes they forget my name and call me Bob, or Norman.' He grinned at her like a naughty boy.

'I don't believe it,' she said.

He was eating her up with his eyes, saying, wasn't it great, wonderful, on the bracken...she hoped.

'It's near enough the truth,' he replied. 'I don't approve of family ties which get in the way. They make you act contrary to your own wishes.'

'That would be all right if you always knew your own wishes.'

'Ah, there you're unfortunate. I have no problem.'

'You may live to regret saying that. You. The great Mr I Am.' She teased him. Yes, it had been stupendous on the bracken. Her skin was still zinging with it, or perhaps more accurately, itching. They should have taken a rug.

Sipping her sherry she glanced across the room and saw a man whose face was vaguely familiar. Young middle-aged. Too old to be a friend of James's. He didn't seem to fit into any group of people she knew, or worked with. She was going through them when she knew who he was. The casual clothes had confused her. Generally he was wearing a black donkey jacket with leather shoulders and a collar and tie underneath. It would be cold in that little wooden box. The thin skull enclosing the narrow face, the water-sleeked hair, the cold eyes...it was Jack Spiers. She kept her own eyes averted while she sipped.

'I've just felt someone walking over my grave,' she said. She shivered.

He was solicitous. 'I think you've caught a cold. You looked pale when we got here. Would you like to go home?'

'Yes, I think I should. I'll go to bed early.'

The joy of the day had gone. When

they went out to the car park the chill wind had increased and was struggling with the remaining leaves on the trees, tearing viciously at them. The sky was grey, sullen, tired of it all, grudging about the wonderful un-Lake-like summer.

'Goodbye,' she said, as he stood by her car.

'What do you mean, goodbye?' His laughing face bent down to her. 'There's our *Death in Venice*. Try and stay the night. I'll be des-per-ate for you.'

'Will you? Desperate?'

She memorized his face as she drove home, the hazel eyes, the dark skin, the white smile, especially she memorized the voice. 'I'll be des-per-ate for you.' She was filled with fear.

Chapter Twelve

It was a crisp enough day with the sky showing deeply blue above the office blocks. Southerners didn't appreciate the graciousness and spaciousness of northern cities, she thought, where the buildings had been in many cases erected by industrialists who'd had a strong wish to perpetuate themselves in stone. Nor did they often appreciate that Manchester was a fine example of a Victorian city except where it had been bombed and rebuilt after the War. Where else would one find a Town Hall which covered nearly two acres?

I'm thinking like a travel guide, she told herself, smiling. The city had been part of the fabric of her young life, the place to go for the annual pantomime, later, concerts, (Barbirolli), shopping, (Kendal's), theatres, for quite simply the best. London was for show only. There you felt like a stranger, here was an extension of your home, a second home.

They had lunch in the Pavilion Room of the Piccadilly Hotel, looking down on to the Gardens which seemed to keep the tall new buildings at bay, the Arndale Centre, hotels and towering offices, stores. Lewis's. Kendal Milne's was the only shop her mother had recognized, in the older part of the city.

'Those lovely teas I had at Kendal's with my mother,' she said to Ben. 'Afternoon teas, a thing of the past. I can scarcely manage a proper lunch nowadays. How about you?'

'Same, more or less. We won't eat much. I'm taking you to Chinatown for an early meal before the theatre.'

'We'll have to walk about a bit, then, before that. Our Lakeland days are over now. It isn't the cold. It's the rain. I'm like a cat. I hate getting my fur wet.'

'We'll meet here in winter.' He was pale. She thought he had a strained look about the eyes.

She said. 'Margaret has asked Alex and me to a party next month, a pre-Christmas party. I can't remember the date. Judith will be there, I expect. Have you had an invitation?'

He shook his head, turning away from her. 'I have a pile of unanswered mail...' then turned back again, eager, but still unusually pale, 'Don't let's talk about people. We never do as a rule. Let's be like what we are at Winster, close, in that pub...' He put out his hand to touch hers, and she thought, but you can't escape

191

people. There had been that man who had looked like Spiers, *was* Spiers. She knew it now with sick certainty. 'This is too formal,' he said. 'We're all dressed up...'

'With somewhere to go. Had you forgotten? Circumstances or places shouldn't alter how we feel towards each other. They are...tests. You look tired, Ben. Have you been working too hard?'

'That wouldn't make me tired. At my age you never get tired.'

'Thanks very much.' She tried to smile.

'Oh, God! That was a clanger.' He pulled a face at her. 'Tell me about this opera. It's from a book, isn't it? I saw the film.'

'Yes, it's by Thomas Mann, a German novelist, about unrequited love. But you know that.'

'You can't say ours is.' He looked at her soberly. You're very special to me, Anne. I want you to remember that, whatever happens, whatever you hear.'

Her heart shook. *Something was different...*

'You have that strained look again. Is it your city look, put on with your city clothes, or fear of being seen with me?'

'You're imagining things.' He was dismissive, 'We'll have to order.'

'Fish. Anything. And coffee.' He summoned the waiter, chose sole for them both.

'You'll remember, then?' he said, sipping his Muscadet.

'That I'm very special to you? What does that mean? Mr Proctor, the fishmonger is very special to me, James is, Marge Braithwaite is—I stay with her sometimes when I'm in London. She's an old school friend. All very special for different reasons.'

'I'll say it, then. I love you. I've never known anyone who aroused the same feelings in me, of...caring.'

She was touched. 'I think love, the word, is debased now. I love beef sandwiches in a pub if the beef is rare. I love going to the opera. "Caring" might be better. It's very comforting to be cared for...in my old age.' She laughed at him.

'For God's sake get that chip off your shoulder! It's the latest thing to have a toy boy.'

'So I believe. I don't "care" for that expression, I don't find it funny, but it might be a sign of age, not "caring" for it.' Was 'hearing' becoming a debased word also?

It was very cold in the streets afterwards, and to escape it they went into the Art Galleries. They confessed to each other it was a cop out, but she became interested in the Lowry show because he seemed to her to be a northern icon.

'I'm glad he wasn't winkled down to London and spoiled,' she said. 'He was a truly northern character, unique.'

He nodded. 'You might be right. I wouldn't know. Heh, do you think I could become an arty type? Maybe we could study art together. That would be nice, wouldn't it? Going to lectures together, earnest little beavers.'

'It sounds idyllic.' She didn't know if he was mocking her. 'Rossetti and Holman Hunt are upstairs,' she said. 'We got lectures about them at school, the Romantic Movement. I even thought of studying art...and then I married Alex.' *Because of Margaret.* Still the old whinge.

' "The Scapegoat" ' Ben was saying triumphantly. 'That's one I remember. Is it up there?'

'Yes, I think so.'

'Lead the way.'

But, when she had done so, she found the frames filled to overflowing with figures and flowers and landscape were too overpowering, and she settled instead for a small sketch by Ford Madox Brown which didn't worry her.

Together they looked at 'The Scapegoat'. 'When someone does something...unconventional,' Ben said, 'do you think it's being ostracized that's the real killer?'

'I don't know. If one was mature enough,

one...' she laughed, 'how Royal one is today...one would realize that it's society which is at fault. It's always needed a scapegoat.' When she looked at him she thought he was paler than ever.

She day-dreamed as they walked back along the streets and through the Imperial Archway into Chinatown and towards the Yang Sing. She and Ben were living together. They both worked—she couldn't decide who would employ her—but they met for swift meals and then set off for some Evening Institute to study art, an Evening Institute with marble stairs and statues in niches of the worthy sons of Manchester. It was a pleasant prospect which she couldn't believe in. They would never grow old together.

When she went to the cloakroom of the restaurant she discovered a cold pinched face in the mirror with reddened nostrils from constant wiping. Her hair, which was soft and of a lively brown had lost its shape and even its colour and clung to a skull which was too small to be important. Would it be like this all the time, a constant dissatisfaction with her appearance, a constant examination for signs of age?

He, on the contrary, looked revivified when she sat down opposite him. The signs of strain were gone. The cold air suited him. His cheeks were coloured, his eyes bright, his black hair crisp. She had been going to say, however lightly, 'You and I could grow old together *caring* for each other.' It was no longer apposite. She would be old long before him.

The opera did nothing to dispel her sadness, although here she was better educated musically than Ben. She had always played the piano, a pleasant necessity in her life, and although she only knew the story vaguely, she was captivated by the role the orchestra played, its harsh cleanness. The stylized nature of the piece increased its poignancy for her. It seemed to go beyond the story of homosexual love to link with her own situation, a struggle to understand herself.

She began to conceive Aschenbach's conflict, to empathize with it. Her guilt about her affair with Ben left her. Conflict was necessary in one's life, she told herself. It was necessary to go down to the depths of experience to discover oneself. Her meeting and falling in love with Ben was part of that discovery. The differences in their ages wasn't the important part of it. Being in love was like being given a key to a door which led to self-knowledge.

She remembered long ago a schoolfriend who had been studying Humanities at her University. She had nodded politely, not knowing what the word meant. Now she thought she did, a learning process concerned with human culture.

'How did you like it?' she asked Ben when they were in the crowded foyer.

He shrugged, then remembering perhaps that he had been a guest, 'Not bad, but it was too gloomy for me. I preferred the film.'

'Did you?' She thought perhaps that she was growing past him.

But in his flat later there was no question of age. He had never been more passionate, nor had she. The days of discovery were over now, they were in a new phase of loving. She gave herself up to him, down to him, sweated in the giving, cried out, and he was no less involved and vigorous. But there was a new quality of despair in his loving.

'Are you happy, Ben?' she said when they were lying quietly.

'Oh, I'm happy with you. *That*'s never been the problem.' She thought how odd it was that they had never used endearments to each other, but how in her own social milieu one could gauge the shallowness of a relationship by the number used. Jan and Mike Saunders fought like cat and dog, but 'Heart's Delight' was Mike's favourite expression for her in company, whereas she usually called him 'Dearest love' while her eyes snapped fire.

She and Alex sprinkled their conversation with 'dears' and an occasional 'darling', 'Bring in the coffee, darling, will you?' It meant nothing, damn all, in fact. She addressed Ben by his name more often than he said 'Anne'. More often they used the ubiquitous pronoun as if they were fearful of other labels.

In the morning she said, 'Maybe I'll see you at Margaret's party?'

'There's not much advantage in that.' He was Welshly morose, deep-vowelled, damp-haired from his shower, dark-skinned against his white business shirt. She loved him very much. She loved him to death.

'Why?'

'Your husband will be with you, won't he?'

'I expect so. He's fond of Margaret.' She paused because there was that stirring inside her, unease, suspicion, no, nothing so strong, dismissed it. 'He always goes to her Christmas party.'

'Two of a kind?'

'Maybe you're right. They think the same way, enjoy themselves in the same way, plenty of booze and food and loud talk. They like partying. How that word has crept into use! I hate nouns used as verbs. I once spoke to a woman who told me she never neighboured. The limit, isn't it?'

He nodded, still morose. This was a facet of young men, she had noticed, to be morose in the morning. James was the same. No social obligations. If she could see any good points in Alex, one was that he was never morose at breakfast. His behaviour was impeccable, if predictable. She had thought of making a tape to save him the trouble of repeating himself.

Phase one: 'Morning. Sleep well? What's for breakfast? Dish it up, then. I'm in a hurry. Where's my paper? God, will you listen to this?'

Phase two: After a rustling silence broken by clatter of cutlery. 'My God, is that the time? Must fly. Chin-chin.' Peck-peck. Slam of front door, garage door, car door, all to background music, 'Hi-ho, Hi-ho, it's off to work we go...'

They said goodbye, lingeringly. He said he would phone. He pressed himself hard and shamelessly against her and said, 'Oh, Anne...' and she saw his face was still strained.

She drove up the motorway towards home, heavy-hearted.

Chapter Thirteen

The house was quiet when Anne let herself in, and cold. She would never stop missing Melissa, her cat, the silky circular rubbing against her ankles, the raised tail above the little button, never forget how she had died. Pets were constant in their affection. That was their appeal.

She turned on the central heating and went into the kitchen to make herself a cup of coffee, then took it to her usual seat at the patio window. Views were constant also. She never tired of hers. She remembered Dora, an old friend who had recently moved to a larger house, viewless, leaving also a delectable view of the sea. 'Won't you miss it?' she had asked her, and her reply, 'I've seen it.' She wished she could be as practical.

Today there was no sea to look at, but the cold winter sun playing on the mole-grey expanse of muddy sand had its own beauty. Deep purple shadows lurked in the hollows between the ridged waves of it, chiselled by the outgoing tide. The white railings bisecting the foreground made a strident contrast, as did the red flag which had been placed there at high water and now waved forlornly.

There were a few fishing boats awkwardly beached, waiting for the incoming tide to release them. They reminded her of the swan at Esthwaite which had looked so queenly on the Lake and how it had turned into a harridan when it had left the water and waddled towards Ben, a metamorphosis.

Aunt Elspeth would have photographed it, she could try and write a poem about it. She mustn't miss the poetry class this week. She had been neglecting it in her obsession with Ben. Perhaps the discipline would instil calmness in her, help her to dispel that unease which was still with her and had been a reflection of Ben's. Could it be that it had only been an Indian summer affair, and now that the cold factual days of winter were with them, he wanted the relationship to end? Had Judith been in the background all the time, Judith of the moist mouth, (and moist thighs?), a young man of Ben's sexual vigour could easily service two women. It relieved her to be bold, Margaret-like in her thinking, crude.

She looked towards the horizon, trying to see where sea and sky met, but it was nebulous, a fusion of feather-soft tones. As nebulous as this affair. The cure for her dissatisfaction in her marriage didn't lie with Ben. In any case he had never suggested that she should ask Alex for a divorce. The solution lay within herself, whether she was able to accept that no marriage was perfect, or if she had the courage to set out on her own.

But did she need to compete? She wasn't 'without'—what a good northern phrase—thanks to Aunt Elspeth's generosity. She was the owner of a valuable house, or a substantial sum of money if she sold it. 'Thank you again, Aunt Elspeth.' She nodded towards the horizon. 'I don't deserve it.'

She heard noises on the stairs and stood up, terror-stricken. An intruder? Burglaries were becoming common in their area with the darker nights. There were constant warnings in the local newspaper to be vigilant. Their only near neighbours, the Browns, were away. They had gone to Australia to visit their son.

The door opened and Alex came into the kitchen, hair tousled, bleary-eyed. Under his dressing gown the silk legs of his pyjamas were crinkled like concertinas. She would never buy silk again for him, she vowed, as her terror subsided, they were too difficult to iron. Her smile trembled.

'What a fright you gave me!' she said. 'I thought you were staying with Reg!'

'I thought you must have gone to church.' She was an occasional early communicant, more from habit than conviction.

'No.'

'Your car wasn't there.'

'What time did you come home?' What should she say to him?

'Around seven-thirty, I think.' He sat down heavily on a chair. 'It was a balls-up last night. Reg was in a worse state than I was. I ran him home, then had a kip downstairs. I thought Jill wouldn't be best pleased if she heard two of us blundering up. She gets ratty.'

'I don't blame her.'

'I woke up around seven feeling damned uncomfortable on his sofa and decided to get the hell out of there and have a proper sleep at home. You woke me up. Where in God's name...?' She wasn't ready yet.

'You must have had some night.'

'I was pissed as a coot. Reg was worse. I'm getting too old for that kind of thing. Sheer murder. I've a head like a football and my mouth's...'

'...like the bottom of a parrot's cage.' Alex's vocabulary was predictable. 'There are some antacid tablets in the bathroom. Why don't you go back to bed and sleep it off?'

'I couldn't put my head down again.

A brisk walk along the prom might be better. You're a great believer in fresh air, aren't you? Is that tea or coffee you're drinking?'

'Coffee.'

'Don't...' He grimaced.

'I'll make some tea for you.' He would ask any minute. What would she say? She busied herself with the kettle, her mind dashing off in tangents. 'I stayed in a hotel...' But that was ridiculous, when she could have been home in little over an hour from Manchester.

'I suppose you stayed with Margaret last night?'

'Yes.' *Oh, God,* she thought. That was a mistake. The question had, all the same, taken her by surprise. She had been so sure he would stay with Reg. He always did after his 'do's'. Maybe that was the reason for Jill's annoyance.

'What were you there for anyhow? Did you tell me?'

'I can't remember. I was at the opera.'

'My God!' She knew his opinion of opera, expressed many times, the screeching women, the posturing men, give him *Annie Get Your Gun* any time. 'Did you take Margaret?'

'No. I had only one ticket. I won it in a raffle at the CAB.' She was amazed at herself, how easily she lied. And why,

204

she thought, a second too late, hadn't she said that an overnight stay in a hotel was included. Make it a whopper.

'I'm glad you *won* it. What would a ticket have cost?'

'Around twenty pounds, I expect. More.'

'Thank God you had the sense not to pay that just to hear men bawling their heads off and poncing around with fat women.' Alf Garnett. She pushed back the dominant Anne.

'There's your tea. Would you really like to go for a walk?'

'No, I was only joking. I'll drink this, then have a bath and sleep till tea time. I have to be fit for tomorrow. Is there anything good on telly tonight?'

'I don't know.'

His voice was quite gentle. 'I like Sunday nights on the telly. Harry Secombe—he doesn't ram religion down your throat —then there's good sports coverage. And isn't there a Command Performance?'

'I think so. We'll look at the paper later.'

Such does married life consist of, she thought, command performances of one kind or another. She watched him drink his tea thirstily, saw that the stubble on his chin was grey. He got up, pulling his dressing-gown cord tighter round his paunch, looked down ruefully at the blue silk which was halfway up his legs.

'I must say you're decent about not kicking up a fuss, Anne. You should have heard the row Jill was making at the top of the stairs. Actually threw a pillow at me. No wonder I cleared out as soon as I could.'

'I'll leave fresh pyjamas out for you,' she said. 'Put those you're wearing in the dirty linen.' The phrase had an ominous ring.

The next morning when Alex had gone off to work, seemingly totally recovered from his excesses, she sat down to think. It was still only eight o'clock. He liked an early start to catch 'those lazy buggers who couldn't get in, in time.' Should she ring Margaret and ask her to say, if she were ever asked, that she had spent the night in her flat?

It wouldn't do, she decided almost immediately. Margaret was bound to say, 'Who's the lucky man?' even if she didn't think it were possible. Her curiosity would know no bounds, nor would her ribbing. The Holy Sister caught in the act! 'Holy' was the word she often used because of Anne's infrequent attendances at early Communion.

Should she, then, repeat her lie, and say she had won both ticket and overnight stay and had quite fancied the idea? That she hadn't liked to tell Alex. 'You,' she could always say, 'would like someone in your bed. To me it would be a great treat to have it to myself.'

No, it wouldn't wash. Margaret hadn't a complex mind. She wouldn't in the first place believe in such an esoteric prize, and if she did, she certainly wouldn't believe that Anne hadn't taken advantage of the opportunity and *not* slept alone.

In the end she did nothing. Far better to hope the lie would die a natural death, and that when she and Alex went to Margaret's Christmas party, the talk would be too general. She set off for Mr Proctor's with her shopping basket, determined to let sleeping dogs lie.

The wind was fresh and the tide now in, the boats were once again swaying gently on the calm surface of the water, once again restored to their natural state. The horizontal lines of shore and sea contrasted with the perpendiculars of the spars and pleased her eye. So much to learn about seeing, she thought, about art. The brief visit to the City Art Galleries in Manchester with Ben came back to her, the rare feeling of pleasure she had got from the small sketch of Ford Madox Brown's, like a window into a different world. That was the advantage of art, the

Alice-Through-The-Looking Glass feeling it gave you.

She walked briskly, head up, a youngish woman having an affair with a younger man, but still interested in other aspects of life. Everything was an experience. Each new day was a fresh experience, an anticipation. You had to travel hopefully, and if Ben decided to end their affair she must not go to pieces about it. She remembered a saying of her mother's, 'As one door closes, another opens.' And, wasn't she a woman of property now? 'Thank you, Aunt Elspeth, thank you again.'

Mr Proctor welcomed her, still in his straw boater. She wondered how she would react if he changed to Russian Cossack headgear in winter instead. The boater evoked sunny days on the promenade, pierrot shows, candy floss, deck chairs, clean sea, a lost world kept alive in a small way by people like Mr Proctor. Even his fishing in a polluted sea showed courage. Perhaps it showed even more courage in her that she should buy his catch. But, if it wasn't polluted fish, it was acid rain, or salmonella—the list was endless. Progress had its drawbacks.

'I saw your boat bobbing about in the water this morning,' she said, after the 'Good-mornings', and the 'Nice days'.

'That you wouldn't, I'm afraid.' He tweaked his scarlet bow tie with a fishy finger, leaving a minute silver scale on it. 'I've given up my anchorage in the Bay. I keep it on the river bank now.'

'Why is that?' The shop was quiet. People were buying packaged fish in Tescos.

'It's more sheltered, and then I do a good trade in shrimps for The Eagle and Child. It's handy for me and Ron there. He'll take anything I get.'

'Do you think I'll just be looking out on a dirty swill soon?'

'You *are* looking out on a dirty swill, Mrs Garrett. It's fact and fiction, really. It *looks* nice on a sunny day with the seagulls flying around—well, we know why, don't we, so better not to think of the darker side, as you might say. As long as you don't eat your fish raw you can't get anything better. And you can't say those are taking much harm.' He smacked a fat trout.

'Those are river trout, though.'

'Same thing. You can't escape it now, river, sea, lake. But remember one thing, you can *gut* a fish. You can't gut a haunch of beef now, can you?'

'No, that's true. I'm rather taken by the look of those trout, but I think I'll have lemon sole today.'

'Southerners, them sole are.'

'Did they swim all the way up?'

'Now, now, Mrs Garrett. You always like your little joke, don't you? Reminds me of a Scotch lady who asked me if my Isle of Man kippers would travel to Glasgow. They could, I said, but you'd be better to go with them. We had a good laugh at that. Two nice lemon soles, is it, then? Expensive, but they're the queen of the sea, sole, as sweet as a nut.'

No, she decided, she wouldn't telephone Margaret. Alex would forget all about her trip to Manchester. It wasn't important to him. Her thoughts turned to Ben with longing. An obsession, an infatuation, lasting love, call it what you liked, took up too much space.

Chapter Fourteen

She was glad when Mr Doldren telephoned her from St Albans to say that matters were more or less finalized legally, and wondered if she could come and see him in his office.

She read the letter to Alex at breakfast one morning, causing him to emerge from behind his *Telegraph*. 'Would you like to take a day or so off and come with me?' she asked. She could afford to be magnanimous since she had been systematically deceiving him for months.

He pursed his full lips in the habit he had and moved them from side to side. 'How long would we be away?'

'I thought I'd go up to London afterwards and see James, stay the night there. I want to hear how he got on with his exams.'

'But he'll be home for Christmas presumably. Is it worth it?'

'It's always worth it to see James, and I might do some Christmas shopping as well.' She didn't say that it would be one way of passing the time until she saw Ben again. I'm like a moon-calf with this illicit love of mine, she thought, me a grown woman, a married woman... 'We could do a theatre,' she offered. She was so magnanimous. 'That new one of Lloyd Webber's.' She was even more magnanimous, downright sacrificial.

'No,' he said decidedly, 'on second thoughts, no. I'll tell you now although I was keeping it as a surprise. I thought I might take you to Lanzarote at the beginning of the year. I haven't spent much time with you recently what with golf and work.' She searched his face for any signs of guilt, but he was bland.

'It's kind of you, Alex, but, Lanzarote?' She spoke consideringly. 'It's so...barren.' She would never have dared to say that six months ago.

'You make the oddest remarks. I sometimes wonder... *Everybody* likes Lanzarote. They don't go for the scenery. They go for the sun and the sea and the life of leisure, to get away from it all.'

'I know they do. Margaret raves about it.'

'Well, Margaret's got some sense,' and then, irritably, 'How should I know what Margaret likes? So where *would* you like to go? It's *your* Christmas present. You might as well choose.'

She considered, head tilted. 'The very north of Scotland, if you could promise me the sky would be blue and there would be snow on the ground. And that we'd see a hare with its winter coat, snow-white, lolloping over the fields. It's a dream of mine.'

'For God's sake, Anne.'

'And come back to roaring log fires and Scotch whisky.'

'With icicles on your eyebrows. Not bloody likely.'

'Or, failing that, the Crillon in Paris for three days, living it up, and taking cabs at night to drive through the streets and see the floodlit buildings. During the day we'd eat at bars or cafés and go to the Cluny Museum and visit Proust's house...' She saw his look of bewilderment. 'The French writer, "Remembrance of Things Past" and all that.'

He made a gesture of impatience, a 'Tchaah!' 'No, definitely not, I don't want to hear any more of your harebrained schemes... Ha-ha!' He remembered the snow-white hare, 'Apt, eh? We're going for the sun, to recharge our batteries. If you don't like Lanzarote I'll stretch a point and go back to St Lucia, although we've been there.'

She gave up the pictures in her mind and came down to earth. Anywhere with Alex would be simply a wifely duty. She remembered how amorous he had become at St Lucia two years ago, and how tired she had been, physically, with his incessant lovemaking. People had asked her when she got back why she wasn't more sunburnt, and she had wanted to say, 'How could I be when Alex blotted it out?'

'All right,' she said, 'I'll go to St Albans on my own, and wherever you want in January will be very nice, if it's sun you're after. Did you know it gives you skin cancer?'

'You're getting positively weird,' he said, shaking his *Telegraph* violently as he resumed reading it. 'First snow-hares and driving in cabs in Paris and now skin cancer. You'll have to watch it.'

Mr Doldren welcomed her with quite a degree of affability. He asked his young secretary to bring tea, settled Anne in her chair and enquired after her health.

'It's good of you to come so promptly, Mrs Garrett, considering we solicitors don't get the name of being speedy ourselves.' She demurred graciously. He was really an attractive young man, as fair as Ben was dark, not nearly as virile-looking and lacking his Celtic mystery. Was Ben going to be her yardstick for all young men?

There were no problems. Miss Craig had been a very businesslike lady. She had made her will some years ago and had never changed it. 'It's such a help when a client knows his or her mind and sticks to it,' Mr Doldren said.

'Yes, she was a woman of character. I miss her very much.'

'She seemed to think a lot of you. Her house is a valuable property, especially in its location, very sought-after. Ah, thank you, Louise.' The young girl, carrying a tray, had opened the door with her knee. 'Put it there.' Louise smiled richly at Anne, the scarcely-contained exuberance of the really young, and went out with a flick of her short skirt above her high boots.

'Yes,' Mr Doldren went on, 'I remember Miss Craig telling me she was a regular visitor to our Museum. Local residents are admitted free, you know.'

'I've visited it with her, and the Roman Theatre. She was very proud of St Albans. "Never a dull moment here," she used to say, "right from Julius Caesar to the Magna Carta. And now the Poll Tax!" '

'Oh, it's the place to be without a doubt.' He wasn't expressing an opinion about the Poll Tax. 'And her house being near the Cathedral makes it very saleable. A prime site. Is the tea to your liking, Mrs Garrett?'

'Yes, thank you.'

Mr Doldren looked engaging, and young.

'I'll be frank with you, Mrs Garrett. My wife and I have been looking for a house in Fishpool Street for some time. We would like to buy Miss Craig's house.' He smiled, still engagingly, 'That must come as a surprise to you.'

'Yes, it does, rather. I hadn't thought...'

'You haven't made up your mind about selling it?'

She sipped her tea. 'Not quite, but I'm almost sure I shall. There doesn't seem much point...' She had an obscure desire not to commit herself wholly. 'My husband is securely based in the North, my son isn't nearly at the stage of settling down. I don't know if I should consult anyone first, my sister...'

'The house was specifically left to you, but, of course, you must speak to anyone you wish, ask their advice. Your husband might have different ideas.'

'I don't know...' Why hadn't they discussed it? She knew why in her case. She had been absorbed in Ben, and she had long since lost the habit of talking over things with Alex. He had probably taken it for granted that she was going to sell it. Perhaps their trip to the Caribbean was being planned on that assumption. 'I told my sister about it, I mean, being left it...'

He nodded, his eyes on her. She had the

216

impression there was a slight struggle going on inside him between Mr Doldren, the judicious young solicitor, and Mr Doldren, the house buyer, that the latter would have liked to say, 'It's nothing to do with her!'

'I more or less promised her that I would...see her all right.'

'Everything is in your name, remember.' He couldn't quite hide the disappointment.

'Yes. I suppose I could dispose of the furniture between my sister's family and my own?'

'It's yours, Mrs Garrett, to dispose of as you think fit. Now, I'll put my cards on the table. If you sell this house to me, it would make it very simple for you. All legal transactions would be taken care of. I would have it valued and give you the agreed price. There would be no quibbling.'

She was greatly tempted to say, 'Done!' She knew if she asked Alex he would say, 'Take his offer,' and Margaret would wonder why she even hesitated since it represented substantial capital. 'What do you think it's worth,' she asked, 'at a conservative estimate?'

'Around the three hundred thousand mark.' He spoke as if it were a fleabite. Their own double-fronted executive residence, as it had been called, had originally cost fourteen thousand pounds. It made you think. She took another sip of tea.

'I tell you what,' she was amazed at the clarity of her thinking, 'could we leave it until after Christmas? That's only a few weeks away. I'm supposed to be going on holiday with my husband sometime in January, and I'll let you know definitely before that. You can rest assured, Mr Doldren, that if I decide to sell, you will be the first to know. I can't think of anyone better to have it than you.'

'Emma's expecting,' he said boyishly. 'She just told me yesterday. We're beginning to bulge at the seams in our little place.'

'Well done,' she said, feeling it was required of her. 'Have you any documents for me to sign, Mr Doldren? I'm going up to town to see my son.'

'Certainly.' He said, as she was signing them, 'If my father had been alive he would have been very sorry indeed about Miss Craig's demise. They were great friends.'

'Did your mother know her?' She looked at him intently.

'Not as far as I know. She never spoke of her.'

'Or your sister perhaps?' She wanted him to say her name.

He shook his head. 'Can't ask her now. She's taken a job abroad. That's why we're rather interested in Miss Craig's house. Later on we thought my mother might come and live with us. That back sitting-room would make quite a good granny flat with the addition of a loo.'

Don't do it. It never works. The dominant Anne popped up. 'What a good idea,' she said, subduing her.

He was growing more like Alex, she decided, sitting across the table from her son. He had none of her reticence. 'What are you staring at, Annie?' he said, tackling his Roulade in the expensive restaurant he had chosen.

'I was just wondering why you decided to come to London at all?' The atmosphere was influencing her. The waiter who had taken their coats had been supercilious.

'Anthony and I applied for the same course at the Poly, don't you remember? We both wanted to shake ourselves free from provincialism. It's a relief to get down south amongst civilized people.'

'You shouldn't fall into that way of thinking. North versus South. That it's more civilized here, softer, warmer.' She remembered poor poignant Aschenbach in the opera who had believed that the South, as represented by Venice, would solve all his problems. Besides Anthony's mother had told her that Anthony had told *her* that James was desperate to get away from Alex. 'I bet you just wanted to get away from us.' She smiled at him.

'Not you. But, Mum, it's the place to be. Life's different here, freer, you can do your own thing, it's the anonymity which appeals to northerners. It's the *metropolis.*'

'It's also becoming sleazy and dirty. Too many people start off thinking like you then they're caught in a trap. I stayed last night with Marge Braithwaite. Do you remember her? They had two daughters...'

'Those frumps! No one would be seen dead with them at home!'

'Lisa is in the City now. In a brokerage firm. She's a power dresser and she wouldn't be seen dead with either you or Anthony. And Debbie's married, rather well, I believe, to a top surgeon in Wimpole Street.'

'See what London's done for them.' He smiled wickedly over his Vodka.

'It took me hours to get to their house. She's on the Northern line. Marge says she would give anything to see the sky over the Bay. It's the *amount* of sky she misses.'

'They can go back when they retire. No, it's all happening here, Annie. Saying you come from the provinces is as bad as saying you've been at the wrong school.'

'You went to a perfectly good one!'

'It was provincial, nevertheless, northern business men's sons. No one's even heard of it down here.'

'I'm sorry we made such a mistake.'

'Oh, I can live it down, not to worry.' He grinned at her, and she had to love him.

'I spent a day in Manchester recently, well, I stayed overnight. I went to the opera and had a lovely meal in the Yang Sing. I bet the food's better there than this place. The streets were lovely at night, not such a hassle as here. They have their Christmas lights up already round the Gardens. And there's nothing wrong with the Piccadilly Hotel, is there? I meet your Aunt Margaret there.'

He shrugged, looking around the dimly-lit corner where they had been guided forcibly by the waiter who had presented them with a menu and said, menacingly, 'Aperitif?'

'Shall we go and eat somewhere else?' she had said. She didn't want James to order another vodka.

They had been given what she thought was an inferior table near the toilets. They had conveyed their order to the waiter, or James had. She watched him doing it with the aplomb of someone who knows he won't have to pay the bill.

'I was just thinking,' she said, 'how like

your father you're becoming.'

'Great! He's a very handsome man, didn't you know?'

'So everyone tells me. They've even said we make a fine couple.' She played with her spoon. She was having Melon Oporto.

'I'm not surprised. I thought you looked like a young thing coming in here. And everything's shorter about you, your hair, and your skirt—it's quite daring, for you.'

'I feel daring these days,' she said, finding she could look him in the eyes.

'Don't tell me you're having an affair?' He laughed incredulously into his smoked trout.

'As a matter of fact I am.' The melon was unripe near the skin. She dug her pointed spoon into it. She would never have served melon like that. She used the whole house to ripen hers, taking it from room to room in a natural progression, according to the temperature. She never put it into the freezer until the last half-hour.

'You're joking,' he said, looking up.

'Why should I joke about a thing like that? With Ben Davies. You met him once at the house.'

'You mean that computer chap?' His knife and fork clattered down. He was bug-eyed with surprise.

'That's what your father calls him.'

'Don't tell me you've told *him!*'

'No, I'm not that daft. But I thought you would understand, James. You're young...'

'But so is he, Ben...'

'Davies.'

'Far too young for you.'

'Do you think so?'

'Well, have a heart, Mum!' (No Annie). 'What's the difference in years?'

'Eighteen.'

'Christ!' He ate rapidly for a few seconds as if to give him strength. Fish was supposed to be good for the brain. He was a handsome lad, she thought, and yet she felt detached. This was her life. She was convinced about one thing, that no one was going to interfere in it. She was amazed at her conviction, just as she had been amazed at her decision to do nothing about Aunt Elspeth's house, meantime...James was back with her, fortified cerebrally.

'You'd never do that to Dad, would you? You've been together now...'

'...for forty years. And it don't seem...'

'Oh, shut up!' He was a boy again, grinning at her, 'It's no laughing matter. No, seriously. You're known as an ideal couple. He's done everything for you, set you up in a lovely house...'

'Everything except make me happy. Are you ganging up with him against me? I always thought you didn't see eye to eye with him. In fact, when you were a little boy I can remember you being very miffed at him, kicking your heels against furniture in your rage, and...' No, she wouldn't mention the day of the party. That was a deeper thing altogether. It should be buried.

'All that was when I was a kid. I've grown up now.' He leaned back, handsome as could be in his dark shirt with the white collar, his handsome sulky mouth. He burst out. 'I can't believe it, that you, my mother!'

'What happened to Annie? I thought I was something else as well, a woman who has kept an unhappy marriage going for twenty years, largely for your sake...' She stopped, seeing the displeasure in his eyes, a frightened disgust. It was all right for men, but women, worse than that, his mother! Was he really so like Alex that he wanted it to 'look nice', to keep the home background intact? Abnegation on her part. That was it.

'You're joking, of course,' he said again, but not too sure, taking a good slurp of wine. 'You're pulling my leg, aren't you?'

'If that makes it easier for you, yes.'

She went on to tell him about the house. She noticed with pleasure that he wasn't avaricious. He didn't say she should sell it and collect the money, nor did he show any interest in the furniture when she described some of Aunt Elspeth's pieces. He was too young to feel proprietorial. She hugged him warmly when she left. He was her son and she loved him.

Chapter Fifteen

The run-up to Christmas. Shopping in crowded stores, planning food—James would be home—stocking the freezer, making sauces and stuffings and mincemeat because he and Alex always said, 'Don't buy any of that awful shop stuff.'

In the CAB, wife-bashing, baby-bashing, incest, attempted suicides, people who couldn't pay their mortgages, people who used credit cards in place of non-existent bank accounts, women who shoplifted through boredom, through drug-taking, through greed, through depression.

And, since they were nothing if not up-to-date, a young man with an old face came in one morning and said he was worried to death because the girl he had had intercourse with several times had just told him she was HIV Positive.

'I didn't know what she meant at first,' he said, looking like Ghandi on a fast, 'I said, "What's that?" and she said "Aids, you fool, I could get Aids. Don't you ever use your brain instead of your..."' He looked ruefully at Anne. 'We were in the same Bed and Breakfast, ditched there by the Government. I'd been up the hill.' This, Anne recognized, as a local euphemism for the Mental Hospital a few miles out of town. 'It was a dingy place, the B & B, as cold as charity. The only way you could keep warm was to...' He stopped abruptly. A poor vocabulary made it very difficult, she thought with pity, when you had to make your meaning clear.

She advised him to go to his doctor immediately. 'He'll explain what you have to do. Don't waste any time. Promise you'll go right away.'

'Maybe it'll get me out of the B & B,' he said, with an attempt at a joke. That evening she gathered up some leaflets and took them home. She wasn't too well-read on the subject herself.

And in the Hospice people slept quietly into death, or held on to a thread of life, and it was the only place she saw joy untainted by materialism. Had you to die to get away from it all?

No matter how unhappy she was she would never want to die. She liked it here. But how would you feel if your inside was being eaten away by cancer or Aids? She felt young and able to cope, and Ben telephoned her when he knew Alex would not be there and made her feel loved.

'Everyone wants software for Christmas. I have to go to Birmingham on a seminar.

I have to give demonstrations in Hull and Wigan, I have to take people out to dinner, I have to induce them to buy. It's hectic. Christmas is hectic. I love you.'

'I love you. Miss you. Is there no hope of a quick trip to our pub even for a Christmas drink?'

'Not a chance. If it's possible I'll ring you again. I have had to put in an answering machine. Don't be alarmed, and don't leave messages on it. It's strictly business.'

'I wouldn't dream of leaving messages on it.' She was hurt.

'Have I offended you?'

'Of course not. I'm busy, Ben. I'm due in town in half an hour.' My work is fundamentally more important than yours. That she didn't say, but it had occurred to her that his was connected with promoting materialism, hers was an attempt to cope with its effects. 'Ring me again.'

'We'll fix something up. It's the one thing I want to do. Goodbye.'

She had to be content with that. She threw herself into her work and only thought of him when Alex made love to her systematically three times per week. It was a guilt-making exercise but she took it as her due punishment and excelled in fakery.

If Alex were only cruel to her, she would

think, knocked her about a bit, it would be easy to leave him. But what to do about a man who provided well for her by working hard, was convivial most of the time, even although he fell asleep in front of television plays she admired?

'What will they think of next?' he would say, opening one eye on a heaving naked couple, the prerequisite of many television plays. As if he had never heard of the practice. As if he had never indulged in it himself, systematically, three times per week.

If only when with him, she didn't feel as if she were constantly firing on only one cylinder. Where were those talks they might have had, now that there was more time, on the state of the world generally, on Mr Bush's attitude to abortion, on the downfall of Communism in Czechoslovakia, on the taking down of the Berlin Wall. Why did he not rejoice when he saw the Eastern Germans pouring through, like children going to a party from which they had long been banned?

But, did she ever have such conversations with Ben? He wasn't insular, like Alex. Although by an odd comment here and there he revealed that he was aware of what went on in the world, he never discussed politics. Perhaps, she thought, it was because their time together was so short, because they were obsessed with loving. That wouldn't last if they could be together all the time. Then would come the sharing of opinions. So she told herself.

She bought a new dress for Margaret's party, a shot silk two-piece in subtle shades of midnight blue and turquoise which set off the soft tones of her brown hair, its shorter length now grown familiar with the contours of her head and clinging to it in a natural kind of way. She bought turquoise enamelled earrings set in heavy silver. They were Alex's Christmas present to her, chosen by her, paid for by him. She felt like a whore when she first put them on but the feeling soon wore off.

They drove up to Manchester through a Lowry landscape in a car which slithered on icy roads and made sickening lurches past giant lorries with Alex cursing their drivers but following again too closely.

She divorced herself from the situation and preserved her sanity by pretending she was in a little private world with peepholes into outer space, except when she felt they were an accident hurrying to happen. She didn't dare say this to the tense-faced man beside her. His reaction to fog had always been to drive faster and get out of it. Anything she said, she knew from experience, would only increase the danger. Meantime, she told herself, she was warm, anonymous, in her steel box with time punctuated by the rhythmic beat of the windscreen wipers.

When they left the motorway and were in the city streets, she allowed herself to return to reality. She saw a young couple laughing at each other at a bus stop, her face raised to his, a Salford Juliet. The deep searing pain slicing through her heart made her bend forward to cover it. She sat with her hands tightly clasped until the suffering grew less, her mouth clamped shut in case a cry would escape it.

Ben's last telephone call had been ambiguous, hurried. 'Haven't time to talk. Party? What party? Oh, Judith's mother's? Yes, I'll be there if I can. Must go...'

Margaret had the capacity for crowding more people into her small rooms than anyone Anne knew. She used every inch of space. People were invited to stand or sit 'even on the loo seat, if you like,' Anne heard her laughingly tell someone who arrived at the same time as they did.

'My little sister!' Clasping Anne's hands, spreading their arms together, 'Oh, very fetching!' Then, standing back, hands on hips. 'Who do you intend to charm tonight? It can't be you, Alex, can it? You're old hat.' She kissed him too, putting her hands on his shoulders. 'Yummy. He's a good kisser, isn't he, Anne? You won't know many people, but just barge. Everybody will be glad to talk to anyone who doesn't live in dreary old Manchester. Grab a glass of that poison and circulate.'

Anne was an old hand at the game. She parted automatically from Alex's side and launched herself into the thick of a group of people gathered round a table with titbits on it, like birds round a bird bath, she thought, fluttering, pecking, turning their heads about, nodding. 'Excuse me! Must get something to nibble. Oh, thanks, I *love* vol-au-vents. I'm Anne Garrett, Margaret's sister. No, I don't look a bit like her. She has all the good looks. Oh, how nice of you to say so. It must be the sea air. No, not the Manchester Ship Canal. I live on the coast. Yes, I'm lucky. Yes, just about the width of the road between our house and the sea. Yes, I love it, pollution and all. Buried? No, it isn't really *buried.* I can drive up here for concerts and things in little over an hour. Yes, actually I did see the opera, *Death in Venice.* Yes, I liked it enormously. No, I don't think it's a disadvantage being in English. You know what it's about. No glamour? Who wants glamour? Plenty of poignancy, and sadness. Well, the sadness of life, the imminence of death. You feel it creeping over your heart...yes, of course, I must circulate too. That's what parties are for, isn't it?'

She kept circulating, kept talking, but saw no sign of either Alex or Margaret. He must be helping her with the drinks in the kitchen. Nor Judith, strangely enough. She felt suddenly as if she were stranded on a barren island with only the chatter of natives around her. Her dress, and the earrings, suddenly seemed grotesque, too much. Why was she here? Where was Ben? If he had really wanted to see her he would have turned up by this time. Maybe he didn't think it worth it. Ben...Ben... 'Oh, thank you *so* much. After this one I definitely go on to orange juice...'

It was half-past eight. Ben looked at his watch for the tenth time at least. To go or not to go. She would be there. Even seeing her in a crowd would be worth it. Sometimes he couldn't understand the obsessional quality of the feeling he had for Anne. It was all against his tenets.

With Judith it had been a game which they both played. Of course she was very beautiful, but her beauty had little appeal for him. What had happened that night he knew had been engineered by her, the short semi-transparent dressing gown falling off her shoulders, the bare feet, too much wine.

He had been a sitting duck, seduced, half-drunk, condomless, presuming, but not asking if she were on the Pill. To admit that, made him grimace with disgust, that he had fallen for the perfume, the moist, beautiful mouth, the moist thighs, old-fashioned trickery because he couldn't think straight.

'Let's hope it was a bull's eye,' she had said when he came back from showering. He had felt the need. And seeing his surprise—and no doubt his half-open mouth—'I thought you knew what I wanted. I've made no secret of it. But, not to worry. It's nothing to do with you.'

He had banged out of her flat in self-disgust after a tirade which she had listened to, smiling. That had been almost the worst part of it. On the way downstairs he met her flat-mate, a girl he hardly knew, and she had the same female smile...

The anger had gone now. The blow, when it fell, had an inevitability about it, almost a relief. Judith hadn't bothered to tell him. It was Jenny Adamson who told him that Judith had left. 'You must know why, Ben,' she had said, hollowing her cheeks, smiling that female smile at him. He had spoken to Judith on the phone, but she had refused to meet him. 'Send me chocolates and some books,' she had said.

The comparison between Anne and Judith was odious, her freshness, her sweetness, her emotional vulnerability. She was always going on about her age, but she didn't realize how *young* she was in comparison with girls like Judith, who were as old as Eve...he wished he could put into words her peculiar appeal for him. Perhaps he had some poetry which would put it better than he could.

In his bedroom he picked up the Larkin which had lain on his bedside table for the last month or so. There was no comfort for him there. It was better to look in some of the so-called love poets. He went back to his bookshelves, knowing he was deliberately putting off time to avoid making a decision about the party.

'O were I on Parnassus hill
Or had o' Helicon my fill,
That I might catch poetic skill,
To sing how dear I love thee!'

Good for Robert Burns, 'Rabbie', they called him. But what the hell did 'helicon' mean? Wasn't it some kind of saxhorn?

'For a' the lee-lang simmer's day,
I couldna sing, I couldna sing,
How much, how dear I love thee...'

That was it, 'How much, how dear I love thee.' Anne. He made an image of her in his mind, the brown, bird-wing hair, the delicate sensitive features, the slimness and winsomeness. Renoir wasn't for him. That flower picture of his they had seen in Manchester, when they had gone in from the cold, had had the same effect on him as a bunch of Renoir's naked women might have had, which was nil. Perhaps Renoir had thought of flowers and fat breasts and buttocks as one and the same thing. They should get up a retrospective and jumble them altogether. One of those art critics could do an erudite piece on it...he flung the book from him and looked at his watch. Nine o'clock. If he were going he'd better go.

He changed his shoes for light-soled ones, found his leather bomber jacket, put it over the suit he had changed into earlier in the evening. He was old-fashioned, he supposed. He liked to party in a suit.

The car park behind the flats was poorly lit. At the last meeting of the owners they had put in a request for a step-up in the lighting. God knows, they were paying plenty for the privilege of living here.

He saw his Volvo at the far end, remembered he had put it there last night because all the spaces had been taken. There was no one about, which was unusual. He supposed that people who were going out for the evening had already done so, either to eat or to go to a movie.

He walked towards the car, his steps dragging, like his thoughts. He didn't want to go to this party Judith's mother was giving. Did *she* know about her daughter? And about him? Would Judith be there? Anne would. Would *she* know? He thought of her eyes turning on him coldly, those eyes he had liked so much, their cool greyness, their brown lashes. Most girls made their eyelashes coal-black, stiff and hard-looking. You felt you could stroke hers. He had, with his tongue. He felt his body move. *Anne...*

He was suddenly taken by the scruff of the neck by a hand, propelled roughly towards the Volvo, his feet leaving the ground, and banged viciously against its side. He came out of shock when he heard something crack. The wing mirror. Not his ribs. Three inches from his there was a stocking-masked face...the cold eyes brought him to life and he threshed violently in the man's grip, kicking, shouting, 'What are you up to, you bas...!'

He was silenced by a vicious cut across the mouth. The quality of expertise, of economy of effort put the fear of death in him. His voice was feebler this time. 'You'll be seen...the police...!' He heard it spiralling thinly round the space, ineffectively.

It was too like a movie, the whole thing, a familiar one, man attacked in car park, generally underground, (the only difference), and then all thought left him as he felt the full force of a fist with something lethal in its core smash into his face. He heard the small tearing noise of his skin ripping from his flesh, tasted the warm saltness of blood in his mouth. Something rattled into it. He spat out a tooth, fell to his knees to try to get away from his attacker, and as he did so heard a north-country voice close to his ear, quiet, almost polite, 'Gerrup and take your medicine now, boy.'

He was dragged to his feet, and his own knee up in the only defensive action he could think of, felt it knocked aside like a ball of paper and an iron knee rammed into his own crutch. Any fight left him. He slid down the smooth side of the Volvo. The vicious kick to his ribs was completely painless. There were no more threshholds of pain. The small rhythmic blows in his head he identified as quick footsteps walking away from him—not running.

He lay there, observing with the small part of his brain still functioning, the reactions of his body to the assault, how it trembled and throbbed, how the small part of his brain left to him could still speculate. Why had the man dragged him to the Volvo? Was his car significant, a part reason for the attack? Cars, power, red, sexual symbol...he and Anne had lain in it...he drifted away into some kind of limbo, deliberately, as an escape.

And then, he was back with himself again, however damaged, his mind clear. Now he had to rally himself, drag himself to the nearest telephone, get himself seen to. He felt ashamed, not murderous. He had had it coming to him.

He was half on his feet, mopping at his face with a handkerchief when he heard the quick tap-tap of heels, feminine heels, the bang of a car boot. He focused on a woman halfway down the space, saw her move towards her car door, tap-tap-tap, open it. In a moment she would be gone.

To shout 'Help!' was too much like that movie he was in. He groaned, loudly, and knew she had stopped to listen, a listening silence. She would be frightened. He called loudly, but tried to make the call reassuring, 'I've been attacked! It's Ben Davies. In the flat above...' The effort made him slump back on the concrete, but he heard her heels as she came running towards the sound, knew that she was bending over him. He couldn't be bothered to open his eyes. The voice was young, familiar.

'My God! Mr Davies! What on earth's happened to you?'

'Who... Is it...' He heard his own voice trail away.

'Yes. Jane Lampson. This is *terr*...ible! Unbelievable!' She was having difficulty in getting into his movie.

'Get someone. You'll need help...' He'd been right. It was Mrs Lampson. The quick tap-tap of heels had told him, a small young woman with matchstick legs, thin, nervous hands, always rushing.

'Right. Right away! I'll get Frank. I was just going to the Take-Away. We couldn't be bothered cooking...right, right away...oh, this is wicked, what's been done to you...lie still,' (that was unnecessary advice), 'I'll get Frank...'

Anne looked surreptitiously at her watch. Ten thirty. Ben wasn't coming. She had had one drink too many which had dulled the pain. She looked around and saw Alex bent over a young girl, exercising his rusty charm. Men nearing fifty reckoned they were irresistible to young girls. She felt fond of him because of this foible. She would give him five more minutes and then sidle up and say, 'I think we should be making tracks now, Alex,' and enjoy the rueful look he would exchange with the girl, 'Wives!'

Margaret was at her side, scintillating in a lame jacket and sparkling, dangling earrings, eyes no less bright. Anne said to her. 'I'm just going to prize Alex away from that young thing he's speaking to.'

'Oh, let the old boy have his fun.' She whirled to look, whirled back, 'You have to give them a long lead. Best way to keep them.' How mischievous her eyes were! What was the joke?

'I thought Ben Davies would be coming.' She tried hard to be casual, thought because of the drink inside her she might be looking lugubrious. 'Isn't he a friend of Judith's?'

'A *friend* she says.' Margaret laughed. 'That's rich! You don't know you're born, Anne. Never have. Haven't you seen Judith?' It was the stance she remembered from the photograph, bold, challenging, but this time a front, surely. Had it always been a front?

'No, I haven't. Has she been here?'

'She's been in and out. Look, there she is, coming out of the kitchen. She's only got one thing on her mind these days and that's food—and keeping it down.'

Anne looked. The short black dress

made her niece look square. Or perhaps it was the straight line from bust to hem, no waist, which gave the illusion.

She didn't believe what she saw, at first. She knew Margaret was watching her, refused to meet her eyes.

'Well, has the penny dropped? Maybe *that's* why your precious Ben wouldn't come. Afraid to face an irate Mama. Although, why should I care? She's got what she wanted. She's single-minded, my daughter. "Don't say I didn't warn you, Mum" she had the cheek to say to me when I tumbled to it.'

Her sister's words were banging about in her head. 'Your precious Ben...' 'Afraid to face an irate Mama...' 'Got what she wanted...'

'I'll have to go, Margaret...'

'What's the rush?' She put out a restraining hand. 'Do you remember what it was like for me? Father half off his head, shouting, wanting to throw me out on the streets. Mother...'

'Mother was all right. She said if you loved Ralph you should go ahead and marry him, but only if you loved him...I must go. Alex...' She shook herself free and began to weave her way towards him, not seeing the people who were making way for her. The worst blows in my life have always come from Margaret. But it isn't

Margaret this time... 'Could you excuse me, please? Yes, wonderful party...'

Judith was standing in front of her, beautiful as ever, her eyes doubly beautiful because they were pregnant eyes, dark-ringed, full, as if they were putting on weight too. 'Hello, Anne. You're not going already, are you?'

'Yes. We have a long way to go...' 'I can drive up here for concerts and things in little over an hour,' she had said earlier in her silly talk round the titbits. She drew in her breath, smiled. 'How are you, Judith? Haven't seen you since...'

'Blooming, as you can see. Oh, come off it, Anne. Always polite...and don't stare at me with those great eyes of yours. You'd think you'd fallen off another planet. I'm pregnant. It's what I wanted. It's not very funny at first, you'll know that, morning sickness, but I'm getting into the swing of things now, or my body is. The end result will be worth it.'

'You always wanted a baby?'

'Not always. But it became a...terrible need, a regret because Jeremy couldn't. The father of this poppet could. And how! You could give him the job of Official Procreator! God, that's good! I just thought it up.'

It was evening, not morning, sickness with her. Anne's gorge rose and she spoke quickly. 'Suddenly desperate to go to the loo. Glad about your...news. Excuse me.' She saw the amusement in the eyes as she turned to push through the groups of people. She was aware of a few glances, only momentary. She was of no account.

In Margaret's cluttered bathroom with its damp, stale smell overlaid with perfume, its peeling paper on the ceiling—she actually noticed that in her rush to the lavatory bowl—she retched her heart out. There was a tideline when she flushed it eventually. Margaret had never been too particular in her housekeeping. The feeling was of being outside herself, noticing everything and yet not believing in the misery she was feeling. In Margaret's bedroom she noticed the variety in the pile of coats and jackets on the bed. She had to root amongst them for a long time before she found her Liberty shawl crushed to a ball.

She found Margaret laughing with a group of people. The party face she turned on Anne was vague for a second as if she hardly recognized her. 'Oh, Anne! Well, if you have to slip off...mind how you go.' She turned back.

'I want to go home, Alex.' She knew she was abrupt in her interruption of his long monologue, but the girl with hair like a prancing pony who was listening, looked relieved. After a few drinks at a party he invariably cornered someone and inflicted on them his complaints, usually about the firm. 'Those buggers never deliver on time. Hold up the whole job. And the men, of course, slouch about, quite pleased...' He had a bee in his bonnet about his staff, about suppliers. It was downright amazing what claptrap women were supposed to listen to from men at parties. 'Are you coming?' She was brief. She forgot her usual politeness.

The girl smiled at Anne and slipped away like an eel.

Chapter Sixteen

She offered to drive on the way home, but he said he knew his own car better. 'Neither of us could pass the test, if it came to it,' he said, 'but women get pissed on less than men.'

'I'm not drunk,' she said. She disliked the word 'pissed', disliked herself for disliking it, 'I went on to orange juice after three.'

'It depends on what the three were. Margaret goes mad with bottles she finds in the kitchen. Talk about a devil's brew! She puts the lot in.'

'I only had wine. I never touch her concoctions. Was that what you were doing in the kitchen, the two of you?'

'Doing? Yes, we had fun sloshing in the bottles. The roads are quiet, aren't they? Thank God the fog's lifted. The main thing is to drive within the speed limit, just.' He sounded amiable, and sober.

She relaxed, but nothing could take away the feeling that her whole world was caving in. Judith pregnant. The square, black, waistless figure topped by that beautiful face, the black ringlets in front of the ears, the rest of her hair swept high, her amused eyes, her *pregnant* eyes. *You could give him the job of Official Procreator...*

She couldn't even tell Ben how badly she felt about it. She had no right. She remembered a story she had once read about a girl whose married lover had died and how her agony had been worse because she could not grieve in public. She was in the same position.

There was a glimmer in the darkness of her thinking. Could it have been Margaret's malicious tongue again? There was no denying Judith was pregnant, looked pregnant, but what proof was there that the child was Ben's? Judith hadn't said it was. And surely he would have told her. Or would he? And wasn't it conventional rubbish to tell herself she had no right to ask him? Didn't being in love give her that right?

Her mind was in a whirl. It was a different world nowadays. She was out of step. Her memory of the Sixties was of girls determined to *avoid* pregnancy. Now they wanted to procreate with or without a stable relationship, far less marriage. If anything made you feel out of step it was to have lived through such a change.

She remembered that her anxiety before the party had been that Alex might check with Margaret to see if she had stayed with her after the opera. Now it had paled into insignificance beside the image in her mind of that black figure with its undeniable look of pregnancy, the sway-back stance, the added bloom. *Why didn't you tell me, Ben?* The tears filled her nose suddenly and she blew it. 'Got a cold, I think,' she muttered. Her mind went to that day they had spent together in the Lakes, and of Ben clambering up the bank at Esthwaite, the menacing figure of the swan at his heels. 'I'm shy but not timid,' she had once said. Was it the reverse with him?

She had a sudden swift longing for the dull but non-traumatic life which she had led before she met him. Was it better to tell him it was over between them, before he told *her*? Her confusion and misery was so overwhelming that she said, unwisely, 'What *were* you and Margaret talking about in the kitchen...for such a long time?'

He didn't take offence. 'Oh, nothing much. Margaret and I always chatter away. We're two of a kind.'

'Perhaps you should have married her rather than me.' She looked at the dark streets as if they represented her past.

'Maybe I should.' He wasn't going to be drawn.

'Did she tell you about Judith's pregnancy?' It was out at last.

He didn't answer. She even wondered

if he could have heard her. He was pretending to peer out of the window. There was nothing to peer at. Salford was more or less asleep, looking better in darkness. The looming bulk of the University gave it a sober and academic air. Many of its windows were lit.

How calming it would be to be seated at a desk in a quiet room, absorbed in the books in front of her. I'm really a thwarted academic, she told herself, remembering the feeling of rightness she always got when she studied for her poetry class. It was an escape route from personal problems, if a dessicated one. Ben had changed her life, but it had proved too difficult. She had stepped out of her role, like wearing a new dress. She had always felt more comfortable in old clothes, clothes she felt at home in. *A married woman...*

The words stopped her introspection. She was back with the present, with her husband, Alex, of twenty years who had never wanted to know what went on in her mind. She had to externalize. 'You didn't answer my question.'

'What question?'

'About Judith being pregnant. If you knew.'

'Yes, Margaret told me. Is that what you asked? It's fairly common now, she says, to want a baby and not the man to go with it.' He laughed shortly. 'Go it alone. Whatever next? But trust old Judy to be in the vanguard.'

'Did you gather Margaret was pleased? Or sorry? What was her attitude? I'm sure Judith felt she had missed out on that short marriage of hers with Jeremy.' *Or I am now.*

'Missed out! That was a disaster! That twister couldn't even make up his mind *what* he was. Better to be an out-and-out poofter like Richard than that. Poor old Margaret. She hasn't had much luck with her family.'

It all depended on your attitude, Anne thought. She had long since given up trying to champion Richard to Alex, and she hadn't even tried with Jeremy Crump. She remembered his sliding shy smile when he had come to visit with Judith. He had brought her a single rose, and Alex had scarcely concealed his disdain. 'What in God's name persuaded a smasher like Judy to choose him!' What indeed? One of life's great mysteries.

'I never realized Judith felt she was deprived of a child in that marriage. She was always dashing about having a good time, but maybe in hindsight... I wonder if she ever talked about it to her mother? I don't know what daughters are like. Do you think she confided in her mother?' Anne asked.

'God knows. Does it matter? Besides, people don't go on the way you do, analysing everything. They accept a thing when it happens. Judy became broody too late, that's all there is to it.' He added self-righteously, 'It's all that voluntary work you do that makes you curious, sitting people down, poking your nose into their private affairs...'

'Thank you very much. It's because they can't manage their own that they come to us. And I don't "poke my nose" as you put it into their private affairs. Often I only tell them where they can get help.'

'Is that so? Well, you're the expert.' Now his urbanity was making her suspicious. Generally he had only two moods, morose, or jolly. Alex was a black and white man. You knew where you were with Alex. Generally. Her mind veered away from him, as from a brick wall.

Cars and planes, she thought, when you're driven or flown, when it's out of your hands and you don't have to concentrate...the effect was soothing, free-wheeling. Perhaps Ben had been too busy to come. She saw him in a strange bedroom in one of those big conference hotels in Birmingham, or perhaps closer by at Wigan, sorting out his computer

251

handouts—he had once shown them to her—major automotive components and accessories, software tools and techniques... Strange that she should remember the jargon when it was so meaningless to her.

Margaret was a mischief maker. It was inherent in her character, those sharp little barbs stuck in randomly wherever she was. She might have picked up something about Anne's association with Ben from Judith, or her friend, Jenny, and passed it on to Alex. Gossip, especially malicious gossip, was the spice of life to her. She wasn't uncomplicated, like Alex. She loved 'situations'. She liked manipulating. Her remark, for instance, about being 'an irate Mama'...was that designed simply to prick, to annoy? She couldn't really know, could she, that her sister was having an affair with Ben? Their meetings had always been in the Lakes, except for that one day they had spent in Manchester.

Now she saw the foolishness of that, no less than the foolishness of going to Ben's flat and saying she had spent the night with Margaret. *Oh, foolish, foolish,* she thought now.

But the Lakes had been safe enough, hadn't they? On their walks in the Winster Valley they had scarcely met a soul. But, and she went cold, a miserable kind of coldness which had an element of nausea in it, in the pub she had seen that man who she thought looked like Jack Spiers. That thin-faced, bitter-looking man whom Alex said had been in prison and 'would do anything for him.' What, for instance? Spy? He would be good at that, a night watchman. She heard her voice, was too late to stop it. 'I wonder who the father of Judith's baby is?'

'Why don't you ask her?' They were on the motorway now, speeding homewards. His touch on the car was sure. They would be all right, and he was keeping well within the speed limit.

'I couldn't do that.'

' 'fraid to?'

'No, it's just...none of my business.'

'Are you sure about that?' He beat his hands softly on the wheel, humming from one of the tapes which had been playing at the party, an old one, 'Are you lonesome tonight?' Lovely. So sad. The poignancy gave way to a new coldness, a new kind of fear, a sword-hanging kind of Damoclesian fear which made her grow rigid.

She felt her blood pressure drop. The feeling was physical, a drained feeling as if her energy was ebbing away, even her life. She had too many worries to cope with, that was it. 'You can only worry about one thing at a time,' they said, but that wasn't true. She could vouch for that.

Generally she liked the last-minute pre-parations for Christmas, but this time was different. She had no heart for it. She bought Christmas cards, half because she liked the pictures on the front, the other half because they helped Cancercare, or Oxfam, or the Blind, or the Spastics, and diligently signed twenty each evening.

It was the only way to get through them. They sent about two hundred each year, and never, even when she had been ill, had Alex offered to help her. Christmas card writing and sending was designated as 'women's work', which was fair enough since she thought of changing light bulbs as men's, although she was perfectly able to jump up on a chair and do it.

She spoke to James on the telephone, and he said, of course he would be coming home for Christmas, where else, which warmed her, but after that he and Anthony were going skiing if they could find a place where there was snow. Anthony knew a place in Switzerland where they had artificial stuff now, but he didn't fancy that. No, they weren't interested in après-ski. They were keen. And girls were out. Or so he said. She laughed at him and then caught her breath. Would he recognize a girl, if he met one, who 'wanted to procreate'?

She telephoned Margaret and asked her to come at Christmas, but she was offhand and said she didn't know if she could. 'You're the limit, Anne. Only people like you who don't work can plan so far ahead. I'm up to the eyes with everything...must go, sorry. *Ciao.*'

Each day became more difficult than the last. Ben hadn't telephoned her, and she had decided she wouldn't telephone him. Their affair was over—or he was allowing it to die a natural death—or he was too busy—or he was too involved with Judith—or he was ashamed—or Margaret had been lying...it was an incredible mishmash in her mind.

She felt herself grow thinner each day. All her bloom which she had been aware of through that wonderful autumn and early winter had gone. Her skin looked grey, she was incessantly cold, she caught every kind of feverish infection which was going, she often crawled into bed after she had made supper, exhausted.

This didn't seem to matter to Alex. The run-up to Christmas was busy for him, always was. All the Do-it-Yourselfers were being urged to complete their projects by their wives, and there was an unprece-dented demand on his stock of builders' supplies, which necessitated him working long hours. He would go off after supper 'to see how they were doing at the Depot.' The Canteen was open for the night shift, and he could always get a cup of coffee there. 'Or Jack Spiers will brew me up one in his box. Cosy little place, that.' He invited her response.

'I'm surprised you fraternize with that man. He isn't your style at all.'

'Isn't he? But I told you before he has been very useful to me. Does all my dirty work.'

She thought, looking at him, that if she had changed, so had he. He had become complex, difficult to evaluate. He seemed devious, and as if he enjoyed this new deviousness in himself which he had acquired. And watchful.

Once he said to her. 'You look different, these days.'

'How different? I've got this sinus trouble. Is that it? It gives me a drawn look. Maybe I'll go and see the doctor.'

'You looked so...on top of the world this summer. And later too.'

'Up to the cold weather arriving. Or the damp. It's the damp.'

'Could be. It was a wonderful summer, all the same. Everyone felt well. It let you see how nice we could be to each other, people, if we had weather like that all the time.'

They were like two strangers speaking.

'Yes.' She was pleased, nevertheless, that he was becoming more sensitive. 'Remember how we enjoyed the sun on the Bay when we were eating? And the sunsets. Now it's shrouded in mist all the time, and when the tide's out it's grey, coffin-grey, like wet clay. It used to have different tones, warm tones like animal fur, fox, and beaver, and mole, a touch of ermine...'

'You're a fanciful little thing,' he said. Her eyes filled with tears. It was the nearest he had got to a real endearment for years.

She didn't say that the sad clay-greyness of the sea suited her mood, that she sat and gazed at it and thought constantly of Ben. She loved him still. Didn't he love her? And if so, why didn't he telephone? He must realize that she couldn't bring herself to telephone him. It was impossible, quite impossible. And having decided it was impossible she rang his office one day and they said he was in London. She didn't know whether to be glad or sorry. Or whether to believe it.

A few days later when she was in the kitchen preparing some food for the freezer, she heard the click of the letter-box and ran into the hall. A single square white envelope lay on the carpet. It was definitely not junk mail which flooded in on the morning post, as well as letters from the Bank, from Insurance Companies, Builders Suppliers, her own mail from CAB headquarters sending the latest leaflets. Alex kept a wastepaper basket at his side when he was opening his.

She took it back to the kitchen table and sat down. Her name and address were typewritten, but that didn't mean anything. Ben kept a typewriter in his flat. She opened the envelope, her spirits falling when she saw the letter-headed notepaper. She glanced at the signature. 'Gerald Doldren'.

'...The legal formalities pertaining to your house are now completed, and it is in your possession as from today.

I wondered if by this time you had formulated any plans regarding it, and wish to put on record that my wife and I would still like to be considered as potential buyers if you should wish to dispose of it. We would, of course, pay the current value.

I do not wish to put pressure on you in any way, but perhaps you could let me know if you have thought further on this matter.

May I take this opportunity of wishing you the compliments of the season...'

She went on with the mincemeat she was making. For some reason, the letter seemed like a light, a very dim light at the end of a very long tunnel.

Chapter Seventeen

It was a quiet Christmas. She had far too much food in the house, and made up her mind that she would take some of it to the Children's Home nearby. Some of the Downs Syndrome occupants had come to know her on her visits. Or perhaps she would offer it to those callers at the CAB whose circumstances she knew. She would be careful, of course, and impress upon them that they would be doing *her* a favour. The more she was involved in voluntary organizations, the more she realized what an insulting downbeat word 'pity' was.

Margaret kept her on tenterhooks until the last minute. She was working late, or she was doing late night shopping, 'not like you who have all day to do it in.' Richard and Con were off to Morocco for Christmas. They preferred souks to stuffing themselves with turkey. 'What a thing to say, don't you think?' Margaret had said. 'He's so unfeeling. Oh, well, it's perhaps better. I can't go on introducing them to my friends. The penny's bound to have dropped by this time.'

'I wish you were all coming to me,' Anne said. 'I've loads of food. I've been making it automatically for the last month. I go into fast forward around November, a form of therapy.' Did you tell Alex I didn't stay that night with you? Did he ask?

'What do you mean by that? You say the oddest things, Anne. But there's Judith.' She became schmaltzy, a new role. 'She needs her mother at Christmas, especially now.'

'She's included in the invitation. How is she?' Go on, ask. Her alter ego had surfaced again. Ask who is the father of her child. If it's Ben.

'Oh, she's positively blooming. Well, you should know as much about it as me.'

'I don't know what you mean, Margaret.' Fearfully. Did she mean as a mother, or as the lover of the putative father? Up till now all she had felt for Ben was longing. Now with this threat hanging over her, there was resentment. It was unfair of him to disappear and leave her to face this alone. She had to know the truth.

'I don't know what I mean myself sometimes.' Margaret was querulous. 'It's all right for you, Anne, up there in the lap of luxury and nothing else to do but make loads of food as "a form of therapy".' She laughed disbelievingly. 'I must say you have acquired some strange expressions since you started doing that voluntary work.'

'Well, at least you're acknowledging that I *do* something, that I'm not entirely bone idle as you always try to make out.'

This time Margaret wasn't prepared to fight. 'Do I?' Great sigh. The cares of the world. 'Well, I assure you it isn't intentional. You're my only sister. I'm fond of you, Solemn Sides.'

'And I'm fond of you, Bossy Boots. Come at Christmas, Margaret. I'd have nobody to squabble with if you don't.'

'Well, I'll see...I'll do my best...' The usual liveliness of her voice had gone. She sounded desolated. 'You're a good sort, Anne. It's a shame...' And then, quickly, as if she'd had an adrenalin injection. 'Not to worry! If I don't turn up, your present will be in the post. I've bought something very special for you, just to show you that...'

'Show me what?' But she had hung up.

There were only four of them at the Christmas table after all, James, Alex, herself and Mrs Parkinson from down the road, Anne's hair shirt. Mrs Parkinson was to be alone at Christmas. There had been a weekly reminder when Anne delivered the shopping which she did for her. She had been worn down. She had said to Alex, 'The turkey would stick in my throat if I didn't ask her to join us, poor soul.'

'You're too soft. You shouldn't let people take advantage of you.'

'I don't do that. I'm fully aware...'

'That makes it worse. I know you, Anne. Once you get the bit between your teeth, nothing will stop you. It's no good arguing. That miserable old hag will ruin our Christmas. We've all to suffer because you have to feel good.' Was that how he saw her, soft and yet adamant? Pig-headed. 'Once she got the bit between her teeth...' Had that been her attitude about Ben? A determined throwing of her cap over the windmill? Well, it had been thrown back in her face.

Christmas Day came and went, with Mrs Parkinson saying it was very nice of Anne to have asked her but Christmas dinners weren't really for her with her small appetite...and there was no call, or sign from Ben.

James packed up his gear and set off after Boxing Day to London with Anthony from where they would fly to the little-known place in Switzerland which Anthony knew about, where they went in for artificial snow.

'I couldn't bear it,' she said to them at the station, 'it would give me an allergy, all that polystyrene. It's as bad as an artificial Christmas tree.'

'Parky,' (this was James's name for Mrs Parkinson), 'thought you would have been far better off with one. Actually that gigantic thing you had, nearly filled the hall. It must have taken you hours to decorate it.'

'It did, but I thought we were going to have a big family party. Nobody wanted to come. Even your cousin and Con are away buying phoney antiques in a Moroccan Souk.'

'And other things. They must want variety in their marriage.' She knew he darted a look at Anthony and heard their sniggers.

She had said to him last night in the kitchen, when he was helping her with the washing up, 'Your cousin Judith's pregnant.'

'Is she?' He showed a cousinly interest. 'Are they getting married, then?'

'To who?' She had held her breath.

'Whoever is the father. Some decide to tie the knot after the baby comes. It's quite common now.' The wisdom of the young...'

'Is that so? And how do you see the girls who don't want the man at all, just the baby?'

'That's got to be kinky. How could anyone want to bring up a child on their own. There's no fun in that.'

'Apparently some do. Your Aunt Margaret says it's the latest thing.'

'Well, I'm not having anything of that sort when *I* meet someone I like. If we're having a baby it's marriage. I'd be quite firm about that. It would be mine too.' It seemed an opportunity and she jumped in.

'Well, I hope you're being careful...safe.' He didn't answer, looked sullen, head down, like his five-year-old stance. 'Are you, James?'

'You're obsessed with sex!' Now he was angry. She knew by the way he was rubbing at the sauceboat. She didn't use the dishwasher for her 'good' set. 'As a matter of fact I haven't...yet...I've been... too busy!'

'You mean you haven't ever...?' She had to stop herself giggling in an embarrassed fashion.

'No, why should I? Abstinence makes the heart grow fonder.' He let out a high hoot at his own cleverness, and then reddened when she tried to hug him. 'Get off it, Mum!' (Not Annie.)

'This is too...you started it all. Get off!'

Now she did hug him on the platform and said to Anthony, 'You take care of my little boy, Anthony. He's too young to be let out alone.'

Chapter Eighteen

The following day the letter came. The envelope had lain on the carpet while she put in her stint at the CAB, had lunch and then tea with friends there, and gone straight to the Hospice. The main thing was to keep busy. There was always a let-down feeling after Christmas, doubly hard in her own case. She took it to her favourite seat at the window and tore it open.

'Dear, *dear* Anne, how to start...

I know you'll be thinking badly of me because of my silence. If it's any consolation to you, I spent a miserable Christmas mulling over everything.

But I want you to hold in your mind while you read this that I love you still, not an easy, throwaway kind of love, but something deeper which has left its imprint on me for ever. Maybe I wasn't ready for it, couldn't cope with it, and that's why I have to put it all down.

First—why didn't I come to Mrs Lang's party?

I know you'll be asking that. Well,

I was on my way and I was beaten up. I hate to have to tell this because I don't want you to be hurt too, but it's all got to come out. I didn't put up much of a fight. Maybe you wouldn't have expected me to, being me, but I never represented myself as a knight in shining armour. My excuse for what it's worth is that I was taken by surprise.

I was in the car park behind the flats on my way to the party when he pounced. It was painful and ignominious, he left me lying there when he had done his dirty work, and sloped off. Luckily a woman in the flat above me arrived just after, helped me upstairs and phoned the doctor.

There was nothing broken except a tooth, and I had a few bruises. I didn't want to tell the police but the doctor said it was my duty to report it. He kept me in bed a few days because of concussion, the police duly came and interviewed me, but didn't hold out much hope of finding anyone. That didn't worry me. I wasn't feeling very proud of myself, felt I'd had it coming to me.

Being in bed gave me time to think. At first I wanted desperately to lift the telephone and tell you all about it, but shame kept me back. And then, as my anger cooled, I began to see it was quite a good thing, being bashed up. It had brought me to my senses.

I realized that all I was doing was mucking up your life. You had been doing all right before I came along, at least you were safe. And then I barged in. But we clicked, didn't we, right from the first? I was completely happy with you, as if you were what I'd been waiting for all my life. You enchanted me. You were with me in my work, your charm, which is a combination of clear-eyed innocence and maturity. The poems I read seem to be made for you.

It was great while it lasted dear Anne, *dearest* Anne. I never had the courage to say 'dearest' to you. That was for married people. My mind is full of wonderful joyous thoughts and images of our short time together, walking in our valley, eating in that little pub, loving. I *liked* you so much as well as loved you. Your persona—great word—is secret, it takes time to unfold, to trust. You're withdrawn to begin with, but how you give when you're sure, a unique giving. You were never a come-on girl, like some...which brings me to Judith and the hardest part of this letter to write.

I had been taking her out occasionally. There was nothing to it. We worked in the same office. It was a feather in my cap, perhaps, with the other men, because she is very beautiful, unattractive, but very beautiful.

One evening we had a blow-out of a dinner together because of a contract she had helped me with, and I went back to her flat. There had never been anything sexual between us before that. I give you my word. Not even in your house that weekend. But that evening—well, she came on in a big way and I was too drunk to resist it.

I should have seen the red light. She had been frank enough, God knows, saying bitterly sometimes that the only thing she had missed in her previous marriage was the chance to have a child. I hadn't taken her too seriously, nor that it might concern *me*. I didn't realize that it was an *idée fixe*. I was too stupid, or too stupefied.

Well, we drank some more, we drank too much, and when I came to my senses I was in bed with her and the deed was done, with no safeguards, no nothing. When I looked at her face on the pillow and saw the smugness on it, I could have groaned aloud. Perhaps I did.

But you know how it is, or do you? You tell yourself it couldn't happen just from one bash. The risk had been

269

minimal. You tell yourself anything, week after week, and just when you have forgotten it, someone, (in this case Jenny, you remember meeting her in the restaurant in Manchester) said to me that Judith was off work, with morning sickness. *Looked at me!*

You must have noticed the change in me. I was spending time with you when I could, in love with you and revelling in loving you, and carrying this black secret around in my heart, obsessed by my own *stupidity*. I wanted to bang my head against my bedroom wall. I think I did.

I went to see Judith in her flat and she was pregnant all right. She didn't deny it. She asked me what was the buzz? She had got what she wanted, and I was to go back to enjoying myself with you—that's what she said—'with Mum's sister'. That was worse than the bashing up, but although I tried to get her to say more, she refused. She said I was to leave her to enjoy her morning sickness and get out of her life.

I had told no one about being beaten up—you're the only one bar the doctor, and the woman who found me. I had a job to hold down, my living to earn. Life had to go on. That stupid phrase. If it has, it's been through no help from me.

Even reading poetry has been no use. I work like a demon during the day, and fall into bed each night and go out like a light. If I stayed up I'd drink myself silly, and I've proved once and for all that's a mug's game. Look where it got me.

Well, that's about it. You can see I'm up shit creek and it's blocked, if you'll pardon the tasteless analogy. One thing is clear to me. I have to get out of your life or you'll be up there too.

Perhaps in months to come, or it may take longer, we'll meet, sadder and wiser, at least I hope *I* shall be, and we'll be able to talk about those lovely times we had without too much bitterness. Thinking about them now is like a bright golden bubble inside me, and as impermanent. I was trouble for you. Even that old swan at Esthwaite who chased me up the bank recognized a wimp when it saw one.

I said I would be completely frank with you, and I haven't been. *I recognized the man who bashed me up, in spite of his stocking mask.* It was the single-minded coldness. I have one attribute, a small one. I don't go around with my eyes shut. I guess I have a camera-type mind, click-click, another one on the film. It works all the time...

If I close my eyes I can see you at the

wheel of your car on the road to that odd place you took James and me, your eyes fixed ahead, the hint of a smile at the corner of that neat, delicate mouth of yours. How well you get on with your son! He adores you, obviously, and admires you. You were such a reliable, good-to-have-in-an-emergency lady that day. The waters parted for you. You were gallant.

And I can see you walking at my side in that lovely Winster Valley, and chatting on in that serious way you have, as if you were mining for gold, then chortling at yourself, like a small girl, pulling down the sides of your mouth.

And I can see your face on the pillow, and those grey eyes with lashes like furry caterpillars—they're brown, too—the smoothness of your skin, the smallness of your ears beneath your short haircut, the smallness of your breasts. Do you remember that word 'gamine'? I think it was used for French music hall artistes, slim boyish ones with long legs. That's you.

You gave me a chance to grow and develop. I wanted it to be permanent but I mucked it up and I don't think I'll ever get over loving you...there I go, avoiding the issue again, and I said I would be completely frank.

Do you remember that weekend when I came with Judith? And that's another image...you and I walking along the promenade about four in the morning as if it was perfectly natural. Some girls would have said it was kinky. It took someone like you...sorry. I'm straying again.

Do you remember that day your husband (I can't bear to write his name. Big, bluff, hard men like him don't seem right with first names...) took me to his Depot on the river to see round it? He stopped at the gates to have a word with the man in the box. I think he was called Spiers. Whatever. I thought there was an odd familiarity between them, as if they shared a secret. I registered with my camera mind that he had a thin face and cold eyes, and that his gauntness was that of someone who had been starved of food at one time in his life and had never made it up.

I have to tell you this. I know it is going to get right down to the core of you, make you afraid. As it does me. But you have to know. Because it means, if I'm right, *that your husband knew about us and got Spiers to beat me up.* And I'm writing this so that at least you'll be able to tell him it's all over between you and me, that he need have no cause for worry. That I'm out of your life...'

The wailing in the room was coming from her, like a seagull circling above the polluted sea. She bent her head to her knees.

She waited, day after day. She worked through the agony, the trembling, the fear, and then something clicked in her mind like a lock, and she became calm, as if she had reached her limit. She didn't know how she could be so calm, and calculating. Ben hadn't worked through all the permutations. If Judith knew about their affair, she could only have known through her mother, or vice versa. Had that man been snooping on her and Ben? He would move like a shadow...through the bracken. Judith and her mother were as thick as thieves, in spite of all their rowing. They thought alike. And Margaret, being Margaret, would have passed on the information to Alex. And he to his partner in crime, Spiers...

Margaret wouldn't be deliberately malicious. When she had got that money from Alex all those years ago, it had not been with malice aforethought. It had simply been expedient. In this present case she would tell herself that it was only fair he should know that Anne was two-timing him, or even more likely, she wouldn't rationalize, she would just *tell* him. That was how she was. Her sister, Margaret.

Alex was playing a cat and mouse game with her. She was sure of that. On the surface his behaviour was the same, the same breakfasts where he read while he got through his sausage, eggs and bacon, his long stints at his office in the town, his frequent trips away from home.

He was in an outwardly jolly phase which increased her suspicions. Business was brisk, he said, taking her out for dinner one night because he said she had worked too hard over Christmas. He looked prosperous, a good match for the expensive restaurant in his light grey suit, striped Rugby tie, gold cufflinks, gold watch. The waiter came running when he lifted his hand. It all 'looked nice'. They finished up at home with the Saturday night bed session, prolonged, with a few variations. This is the nadir, she told herself, lacking the willpower to stop it. I am worthless.

A few days later, when he came into the sitting-room and found her listless at the fire, he commented in a kindly tone, 'This isn't like you, Anne. You're always busying yourself about.' His smile came and went, unanswered by his eyes.

'After Christmas blues,' she said. An

automaton spoke for her.

'Not to worry. We'll soon be going off to St Lucia. That will buck you up.'

He became even more masterful in his incursions into her body. There was a kind of ruthlessness. She submitted because she wasn't there. Her life and love were over. Only her mind was alive, stirring, beginning to plan...

Slowly, the shock of Ben's letter went. What he had revealed to her began to fit into place. It was like a ritual dance, or a play where they all had parts, Alex, Judith, Margaret, Ben and herself, even James, a walking-on part.

Her lethargy began to be replaced by hate such as she had never known. It had been slow-growing, and now in its full flowering it swamped her, demanded some expression. She could barely look at Alex, or speak to him. She wanted to shout her head off, to scream at him, 'Why are you torturing me? Why did you get Jack Spiers to do your dirty work? Your...thuggery? Was it jealousy of Ben or your proprietorial rights on me?'

Property, she thought, was the key word, his leitmotif. She was property, just as the Depot on the river was property, his. Just as Jack Spiers was his property. She dished up his sausage, bacon and eggs each morning, and thought that it was only there in that gaunt cobbled place on the marshes, with its freshly-painted white sign-boards, 'Tiles', 'Concrete', that she could challenge him, tell him what she knew, since it was *there* that he had arranged with Jack Spiers to beat Ben up.

She recognized that her thinking had all the awful reasonableness of the obsessional. She knew she was not in her right mind.

She telephoned the Citizens' Advice Bureau and said she would have to take a week's holiday, that she was run down. It would have been more accurate to have said that she was wound up.

When Alex said he was going to the Depot that evening and not to expect him home until late, she realized that this was it.

'Why?' she asked calmly.

'Why am I going to be late?' He humoured her. 'I told you I was going to the Depot.'

'Has something blown up?'

'Yes, since you ask,' still humouring her, 'there's a big shipment of tiles arriving from the south. They try to avoid the peak times on the motorway. I have to be there when it arrives.'

'Couldn't Jack Spiers check it in?'

'Oh, yes, he'll do his bit, but he likes having me around. It's a valuable delivery. I give him...authority.'

'I didn't think he needed that.'

'Yes, Jack needs it. No initiative, but carries out instructions, to the letter.'

'He always does what you tell him?'

'Always.' His eyebrows raised. 'I told you he owes me.'

'I'll go to bed, then,' she said, 'I'm perpetually tired.'

'You'll be all right when you get to St Lucia.' There was no sympathy in his voice.

'Yes, I'll be all right then.' By that time it would be over...she didn't know what she meant, but it would be over.

She did go to bed early to weep and let herself go to pieces, then she got up, showered and dressed, got out her car and drove to the Depot.

Chapter Nineteen

A dirty night for dirty work. Where had she heard those words before? Yes, in Ben's letter. Jack Spiers had done his dirty work on Ben, left him lying bleeding in a car park and walked off, satisfied. He had done what the boss had told him to do. 'He owes me', Alex had said to her of his henchman, the night watchman, the man in the stocking mask.

She saw herself as more reprehensible than Alex, or Spiers, or even Ben, who had been foolish, that was all, a young twenty-four going on for twenty-five who had allowed himself to be trapped by a young beautiful woman with an *idée fixe*. An intelligent young man, who read poetry, who was a computer expert with a creative mind, who drank too much one night and walked into a trap. 'Will you walk into my parlour?' said the spider to the fly. But could Judith be blamed either for her obsessive wish for a child?

Yes, *she* was the more reprehensible for going on year after year with Alex, as a whore, a kept woman, submitting to his sexual advances in payment for bed and board, telling herself that if she did voluntary work for the good of the community it would benefit her soul as well, make a wrong, right.

A strong woman would have moved out long ago, made her own life, not been a chattel. The marriage had been wrong from the start, embarked upon because of a wish to balance the shame she had felt at Margaret's request to Alex. There had been no need for that shame. Her vulnerability was not an attribute. *Your life has been built on misconceptions and false premises,* she told herself. *After this you have to get out, or end it...*

'It degenerates into a marshy, dismal-looking area,' she remembered telling Aunt Elspeth. 'Sometimes there are one or two caravans on it. The Town Council likes to keep them out of sight.' The town's dirty linen. No one likes to wash their dirty linen in public. She had pretended that she and Alex were a well-integrated couple, pillars of the community, she a good wife and worker, devoted to good works...but not any more.

She passed the Blue Dolphin, at the 'posh end', James's words. Did he really admire her, as Ben had said? She felt a small glow. That was where Alex had taken her to dinner the night he had told her about giving Margaret the money she had asked for, the night her own sentence had begun, a self-imposed sentence which no one had asked of her, which made it worse.

Alex would have been far better off with any other woman she could think of. She was not his type. His type shouldn't cringe at some of his remarks. Margaret enjoyed his *bon mots,* laughing uproariously at them, and with him. *She* was his type.

It was dark, with a mist from the river. The railway arches swam out of it, lending substance, slowly the old warehouses came into focus, their edges undefined except where the light from the lampposts caught a corner or an angle.

At the foot of one post the light splayed on the cobbles, highlighting their pleasing shapes. 'You need cobbles for atmosphere,' Aunt Elspeth had said, making a frame with her hands. Ben had written that he had a mind like a camera, but whereas his recollections remained as bright images of the mind, she tried to pin hers down in words, in poetic words. She would have been better to scrap the do-gooding and concentrate on writing. She might have discovered herself in the process.

But, by God she had discovered herself tonight, she thought, driving carefully along the quiet road by the side of the river, seeing the boat spars swaying behind the wall. Would Mr Proctor be going out tonight? How lucky he was to be able to shake off the daily worries and sail forth into the darkness, be welcomed by it, a new beginning. *He* could write poetry if he sat down and tried, about his 'nightly sojourns into the Infinite', but not in *these* terms. She grimaced.

In her own case it had needed a trauma, a love affair with a young man who had shown her what love meant and what she had been missing, an idealized love because ideals by their very nature were unobtainable, and it had needed his letter to show her how unobtainable they were. Her future didn't lie with Ben. He was far too busy with the process of discovering himself. He had to sort out his own not inconsiderable problems first...

'Not a nice place to be at night,' Aunt Elspeth had said. 'You could imagine all sorts of things. Atmosphere, though. I hope I caught it...'

Aunt Elspeth had sorted out her own problems before she took up photography with Mr Cholmondley-Brooks. They had not been inconsiderable either, her affair with a married man, her solicitor, the father of that nice young Mr Doldren. She liked that interpretation anyhow. It was better not to know definitely. Aunt Elspeth had been able to put it on one side, get on with her life.

Now she was coming to Alex's 'place of business'. How people left their personality in remembered words and phrases! 'The heart of the operation', she had said. The *mot juste*. But the heart of Alex's most recent operation had been the plan laid to intercept Ben, the careful directions given about his address, how the car park behind the flats was poorly lit, how he should first take up a position where he could watch the comings and goings of Ben.

Alex would have known through Margaret that she had invited him to her party. There was a fair chance he would go. Alex would know it was only a fair chance, as he might not want to be seen, but it was a sporting chance. It might not be the first time that Spiers had sat, patiently waiting, parked in the street outside the flats so that he could make a quick getaway.

Everything would be arranged between Alex and Spiers, even to a stand-in at the gate. Ben had noticed the familiarity between them, old buddies. 'He owes me,' Alex had said. If ever a man extracted his pound of flesh it was her husband. He owed his success to it.

Now she had reached the box, a little lit wooden box with Spiers reminding her momentarily of Punch, his head and upper part of his body outlined by the light above him. No baton. *He* depended on the loaded fist.

The bar was down, stopping her progress. She braced herself, drew up the car confidently at the counter—it would have been bad policy to crawl—and said in a firm voice, 'I'm going to see my husband, Mr Spiers. I have an urgent message for him.' She waited, gathering her strength. The first move was the crucial one. Obedience had been instilled into him, she hoped, in his 'place of retention'—a phrase worthy of Aunt Elspeth—and Alex had said he needed authority.

'I'm not sure he's in his office.' Cold, watchful eyes. no stocking mask.

'I know he is.' Don't ever say too much. It's fatal. Don't explain.

'I'll phone him.' The man put his hand on the telephone beside him. 'To make sure...' She cut in.

'Perhaps you didn't hear me the first time. I have an urgent message for my husband. Do you want me to get someone else to make it clear, the...' she raised her shoulders impatiently, '...police?'

He hesitated. She thought she saw, mixed up with the sullenness, a quick gleam of pleasure in his eyes. *Strange...* 'If that's the way you want it.' He pressed a lever and the bar lifted.

She said, leaning forward before she

drove through, 'And I wouldn't phone him, if I were you.' She put an authoritative rap in her voice, but instead of answering sullenness, there was again the gleam of pleasure, lighting up the cold eyes. She could not understand it.

The road between the various sections was broad and empty, not like during the day when it was cluttered up with other vehicles loading and unloading. 'Paving Stones'. She saw the white notice board on her left, the square, house-like erections of them, then, rearing in the darkness, small mountains of sand or cement with barrows upturned at the foot of them, left by the workers, no doubt, when the buzzer had sounded.

The layout was familiar, the storerooms with their huge doors, the Glass Department, the Tiling Department under cover, the precious stones of the Depot too valuable to be left out in the rain. She drove slowly along the road, clearly delineated by its pale colour, the result of cement dust having been ground into it for years. It shone bone-white in the darkness.

Now she was approaching the brick building where Alex's office was situated. Only the sandstone trim of the windows showed, and the three sandstone steps up to the heavy front door. The rest was a non-reflective dark brick.

She stopped the car at the foot of the steps, surprised to find that she was shaking violently. She sat, clenching her hands in her lap to steady herself, her shoulders rigid, before she got out. With the fresh air she felt a new rush of anger, as if to give her courage. She was here to tell him their marriage was over, that the beating up of Ben had been the last straw. She had no guilt about their affair. That belonged to the past, along with the creeping sense of shame—now she saw it had been the blow to her self-esteem which mattered more to her.

This was the right place to let it all come out, not in that house where she had lived with him for so long and where she automatically took up the role of dutiful wife, soft-spoken and polite. This time she would not be polite. This time for the first time, he would really know what she thought and felt. She would be able to say it all because she was clearing out. She would at last be honest.

She walked up the three steps and found the door securely locked. Panic rose in her, that she might at this stage be thwarted. Had Spiers telephoned him after all, and was this to be a further, a final ignominy? It was necessary that she should burst in on him, a new Anne, tell him that it was all over, that it had taken the assault on Ben to bring her to her senses.

Should she drive back to the box? No, that would be a mistake. She had taken Spiers by surprise once, but he would be prepared this time, especially if he *had* telephoned Alex. She stood irresolute, then went down the steps again, turning at the bottom to survey the dark building. No lit windows. Alex's office was the big room on the left of the door. Utter darkness. But, as she turned once more, she saw the bulk of Alex's Mercedes, tucked in at the gable wall. He was inside the building. He was there all right. Somewhere.

Like a shaft of light, she remembered that at the back of the building he kept a small room which he had furnished years ago as a kind of waiting-room. There was even a camp bed in it. When he had been building up the business he had sometimes slept there if he were taking all-night deliveries and there was no one on duty. 'I owe my success to lending a hand wherever it is needed.' He still used it occasionally to interview contractors on the site.

She made her way round the corner of the building. It was darker than ever there, and she stumbled once or twice over odd pieces of flagstones, or possibly corners of cement blocks. Then, a Diesel tin. The rattle it made caused her to stop fearfully. Surely it had been heard. Now she saw the lit window, a louvred blind lowered over it, the chinks of light showing.

Elation gripped her, mixing with anger, a heady concoction which gave her renewed impetus. She would bang on the window until he raised the blind. When his face showed she would call, 'Let me in! I have something to tell you...' She should have brought a weapon, anything, something to frighten him with. But, oh, the satisfaction of letting it all spill out, the years of meaninglessness, the waste of valuable time...except for James. 'He obviously admires you.' Only a parent could know the particular pleasure of such a remark.

She went towards the window, then disappointment drew her up short. It was too high for her! Her eyes didn't come up to the level of the sill. Possibly the ground at the back sloped away towards the estuary. No, it was too much to bear... She stepped back and her heel struck against something bulky. She turned and saw dimly that it was a sack, torn in places, with a greater darkness spilling out on to the ground. She bent down to feel.

A gritty kind of sand. She felt the grain between her fingers and under her feet, and made up her mind instantly. She took hold of the sack and began to heave and drag it slowly into position beneath the sill. Its damp weight dragged on the muscles in her arms and legs. She had to stop from time to time to get her breath back, but she went on, inch by inch. 'A good-to-have-in-an-emergency lady', Ben had called her. Slowly, slowly, she got it placed under the window. When she paused for breath she heard a woman laugh.

It seemed like hours before she could stir herself. Perhaps she had been mistaken. It might have been the night screech of a seagull—did gulls screech at night—or a cat from one of the gypsy caravans being attacked, or attacking... She felt suddenly afraid, felt the loneliness of the place press in on her, imagined the dark stretch of the marshy ground towards the estuary. She remembered the torso found in the river. Had the murder taken place near here? Her purpose evaporated, but only for a second. The idea of knocking, or even shouting, however, now seemed pointless.

The sack was a fraction too far from the wall, but it would do. She climbed on it, wobbling a little, and to steady herself, leant forward, supporting her slanted body by her hands on the windowsill.

If the sand ran out through the holes she would fall ignominiously. But now the whole venture seemed ignominious, 'painful and ignominious'. Those were Ben's words describing the assault on him, when he had castigated himself for not having courage. What was courage, after all? It was no good against cunning nor malice aforethought.

Her eyes were level with a slit in the louvred blind.

At first she couldn't see properly, and then her eyes accommodated to the restricted view. The room was lit. It was a surprisingly comfortable-looking room, even cosy, furnished with easy chairs and a divan in the corner. The divan was not being used, which would have been more sensible.

Two half-dressed figures were rolling on the floor, no, not rolling, because one was astride the supine figure of the other. The seated one was a woman, practically undressed—at least what she wore was falling off her, revealing the upper part of her body—her head was thrown back, her black hair was falling backwards, her throat was stretched, her mouth was open. She was laughing. It was Margaret.

Anne's feet rolled off the sack as the sand ran out and its bulk redistributed itself. She fell awkwardly, bruising her knees badly and lay where she fell, feeling the pain and the wetness of blood. Apart from that feeling, nothing. She was a ball of nothing, an object, like the sack, drained of feeling.

After a long time she managed to get up. Her tights were torn at the knees and sticking to the oozing blood so that it was agony to move. At least it was a relief to feel the stinging pain than that awful emptiness of soul.

She took out a handkerchief from her pocket and tried to wipe her knees, but it only served to push grains of sand or dirt deeper into the flesh and she gave it up. They would have to be picked out with tweezers. It didn't matter. Nothing mattered except the memory of Margaret in her nursery position, 'Ride a cock horse, to Banbury Cross...', the head thrown back, the laughter, the stretched throat.

Somehow she was in the car and starting it up. She drove slowly because of the stiffness and pain in her knees which made it difficult to operate gears, but the road was easy to see, even if it had not been delineated by the white notice boards, now she was at the lit box. The bar was down. She stopped. Sat looking straight ahead. Waiting.

'Did you find your husband?' Spiers said. Something in his voice made her look at him. The look of pleasure in his eyes was more than a gleam. He lowered them quickly, but she had seen it, 'Got you, boss!'

He had *wanted* her to go through. He would concoct up some story should he ever be challenged by Alex—and how could he, since he didn't know she had been lurking outside his room—that she had insisted. 'Authority,' he would say, 'you know what I'm like, boss, a sucker for authority.'

She didn't answer. She continued to look at him and heard the creak, saw the bar rising. She drove slowly through.

The mist had grown thicker, and she went even more slowly, using the looming bulk of the wall running by the river as a guide. It was only the 'posh end' which had railings. A wave of nausea and reaction suddenly overwhelmed her so powerfully that she had to draw into the side of the road and put her head down on the wheel. She heard her own voice, half-sobbing, 'She's done it again, the bitch, she's done it again!'

Long, long ago she had been obligated (what a strange word), to marry Alex. The blow to her pride had been all-consuming, that she, the perfect secretary, had gone home and blabbed about her employer's wealth, his car, his luxury flat by the estuary. She had punished herself by marrying Alex, her method of doing penance.

Oh, stupid, stupid! Did this situation she now found herself in spring from that ridiculous idea? She certainly wouldn't be in it if she hadn't married Alex. And by doing so, had her affluence always been a pinprick, or maybe a running sore to Margaret who had had a failure of a husband, in her own estimation, in poor Ralph who had quietly died to get out of the way?

'Who had quietly died...' How attractive that sounded. In this lonely place, the mist swirling round her, there was very little difference between living or dying, a limbo. The river would be deep and dark, and welcoming... She moved restlessly, and the torn edges of her tights caught on the torn flesh of her knees, causing fresh shafts of pain to shoot up into her groin.

The river water would be soothing. If she at least bathed her knees in its coolness, the nylon would be softened and would release its hold. She imagined the small pleasure of gently bathing the bruised flesh, the relief from those excruciating jabs which were becoming unbearable. And if she felt that to slip into the water would be even more pleasurable, what would be the harm in that?

Her life with Alex was finished. She

could not go back to that house with its view of the Bay—a small sorrow, the view—go to bed as usual, move over to let him in beside her, perhaps submit to his presumptuous embraces. How often had he made love to her after having been with Margaret? How dull it must have been in comparison, the marriage bed, after high jinks in the Depot or wherever they had been meeting.

And for how long?

The shaft of pain which went through her this time was not from her knees. Aunt Elspeth's photograph! The white Mini under the arches! Periodic trips made by Margaret, assignations at the Depot. Spiers lifting the bar for her, clocking the visit up in his evil mind. Oh, it was all painfully clear now!

Had she been a dupe for years, had they been laughing at her, saying, 'Poor Anne, it's really comical, isn't it? And have you heard the latest? She's got herself a toy boy, eighteen years younger.' 'I never thought she had it in her,' Margaret would have said, 'Miss Prim Pants.' But Alex would have gone morose and say, after all he had done for her, that she should make a fool of him.

And when Margaret dropped the bombshell, the big one, his self-righteous anger on her behalf. 'I can hardly believe it,

294

that Welsh kike two-timing her on the sly! Having it off with Judith at the same time and now she's got a bun in the oven...'

No, she was no good at reconstructions, 'bun in the oven' was Sixties talk. More likely they would exchange strong Norman sounding words which seemed common parlance now and which she saw often in novels written by people of her own age. Yes, she was prim, or inhibited, or both...but she hadn't been with Ben.

Black depression washed over her. She was a misfit, a failure. She could see now that she had made a complete balls of her life (was that modern usage or dated), beginning from her marriage, no, long before that, back to when she had allowed herself to be bullied by Margaret, had had no worth of her own...

No worth. Another great shaft of pain shot through her, this time from her knee, shot into the woman's core of her, and the agony was such that it made her open the door of the car and stumble out into the darkness. She heard a soft, clicking noise, and she came back to the world for a moment, to realize that it was the spars of the fishing boats knocking rhythmically and quietly against each other because of the pulling of the tide.

She must be near the steps down to the river. She went slowly towards the wall and saw the gap. She went through it and stood on the stone platform at the top. The dankness caught in her throat, but the cool night air reduced, somewhat, the pulling pain in her knees. There had always been virtue in the elements for her. She remembered that early morning walk with Ben on the promenade, striding along, hands in pockets, the freshness, the simple joy of it. That was before it all started.

She could see nothing. At first she thought she could discern the faint shape of a boat at the foot where the darkness intensified, and perhaps a dim light, like that of a lantern. Perhaps a riding light. But a swirl of mist blotted it out, the light disappeared and she decided there was nothing there to impede her. The other boats would be uninhabited. No one in their senses would go out fishing on a night like this. And the fish, if they had any sense, would be lying behind their rocks waiting for daylight.

Slowly, slowly, feeling her way, she went down, step by step. There was a soft lip-lip, a soothing whooshing. She liked the sound. 'Be still my heart...' Why was one's mind full of useless phrases? That was what the tutor in the poetry class was trying to get them to understand. *Fresh* language. You must search for fresh language, your own language, newly-minted, and that, by the way, is old language. See how easy it is to fall into the trap?'

She had fallen into the trap all right. A loveless marriage and a love affair which had gone wrong. Really, at some stage you had to say enough was enough. Bruised knees were only the beginning of it, there was a bruised heart, a bruised psyche, soul, whatever, bruised self-esteem, there was no end to it. If you were equipped like James with his practical approach to the world, you were better at it. 'Somewhere...over the rainbow...' Oh, the corny phrases and songs you picked up in the course of your travels! It would take more than a broom to sweep out all that rubbish, there was only one cure, to wash it out...

A man loomed up in front of her, a man holding a lantern high up, a man who looked like Jesus, a thin, noble face, abundantly hirsute, but with, incongruously, a fisherman's cap, (or perhaps not so incongruously) stuck on the top of the flowing locks.

He peered at her, leaning forward to where she crouched, cowered, against the wall, her arms in front of her.

'Mrs Garrett! What on earth are you doing here?'

It was a good question.

Chapter Twenty

He had come towards her, two further steps, to where she was still cowering against the wall, and said, 'Can I do anything to help you, Mrs Garrett? It's Albert Proctor, you know, from the fish shop.' His voice had lost its behind-the-counter briskness, and was gentle.

'No...it's all right...I came to deliver a message to my husband...I had an accident...fell...'

'Ah, that explains it!' He sounded relieved, as if, giving the circumstances she had described, it was quite reasonable for her to be half-down those steps leading to the river on a dark January evening. 'What did you hurt?'

'My knees.' Her voice sounded to her like a small child, like James's. He still had a scar on his right knee where he had opened it to the bone in the Junior School playground. 'I came down on my knees...'

'I have a First Aid kit on the boat. If you like, I could bandage them for you. And maybe a cup of tea?'

'No, no, thank you. It's all right. I'll... I'll...' She didn't know what she would do if she retraced her steps, except that she knew she was never going back to that house, no longer her house, Alex's.

'It will only take a few minutes, and then you can be on your way. Come on, now.' His arm was round her shoulders. Holding the lantern aloft, he was leading her down the remaining steps, across a small gangway, along a boat deck—she felt all this rather than saw it because of the mist, (and the mist in her mind), and into a snug cabin.

There was another man there, smoking a short pipe, which made the smoke whirl around a hanging lamp. The smell caused her head to swim, and looking around quickly, she saw a bunk and sat down on it. It was better than fainting.

''Evening,' the man said, as if her appearance was quite run of the mill. 'Murky night.'

'Yes,' she said, forcing herself to sit upright, 'murky night.' She was glad to see he knocked out the dottle from his pipe and stowed it away in his pocket.

'Met Mrs Garrett on the steps,' Mr Proctor said conversationally. 'Had a little bit of an accident, it seems. You get a brew-up going, Ron. You'll know Ron, Mrs Garrett, Mr Ron Moseley, landlord of the Eagle and Child. We were going fishing.'

'Fishing's off,' Mr Moseley said. 'My, your knees look in quite a state, if you don't mind me saying. Been in the wars by the looks of it. Tea, then, is it?' He disappeared into what she presumed was a small galley.

The warmth and the fug were having the effect of bringing her back into the world again, or into this other strange world, a small fishing boat anchored in the river where those two men seemed as snug as bugs in a rug. She liked that, 'snug as bugs in a rug.'

But only for a moment or two. It became suffocating, there was a faint smell of petrol mixed with the smoke and the fog which had seeped in, and again she felt a wave of faintness creeping over her heart, then her brain.

Mr Proctor's hands were on her. He was lifting her legs on to the bunk, tut-tutting. 'You have a stretch-out there. My, my, you *have* done yourself an injury. But I'm not going to touch those knees until you have a cup of tea with a good drop in it. Helps the shock. Put a tot into it, Ron,' he called, then sat down at the foot of the bunk. 'You just rest, Mrs Garrett, just rest. You're in good hands now. We'll see you all right.'

'I feel...so stupid...' She put her hands over her eyes. 'You must be wondering...'

'I never wonder. "Mine's not to wonder

why, mine's just to do or die..." '

' "Into the valley of death rode the six hundred." ' Mr Moseley was there holding a mug of tea. 'A sip of this will make all the difference.' He handed it to Mr Proctor.

'Take this cup...' Mr Proctor intoned, or did he just speak? 'Can you manage, Mrs Garrett?' That was what he often said when he wrapped up her fish and handed it to her. 'Are you *sure* you can manage, Mrs Garrett?'

She took the cup from him and drank, deeply, so that it would not spill. Immediately she felt the warmth of the brandy or rum or whatever it was, slip its warm way round her chest, finding the sore place which was her heart. She drank again, and her ears grew hot and she felt the blood returning to her face.

'That's better.' He took the cup from her. 'Bit of colour now. I tell you, Ron, when I met Mrs Garrett on the steps I thought she was a ghost. Do you think you could bear a spot of first aid now, Mrs Garrett? We don't want any poison to work its way into those knees.'

'So sore.' It was the little boy voice again, James's voice. 'So sore, Mummy.' All that love which had flowed between them, still did. 'He obviously admires you,' Ben had said. Balm to a mother's heart.

Mr Moseley was there again with a basin of steaming water. Mr Proctor was on his knees beside her. He had put a grey blanket over her, up to her armpits, and was smiling at her. How noble he looked in this yellow light! She couldn't think of a better word. Why had she not noticed his nobility before? And those eyes...full of kindness and understanding, as if he could see round the corners of her mind.

'If you could just manage to winkle off those stockings of yours,' 'winkle', she thought, is good, 'we could begin operations,' he said.

'Begin operations,' Mr Moseley repeated, who had now put the basin of water on a stool at the side of the bunk.

She 'winkled' and wriggled the tights off, put the soiled ball shamefully on the floor. 'I'll take them with me, dispose...'

Mr Proctor had gently folded back the blanket to just above her knees, and was just as gently bathing them. 'We'll swill out the dirt first,' he said. He wrung out the cloth, immersed it in the water, and then held it, dripping above her knees. They stung. She winced, turned her head to the wall.

'A touch of disinfectant,' Mr Proctor said.

'A touch of disinfectant never hurts,' Mr Moseley confirmed. He had sat down on the stool now and was holding the basin on his lap, as if to get a better view. 'You're getting it away, Albert.'

'Sand, mostly. But there's grit in it. Fell over a bag of aggregate, did you, Mrs Garrett?'

'I don't know,' she mumbled. The pain was less now. She moved her knees. They felt supple again. There were no longer the shafts of pain.

'Now, bandages,' Mr Proctor said. 'I've put plenty of ointment on them so that they won't stick. I shan't make them too tight. You want comfort when you walk.' He was working away deftly. 'How's that? Do you get the comfort?'

'Yes.' She flexed her knees. 'It's much better. I must say it's better. Thank you very much.' She sat up straight, her head against the wooden planks behind her.

'Soon be able to get you home.' He was strapping the bandages with tape, 'Then your own bed. There's nothing like your own bed.' It's never been my own bed...

'I'm not going home,' she said, and putting her head in her hands, she wept. She was surprised at herself. She had thought she was completely in control now. The silence was river deep. She heard the slip-slap of the water in the bowl which Mr Moseley was holding because of the small movements of the boat.

'She's not going home,' he said. The silence lapped again. She knew they would be looking at each other. She wept on and on, then lay back, exhausted, her throat throbbing, and fumbled for a handkerchief in her jacket.

'So silly,' she said, in her polite shopping-for-fish voice, 'so silly...'

'It doesn't sound silly to me,' Mr Moseley said. 'That's serious, not wanting to go home.'

'And her husband wondering where she's got to.' Mr Proctor agreed.

'He won't be at home yet,' she offered.

'But when he does?'

She thought of him, coming upstairs, getting in beside her after all those late nights. All of them, of course, would not have been spent with Margaret, but some. Her anger rose again, choking her. The nerve, the bloody nerve of it... But, hadn't she felt the same about Ben? Wasn't that why he had got Spiers to do his dirty work?

The anger subsided as suddenly as it had come, and she felt cold and lonely and wished she was not in this strange lamp-lit space with those two strange men, that Mr Proctor hadn't found her, that she could just be again on the steps, walking slowly into blackness and nothingness.

'You mean what you say, Mrs Garrett,

don't you?' Mr Proctor sounded business like, his behind-the-counter briskness. She nodded, her eyes closed. She didn't have to face the world with them closed. 'Well, I have a suggestion to make. You know my missus runs a B & B on the promenade?'

'Yes, I believe she once told me.' She thought it was irrelevant at the moment.

'We have a nice front room vacant, in fact, we're empty just now, but Ada's proud of that room, double bed, pink eiderdown, pink shades, white rug. She keeps it heated for the unexpected guest, so to speak. How would you like to stay there tonight, get yourself a good sleep?'

'Everything looks better in the morning,' Mr Moseley said. 'That's a good idea of yours, Albert.'

'Would that appeal to you, Mrs Garrett?'

The pink shades sounded restful. And she had a feeling the bed would be comfortable. Perhaps it was meant for a honeymoon couple. Mrs Proctor was an efficient woman who could gut a fish in the twinkling of an eye, wrap it up in shining, slippy paper which didn't absorb the blood, then pop it into a plastic carrier with 'Proctor, The Best Fish In Town' printed on it in blue letters.

'Yes...' she laughed apologetically, 'I'm actually quite tired.'

'Who wouldn't be?'

'Who wouldn't be?' Mr Moseley echoed. 'I think all the same we should let your husband know you're safe.'

She shook her head impatiently. Why should she? Let him sweat, and if Spiers hadn't been able to withstand authority and had told him she had been in the Depot, let him sweat all the more.

'Not to tell him *where* you are,' Mr Proctor said, 'just that you're safe. You don't want a hue and cry, do you?' Hue and cry. It made her think of the estuary, the dank marshes, dogs racing, low-nosed over it, looking for that poor lost girl who had been raped and then found headless in the river. You wouldn't wish that on anyone.

'No, that's true.' She felt sleepy. Her eyelids dropped.

'Supposing you get the car started up for us, Ron,' Mr Proctor said, 'Let the engine run to heat it, then come down and help me with Mrs Garrett?'

'I'll do that.' He got up, holding the bowl. 'Then I'll make the boat ship-shape when you've gone.'

'Shut up shop,' Mr Proctor said.

'Count the takings,' Anne murmured. She couldn't keep her eyes open.

Her drowsiness made the next part easier. They helped her across the narrow gangway, one in front, one behind, up the steps slowly, across the road to the car where Mr Proctor went round to the driver's seat and Mr Moseley helped her in beside him. Then he said, 'Good luck, Mrs Garrett,' banged the door and they drove off.

'He won't blab all over the town?' she asked Mr Proctor.

'Ron? No, he's as close as a clam. I've never met anyone like him. He can talk and talk and yet say nothing. Utterly reliable. He'll phone Ada to warn her, then he'll keep phoning your house till he gets an answer.'

'Just to say I'm safe.'

'Just to say you're safe,' Mr Proctor's voice was gentle. She stole a look at him, and saw again the nobility of his profile, the abundant hair which grew nobly back from his brow. A Triton. Or even what she had first thought when he came towards her, like Jesus. 'Come unto me all ye who are heavy laden and I will give you rest...'

He did, with the help of Ada and the guest bedroom. The bed was pinkly sumptuous, and there was a bowl of dried rose petals from Boots on the side table which smelled pink. Mrs Proctor had provided a pink brushed nylon nightdress. 'Soft to the touch,' she said, slipping it over Anne's head. 'You need a good sleep,

307

my dear.' She was in a towelling dressing gown which added inches to her all over, fur slippers which broadened her feet and curlers which heightened her. 'Things will look better in the morning.'

Since they all seemed convinced about that, she slept.

Chapter Twenty-One

She woke in a pink haze, and then, as her vision cleared, saw why. She was in Bella Vista, she had noticed the name above the door last night when Mr Proctor had taken her to his Ada. The pink faded slowly to black, an internal darkness, and she lay in misery until there was a brisk knock at the door and Mrs Proctor, a transformed Mrs Proctor in a smart tight skirt and bulky sweater, high-heeled and tightly-curled, came in with a breezy 'Good-morning!' and put a tray on her knees. 'If you're like me, you're never anything till you get that first cup.' She had Ron Moseley's capacity for treating unusual happenings as usual.

She was suddenly calm and resourceful, not even embarrassed. It must be catching. 'Thank you very much. I can't thank you and Mr Proctor enough, and his friend. I don't know what I should have done without them. That accident...' She didn't specify it. Don't explain...

'They would be glad to help. They're a comical pair. Been bosom friends for years, although maybe you can't say that about men.' She gave a high, jolly laugh.

'They couldn't have been kinder. Nor you.' She met the woman's brown eyes. They were certainly kind, like her husband's, but there was a lively curiosity in them, like two little birds sitting in their nest with their heads cocked.

'You looked really white and tired when he brought you here. It was the least I could do. I've been married a long time...drink up your tea... I know there can be little difficulties. Men...they're different, at least most men. I can't say that about my Albert. I used to wonder how he could *bear* to gut a fish.' She laughed. 'If I didn't trust him absolutely I might get annoyed at the amount of time he spends fishing and sitting in that old boat with Ron Moseley.' The two little birds cocked their heads further, two warm brown wrens. Don't explain...

'Did Mr Moseley get my husband last night on the phone?' she asked. The breakfast tray was beautiful, orange juice, thin toast, butter made in careful whorls in a shell-shaped dish with a silver butter knife, a crystal dish of marmalade, a pink napkin with flying cupids on it. Mrs Proctor was faithful to her pink theme. If it had not been January, there might have been a vase with a pink rose in it. She sipped her tea, her heart beating loudly, clattered her spoon to cover it.

'Yes, he did. Albert left a message for you. He goes to the shop early to lay the fish out.' (It sounded like a funeral parlour.) 'He was very distressed, your husband, and he wants you to go back home. He said to tell you.'

'But Mr Moseley didn't say where I was?'

'No, he wouldn't do that. Albert said you didn't want your husband to know.'

'I don't.' The toast crackled as she buttered it. 'How nicely you've done the butter, Mrs Proctor.' When she looked up she saw the two little cocked heads, waiting. 'Sometimes, perhaps you know this, you need time to think. You'll understand. I've been married twenty-one years. I never had time to sit back and look at myself. Last night decided me.'

'Well, maybe you're different from me.' Mrs Proctor sat down on the edge of the bed, partly satisfied. 'I'm not of a thinking nature. But then I'm lucky with Albert. He's special. I can think enough to recognize that. I've a man in a million. I can trust him.' Her brown eyes were level with Anne's. Definitive eyes. Had she heard anything about Alex? Had he a reputation in the town as a lecher, a man who took women to his little parlour on the river, not only Margaret? A wife was the last to know.

'What I need, Mrs Proctor...' Don't confide. Mrs Proctor could give away titbits with the change... 'what I need is a few days of rest. I hurt my knees last night when I fell. They're still stiff.' She could offer that.

'Yes, Albert told me. And I saw the bandages.' She drew in her breath, a practical woman, if kindly at heart. 'You're very welcome to stay here, but one thing, Mrs Garrett, and I know you won't mind me saying this, I don't want to be involved in anything to do with the police. I think your husband mentioned something...' Her expression softened. 'I was real sorry for you. You looked a poor little thing last night when Albert brought you in.' Like a drowned rat? She must dispel that impression, become calm and resourceful again. The dominant Anne was at her shoulder.

'That's the last thing I want for you, any trouble because of me. Supposing I get up and dress, then telephone my husband? That'll set his mind at rest, and I'm sure he'll understand that I need a day or two to...recover.' She smiled at Mrs Proctor, 'He'll understand that I need a little break.' Aunt Elspeth.

'Well, it isn't exactly the Caribbean

here,' the woman gave her high jolly laugh, 'but if you make it all right with your husband, I'm more than willing to put you up. You've come at the slack season for your break.' The brown eyes danced. She had a sense of humour.

'I haven't my handbag with me to pay you...' She looked around and then horror struck her. She wasn't as calm and resourceful as she had thought. 'It's in my car. I left it!'

'That's been taken care of, not to worry. Ron brought it here. It's in the wardrobe. He locked up the car you'd left the keys in it—and he's put them on a nail in the Eagle. Your husband said he would pick them up and have the car driven home. They'll probably have a drink together.' Her shoulders went up. Men...

'I could have done with it here. Never mind.'

'I'll lend you mine.'

'Is there no end to your kindness? I'm going to rest those old knees of mine and write a few letters and enjoy myself. Have a Kit-Kat, have a break.' She smiled at Mrs Proctor and suddenly they were two girls together—they would be about the same age—untrammelled by families or errant husbands or deceitful sisters, or anything else, as green as hazel twigs.

'Move over,' Mrs Proctor said, giggling, 'that would suit me fine.'

Alex was at home although it was after nine o'clock when she eventually spoke to him on the telephone. It had been engaged earlier.

'It's me,' she said. 'I couldn't get on to you. I hope you weren't telephoning the police.'

'Anne,' he sounded fairly reasonable, 'what is this caper? I've been at my wit's end. I never got a wink of sleep all night. Of *course* I phoned the police.'

'Well, I want you to ring them again and tell them I'm perfectly all right and that I've been in touch with you.'

'Where are you?'

'You don't tell me where *you're* going every minute of the day, or night. I'm having a rest for a day or two.'

'What's got into you? Having a rest for a day or two! What's wrong with your own bed?'

'It's quite simple. I fell and hurt my knees last night and I couldn't drive so I checked into the nearest hotel. You could find it if you systematically phoned round, but would you please just content yourself for the time being?'

'You must be out of your mind. I don't understand. I've got your car. It was found down by the river. What were you doing there?'

'I know you won't believe this, but I wanted to see it at night.' She was thinking creatively, or the dominant Anne was. 'I was bored at home. I'm thinking of taking up photography. Aunt Elspeth thought it was very atmospheric there...' The name was like Tinkerbell's light in her mind, flickering, significant. She would come back to that later. Meantime she must stop this nonsense.

'I never heard such nonsense in my life.' He agreed with her. 'Do you expect me to believe that? You're reliable. You don't go out at night just when the spirit moves you, alone.'

'Do you expect me to believe that you're working all the time when you say you are?' Oh, that was foolish, foolish... Now he'll bluster, his mind will start working, being suspicious, if it isn't already.

'I don't know what in God's name you're talking about! I was working at the Depot, for instance, last night until all hours. If you had come in when you were so near you'd have seen that.' The arrogance! So Spiers hadn't said anything. He had sat in that little lit box when he and Margaret drove away and laughed. 'Got you, boss! Now *you* owe *me!*' Revenge had won over authority. It could be slow

315

and sweet. She felt a new rush of calmness and resourcefulness.

'All I need is a few days' rest and then I'll come and see you. We have a lot to discuss.'

'What do you mean, "We have a lot to discuss?" ' He was shouting. She held the receiver away from her ear. 'All we have to discuss is your crazy behaviour, going out at night, staying away in some down-at-heel place wherever it is, worrying the life out of me. I can't even begin to understand it!'

She took advantage of the pause. 'I'll be home,' she said. 'We have a lot of talking to do.' She hung up.

Mrs Proctor wasn't in the bright plastic kitchen when she passed it. She must have gone out shopping, or perhaps she did a stint for her husband. It was a cheerful house, white Anoglypta from top to toe—easy to touch up—with a narrow corridor and stairs which were flooded with sea light. There was a gong at the foot of the stairs, and notices which said, 'Please Ring for Attention', and 'Breakfast in Rooms, Fifty p. Per Person Extra'. There were photographs of faces bursting with smiles, 'A happy crowd at Bella Vista'. She was a crowd of one.

In her pink room the bed was neatly made, and some pink notepaper and envelopes had been laid out on the table at the window. There was also a pink crinoline china lady on it, and she lifted it carefully and laid it to rest on the eiderdown where it looked more at home than possibly she had.

She sat looking at the wide expanse of the Bay. The tide was out, but the fur colours were there, with a band of platinum ermine on the horizon. Mrs Proctor had also laid out a pen for her, mercifully white, but the pink notepaper had pink cupids cavorting on it. Still, it was a kind of honeymoon. A honeymoon of one. She began to write.

'Dear Ben,
You will be surprised at the pink notepaper with embellishments, but I had to get away to feel able to write this. The fleeing wasn't premeditated, events ran away with me, and I'm 'holed up', I think that's the usual expression, in the Bella Vista on the Bay. I had a little accident, fell and bruised my knees, and was obliged to stay here. When I'm strong enough I'm going home to pack my bags and leave Alex for good. It's not because of what he did to you. That was only the trigger.

I couldn't believe he would have you beaten up. When I read your letter I felt the blows that landed on you, felt the pain. I was so upset that I went out one night when he was working late (such an euphemism), at his precious Depot *because* I couldn't believe what you told me, but when I saw Spiers I knew it was true. Everything about his demeanour told me he was perfectly capable of it.

I don't think Alex realized what he was doing to *me* when he arranged with Spiers to beat you up. With him, all his reactions are simple. It would be "to teach you a lesson". The very idea of you breaking and entering *his* property, i.e., me, would bring out all his, to him, natural instincts. Alex is the last of the cave men—no wonder he likes golf where he can brandish his club. And what a poor joke that is.

I don't blame you about Judith. Nor have I any right. She's a very beautiful girl. I couldn't resist her if I were a man, and if you find the stirrings of fatherhood in you, who knows, you might persuade her to marry you. Women get very protective when they have a child. I know I did. I think that's got a lot to do with me staying on with Alex. I needed the protection he could provide for James, and I didn't want to deprive James of a father.

And time wears on, even in unhappy marriages. Things don't hurt all the time, even the bad things. I made the best of a bad job...'

She put down her pen and stared across the Bay. The band of ermine had gone, now there was a broad silver strip which was the tide rushing in for its daily wash over the mud. If it was calm, the sea would be blue, if choppy it would look brown and polluted and remind you what it must be like to drown in it...a race between poisoning and asphyxiation. Still, it *looked* nice...

Should she tell Ben about Margaret, that she had seen them together? Ben had been completely frank with *her*. She ought to reciprocate, wipe the slate clean. But had it anything to do with him? Perhaps she would become simply his mother-in-law's sister in time. Better not to realize that this was Margaret's forte, upsetting the apple-cart, and that the only way to avoid it happening yet again was for she, Anne, to cut herself free from her and Alex.

No one wanted to become punch drunk. Her emancipation lay in getting away from both of them. Ben had shown her how to do that, but she had always known it was only a temporary solution. Had she? Hadn't she sometimes hoped?

She looked at the Bay fixedly, to prevent herself from weeping, saw the tide had done its work again, was busy filling up the channels with a smooth metallic sweep of water. Oystercatchers re-inhabited the islands it made for them, the dunlins took a last run along the shallows.

She didn't blame Ben for being caught by Judith, if 'caught' was the right word. It takes two and the door wasn't locked. And perhaps it showed her that in the long term she couldn't have been any surer of him than Alex. She needed a commitment, either in marriage or in an affair, and if that weren't forthcoming, surely it would be better to stand on her own feet? It would be difficult, but a few days in Ada Proctor's pink bower might get her used to the idea.

Now she saw in retrospect how easy it had been to settle other people's problems at the CAB...she took up the white pen, saw it had a tiny black and white Panda on its end. *Pity*...

'I can't begin to tell you of the joy you gave me, Ben. I was like the Sleeping Beauty—I'm sorry, but my setting here inspires me to such flights of fancy—but it's true in a way. You woke me to happiness and love, and laughter and companionship, all the missing

320

ingredients of my life with Alex.

I wonder how many women exist in marriages like mine, outwardly well-adjusted, inwardly resentful, compensating with 'good works', the trivia of running a house where no love exists, dreading the necessity of sexual submission, or, worse, becoming habituated to it—faking was invented by women like me. We do it very well, I guess you could say we've a call, to paraphrase that poor, sad girl whose poetry we admire. The marriage service must have been written for people like Alex.

I'll never forget our Indian summer. I'll weep if I see again the sun chasing the wind over our valley in those long, dramatic sweeps of light and shade. I don't think I can bear to go there for a long time.

And I'll never forget but I'll avoid our pub. Do you see how I say "our valley", "our pub", the only thing we didn't have was "our song"...thank God.

And being in bed with you... I can understand Judith enjoying that, even if she had other ideas. The pain is going now, and I don't mind sharing you with her. Not much. At least she'll know what I had. Keeping it in the family. Maybe *she'll* mind. I don't expect so.

She's like her mother. She's got what she wanted.

I am not making any vow never to write to you or see you again. When I've left Alex and I'm settled down somewhere, I'll let you know where I am, and some time we might even meet. But our...episode? Encounter?...call it what you will, is over. I'm moving on. You may remember that my aunt left me a house...'

She stared at the words. Automatic writing. Should she clap her hands for Tinkerbell?...

I've wondered for some time whether or not I should sell it, and indeed, the solicitor dealing with her affairs wanted to buy it from me. But I've decided to go to St Albans and live in it.

Alex and I will get a divorce. Oh, there will be days of altercations and speaking one's mind, all the old wounds and scars will be shown, but in the end I hope we'll be sensible and let a solicitor handle it and keep us apart.

I'll go to St Albans and settle in there on my own.

It will be a big move, from the north to the south, from being one of a pair to being an entity. I'll study something.

I've no desire to do an uninteresting job. My do-gooding will be confined to myself. There's a lot of work to be done there. I rather like the idea of becoming a mature student.

I'll be near James, and if he stays on in London after he gets his degree, it will be a good *pied-à-terre* for him. In any case I'll make a little suite in the house for him, and of course, he'll be left it in my Will. Property, as Alex often said, is the best investment. Well, he ought to know. I must be his only bad one.

I'm lucky to have James. You'll have that too, or a daughter. So tangible. I wonder what difference it will make to your life. It would be interesting to know. So much I'll miss, being a northern girl. The hills and the sea and the people, but I'll try to fit in with 'down there' and let the southernness wash over me, soften the edges. I think I can do it.

Au revoir. We don't have anything in our language quite like *au revoir,* and that's something I might do in my new life, study another language. I'm suddenly very happy! Just a few hurdles to get over and then I'll be free. Now I know how the dissidents feel. Thank you for helping me.'

She sealed the envelope, and thought she would walk along to the post office and get some stamps. Alex never came to this part of the Bay. At the foot of the stairs she realized she hadn't any money. She saw she had stopped beside the telephone. There was just a slight chance James might be in. It was nearly lunch time and sometimes he came back to the flat.

She was lucky, which she took as an augury. 'Hello, James,' she said, 'It's Mum here.'

'You sound perky. Look, Annie, I've just dashed in for some books. Got to get back.'

'It won't take a minute. James, I wanted to tell you. I'm going to live in Aunt Elspeth's house. At St Albans. It will be your house too, if you like.'

'What the hell are you talking about?' (So polite, the children of today.) 'Dad would never shift his business down there. You know what he thinks about the south. Says they're all queer.'

'Dad's staying put. We're getting divorced. At least, I'm going to see him...'

'Look, I'm terribly rushed. Must get back. WHAT?' The word jumped along the wire and crashed in her eardrums.

'You heard me. We've both been unfaithful. I told you about Ben Davies, and he...'

'I know, but it doesn't count nowadays. Not with married couples.' He was hardly twenty, bless him.

'It does with me. Some day I'll tell you the whole story. When you grow up. Are you surprised, I mean, at me?'

'Not a bit. I've often wondered how you stick him. I really must go, Annie. It was just a fluke, catching me.'

'I'm glad I did. I'll be in touch to tell you how things are going. Do you intend to come up soon?'

'I've *been* up, at Christmas. And I'm just back from skiing. Had you forgotten?'

'I'm afraid I had. How did it go?'

'The artificial snow was a flop, but luckily they imported a few tons. We didn't mean to fraternize—we'd had it up to here with women, but on this morning there were these two on the piste...' He had forgotten he was in a hurry. She listened patiently.

'*Ciao,*' she said at last. Maybe that was what she should have said to Ben.

Chapter Twenty-Two

It had been a surprisingly easy transition, Anne thought, or so it appeared now, sitting in Aunt Elspeth's drawing-room in the quiet Fishpool Street terrace. She was only beginning to regard it as hers. And it was easy enough to think, on this pleasant May afternoon, that it had been easy, with the sun slanting onto Aunt Elspeth's Delft vases, her Cloisonné ware, her girandoles on the mantelpiece and her silver candlesticks with the beaded lampshades.

'Don't change a thing,' Richard and Con had enthused, 'it's perfect. One Braque print would ruin it, and a David Hockney would cause the heavens to fall.' There was no doubt it was a charming house, still smelling of Aunt Elspeth's pot pourri bowls in every room, and more than that, a happy house. She had settled into it like a bug in a rug.

Truthfully, the leaving of Alex had been hell. When she went back from the Bella Vista, knees in working order and able to tremble, he had greeted her morosely, head down. 'If you had stayed away any longer,' he said, following her into the kitchen, 'you were well on the way to making a damn fool of me.' By habit she was filling the kettle, still with her coat on. Every housewife did that.

'Didn't you think you were likely to make *me* the laughing stock of the place?' she said, banging the kettle onto the stove to give her courage. He came to her and whirled her to face him. His face was a dull red, his bottom lip stuck out. She had been dreading the rows. Better to get them over quickly.

'What the hell are you insinuating?'

'If the cap fits,' she said, inwardly shaking. She wished she felt angry, the way she had felt when she read Ben's letter. If she had been boiling with rage she would have said she had seen him with Margaret, in action, she might well have used the four-letter word, but her pride forbade it. The scene in her mind was too undignified, farcical, she peering into that room perched on a sack of aggregate, as Mr Proctor had called it so knowledgeably, falling off it with shock, *Feydeauesque*. That image had to be kept a secret. It was too shame-making.

'Ach, you...!' he rejected the challenge, she noticed, pushing roughly past her and going to sit down heavily at the table. She made the tea, poured it into mugs, and sat down opposite. She pushed a mug towards him, thinking, I have my coat on. I'm ready to go...

'I'm leaving you, Alex,' she said. 'I've had enough. I know what you did to Ben Davies...'

'What are you *talking* about?' His indignation, his raised hands, were the essence of falseness. Did he fool people with performances like this? Business people?

'Ben Davies. It's no good denying it. Oh, yes, I was in the wrong. I broke my vows, my holy marriage vows.' He was listening, agreeing with her. Words like 'vows' and 'holy' were words he liked. 'Once after twenty years isn't bad when you've been breaking yours systematically over that period. Don't bluster. Don't even bother to deny it. I have proof, undeniable proof.' That made him take a quick look at her.

'I'm not denying it. I'm no angel. Hell, I've never pretended to be. We've both had a bit of a flutter, but let's forgive and forget, *quid pro quo*. You'll always be first with me, Anne, you know that. And for Pete's sake,' he was boyish, 'Davies must be pretty lily-livered if he was put off by Spiers laying into him...'

'Laying into him?' Her anger erupted. She was shouting. 'You and I just don't

328

speak the same language! You don't think like me, you're an arrogant bully and a coward into the bargain! Well, it's over for me, finished, *kaput*. I want a divorce. I'm going to live in Aunt Elspeth's house. In St Albans,' she added, seeing his total lack of comprehension.

'St Albans? You are bloody well not. You are not going to shame me in front of all our friends...'

'Would it have made any difference if it had been Tunbridge Wells? I've a house at St Albans. Had you forgotten? Mine. Look, Alex,' she pretended weariness, 'half of our friends are divorced. Haven't you noticed? It's been like musical chairs amongst them for the last ten years at least while you've been putting up your smokescreen. We must be about the only couple who are still with their first partners. I've had enough. It's nothing to do with *quid pro quos*. I want to live on my own. I *have* to.' She spoke the words slowly.

He stared at her, unbelievingly, brows together.

'Alex,' she put her hand across the table to him, 'I'm sorry, really I am, for everything. It goes back for years. I know it's mostly my fault, but my mind's made up. That's why I stayed away to think. Try to understand...'

He interrupted her. 'I don't want to hear

329

this.' He pushed his mug aside, put his head down on the table and wept. It broke her heart. Or perhaps only bruised it, like her knees. She would have to find out.

She sat, looking at his bowed head, sorry, very sorry to see him reduced to this, and knew she had won. It was a small feeling compared with his distress. There would be more recriminations when he had got over his disbelief, his hurt pride, more rows, accusations, pleadings, but she wouldn't give in. It was a hard-earned first round.

She sat, waiting for him to stop. It was more snuffling than sobbing. She couldn't believe her own coldness. She sipped her tea, watching him in a detached fashion, and thought of their life together.

Oh, she could find excuses for him, for his ignominious smacking of the small James, for his throwing the cat out of the bed, for having Ben beaten up. None of them were malicious. They could be put down to quick temper, sometimes justified.

But the trouble was there was no moderation in his behaviour, always too much or too little, too generous or too mean, too obstreperous or too morose, too loving or too curt, but always the urbane public image to the forefront which had to be kept polished by her so that it 'looked nice'.

There was, of course, the other side of the coin, that she was too sensitive, too prissy, too vulnerable, too easily ashamed, too worried about *her* public image. Wasn't that the core of the distress she had felt when she saw them together on the floor at the Depot, that she, Anne Garrett, wife and mother and voluntary worker for the good of the community should stoop, (or in this particular case climb up, on a bag of aggregate), and take part in a licentious peepshow?

When she had finished her tea and was still waiting, he at last looked up, his eyes wet and reproachful, his cheeks flushed, reminding her of James after a tantrum. 'Drink some tea, Alex,' she said, 'you'll feel better.' But not, 'Come to Mummy.'

'This isn't happening,' he said, his lower lip trembling, 'it isn't happening. I love you. You're my wife.' He was exposed, vulnerable, his urbanity gone.

'You only love the wife you have constructed in your own mind. I'm not like that. I'm tired of being a sham. Honestly, you'll be better off without me. You'll find someone else. And don't think I'm going off with Ben. That's over. He was only the trigger. I think I can live alone. I don't think *you* can. You're hopeless,' she shrugged, smiling, housewifely, 'absolutely hopeless in the house.'

He shook his head, his eyes on her. 'It isn't happening.' The words had an absent-minded sound. He drank his tea, braced his shoulders and got up. 'I have to go out. I've an appointment. I expect you to be in your proper frame of mind when I come back.'

'This is my proper frame of mind,' she said, but he wasn't listening.

He refused to have any more discussions, withdrawing into himself, moved into the guest bedroom, was scrupulously polite to her. The misery in his face almost made her give in. She felt their problems hadn't been talked through properly.

She wanted to say, 'You see, it's the violence in your thinking which disturbs me so much, having Spiers beat up Ben, for instance.'

She wanted to hear him say, 'It was my love for you which drove me to it, my jealous love,' anything which would explain his motivation, and on her part she would have liked to convey to him the humiliation she had felt when she had spied on Margaret and him, a crawling disgust in *herself*, as if she had been playing a part in a bad film.

But they didn't talk, and after three days of his injured silence, she packed her bags when he was out at work and put them downstairs in the cloakroom. That day she saw their solicitor and asked him to start proceedings. She said they were equally reprehensible, but he looked at her as if she were to blame. He was a friend of Alex's.

She filled the refrigerator, cleaned the house, made arrangements for Nan's niece to come in and prepare his evening meal.

'Things won't be the same without you,' the old woman said, 'maybe I'll let Brenda take over me mornings. It was only to get away from him that I came to you. Made a nice change from his grumblings.' The Nans of this world, Anne reminded herself, had to stay put.

She had telephoned Mr Doldren to tell him she had decided to take over the occupancy of Aunt Elspeth's house, and to her surprise he had professed himself delighted. 'I hope you're not disappointed,' she had said. But apparently not. The house was charming, but while they had been waiting for her decision, another one had come on the market on the way to Hatfield which had the added attraction of a paddock behind, and as they intended to buy a pony for the children...

'Is your husband in need of help, by the way?' he had enquired, 'Perhaps I could...'

'Oh, no, thank you, he's wedded to the North,' she said, and summoning up her courage, 'We're being divorced.'

'I'm sorry.' It sounded perfunctory. He must deal with divorces every day of the week. 'Perhaps you're making a wise decision to come to St Albans,' he said, 'a new life for you. And nearer London.' He had the popular belief that it was the only place to be near and that everyone else lived on a cultural dialysis machine.

She braced herself. When she and Alex had breakfasted together for the last time (although he was unaware of it), she had told him she was leaving that day, that she wouldn't be here when he came home.

It was the hardest thing she had ever had to do in her life. Its enormity struck her even more than it seemed to strike him. She half held out her hand—a useless gesture—but his face was expressionless as he rose, noisily pushing back his chair. His look was full of contempt. 'You'll regret this,' he said. He was a stranger.

She had left a short note—adding insult to injury, she realized, but unable to metaphorically close the door.

'I'm so sorry, Alex. We haven't even parted sensibly. We ought to have talked, tried to understand each other, but that's been the fault all the time we've been married. We've never really talked, explored each other. If it went on any longer I feel I'm in danger of becoming what you have made me, a pleasant woman without opinions, dressed by Alex Garrett, kept by Alex Garrett. I'm sorry about St Lucia. Maybe you can cancel the tickets—or take someone else.

  Anne.'

She wasn't good at this, she told herself. You read every day of marriages breaking up, but the actual mechanics were never mentioned, the last-minute looking around the house to check that nothing had been forgotten, that the table had been set for the husband's first solitary meal—and sitting down to weep at this point—making sure that the timers had been set to bring on the lights in various rooms—burglars and their proclivities must never be ignored—last-minute tweaking of curtains for a natural, lived-in appearance, neither wide open nor fully closed...

  When at last she was in the hall surrounded by her bags she sat down at the telephone and dialled Margaret. She hoped she wouldn't notice that her voice was thick with tears. The reaction when she told her she was leaving Alex was a horrified silence. At first.

  'You're *what?*'

  'You heard me the first time. Leaving

Alex. I've asked him for a divorce. I'm going to live in St Albans, in Aunt Elspeth's house.'

'I can't believe it! I don't know what to say.' It was the first time in her life that she had been able to take the wind out of her sister's sails.

'Aren't you going to wish me all the best?'

'I think you're off your head,' and then reverting to type, 'Trust you to fall on your feet. Decent house to go to anyway. No sleeping in cardboard boxes for you!'

'That's true. I'll write or phone when I'm settled in.' She hung up.

She telephoned Mrs Proctor who wished her all the best. 'I thought you would do it,' she said. 'I knew when you walked in with Albert that you'd had enough. Good luck. You're young enough to bolt.'

That was the sentence which surfaced in her mind as the train took her southwards—she hadn't taken the car since it was Alex's possession. Perhaps she had been too old for Ben, but she was young enough to bolt. A good-looking young man opposite her asked if she would like to read his paper. She accepted with a smile.

Her first week in St Albans had been like a waking dream. She knew now how

Alice felt when she went through the looking-glass, an 'otherness'. St Albans was different, it looked different, smelled differently, its inhabitants acted differently. They weren't as friendly as the Bay people. Their voices were sharper. They didn't take a personal interest in her in shops as they did at home (she still called it home), but then it was unfair to judge them all by Ada and Albert Proctor.

It had the slightly smug air of towns with a rich history, especially cathedral towns which have been made cities by virtue of their charter and their alternative Roman nomenclature. She could not imagine Nan Ward feeling very much at home in a town which had once been called Verulanium.

She had been several times to the Museum which was probably more than most people in the town, she'd had a morning sherry in Ye Olde Fighting Cocks, she had seen the almshouses, the clock tower and French Row and she could have written a small essay on the Peasants Revolt. She was also desperately lonely.

Each morning she went into town to be amongst people and to get to know its streets and shops, then went back to the house, had a frugal lunch and spent the afternoon making new curtains which were needed, writing letters, and on fine days working in the garden. Aunt Elspeth had had a part-time gardener who kept it in order, but after her death he had departed to fresh pastures, and she had decided not to pursue him.

She had to economize. With Aunt Elspeth's legacy of two thousand pounds and a similar sum she had in the Bank, she thought she could scrape by for the best part of a year. There had been no communication from either Alex or his solicitor.

There were some days, in the first few weeks, when she felt like crawling back. She was desperately homesick for the northernness of what she had left, especially the wide skies—she wondered if they were more important than the sea—while realizing you couldn't have one without the other. She felt closed in, an alien. People seemed to look through her. Their voices were strange, high-pitched. She felt like an 'Erewhonian'.

She knew she could have got a job as a personal secretary again, but she was keeping that in reserve. The daily newspapers told her there was a constant demand. She wanted time to think, to study English. It was a burning desire which would give point to being here at all. Before hardship drove her to answer advertisements, she enrolled in the Open

College in the nearest Polytechnic to work for a degree.

Ben hadn't written to her. She went through expectation, disappointment, resentment, hate, love, then reached a status quo. He had more sense than she had. He knew when a thing was finished.

She had only been attending classes for a few weeks when she was asked if she would go and see the office supervisor. She went, inwardly trembling, convinced that they had found some flaw in her being there. Alex had got at them... Miss Mappin was an elderly woman vaguely reminding her of Aunt Elspeth in her manner, or perhaps it was that St Albans voice with its faint hint of Cockney. She asked Anne to sit down.

'Mr Stobo said you might be interested in some part-time work here, Mrs Garrett,' she said, looking over her glasses. Anne's relief was great, making her rush to agree.

'Oh, yes, I would. But I wonder how he knew that?'

'From your Application Form, I expect. You're experienced in office procedure, he says, and we like to give students the first opportunity.'

'How much would there be? I'm rusty. I need time to study.'

'It's basically two afternoons a week, or evenings, if you prefer. That can be

339

negotiated with the rest of the staff. Fifty pounds per week, typing, keeping records, window work. They keep knocking, always asking something...' she sighed, 'morning, noon and night.'

'I'd be glad to take it.' She smiled at the woman. 'It would make all the difference to my finances. Thank you.'

'Don't thank me. Thank Mr Stobo. It was his idea.'

You had just to push the boat out, she reflected, going back to her class, take the plunge. The analogies made her think again of the sea, how she missed the view of it from High Croft, the view from Mrs Proctor's pink room. She missed it more than Alex—she was still unused to living alone—but far more immediately she missed Ben, the excitement he had brought to her life, new sensations, anticipation, how her love of him would permeate everything she did: ironing, gardening, shopping, sitting behind her desk at the Citizens' Advice Bureau.

She missed his broken vowels, his dark hair, his thin eager body, his youthfulness, his youthful smell, the half-moon crease on the side of his mouth when he smiled, she missed their walks and their beddings in the pub. She thought of their picnic at Esthwaite, and how he had clambered up the bank to get away from the swan, how he was still metaphorically doing it. Even impregnating Judith was a get-out clause from his involvement with her. So brave in love, so timid in battle...it was better to end.

In April Margaret wrote her a brief letter, the first communication which had passed between them, a terse note. 'Judith's had a little girl. Thought you would like to know. Are you not talking any more to your big sister? Give me a ring sometime.' She must suspect that she knew about her affair with Alex. They would have discussed the possibility many times. But, typically, she was ignoring it.

She got used to living alone. She bought a cat as near in appearance to the beloved Smoky of her childhood and had a cat-flap cut in the back door.

And as well as Richard and Con, James began visiting her occasionally at the weekend, sometimes bringing Anthony. The weeks in between flew. She had classes to attend, work to prepare for them, her part-time work which she enjoyed as she got to know the other students, and there was the garden, which was a challenge to her.

She was persuaded to join a Debating Society in connection with her course. Garth Stobo turned up one evening, seemingly very much at home. She found it quite easy to think of him as Garth. He was young middle-aged, possibly near her own age, his hair was grey and thick like a pelt, he was stocky with a slight pot belly, quizzical and not very well-groomed. His shirts were clean but not well-ironed. She thought he looked like the archetypal teacher, imagined the pads of his fingers were permanently white with chalk dust.

'How are you getting on, Anne?'

She was wrongly effusive. 'Oh, splendidly. I can make the hours to suit myself and I quite enjoy my window work.'

He looked surprised, then his face cleared. 'I didn't mean the part-time job.' He smiled. 'I meant your real work.'

'The course? Sorry. I like it.' She felt young, a different person from the wife-of-Alex Anne, in her tight black trousers and sweater, high boots, her hair tied back. Her hips were slim enough because of her frugal eating. 'I basically like it, in spite of its difficulties, because I've always wanted to go back... You don't think I won't manage it? I know I've been a long time away.'

'No, no. Motivated mature students are never any problem. Come and have a coffee.'

They went to the counter, then stood in a corner with their cups to get out of the crush. 'What a din,' he said. 'Thank God they're not like this in class.' He grinned at her. 'I'm desperately curious. I always want to know what brings people like you to the point of wishing to go back, just as when I see people who are married I always want to know how they met.'

'And how they got divorced? Or, why?'

'That's it. I'm divorced. My wife found someone she liked better.'

'So did I. But it's over now.'

'And you're not going back?'

'No.' She shook her head. 'This coffee's good.'

'I'll take the hint. Well, what you lose on the swings...your work shows promise. Perhaps because you come to it fresh. I'm surprised you were content working in an office, that's right isn't it?'

'You know it is. You read my C.V. Lots of people work at what they don't like. I fell into it, found I was efficient and stayed on.'

'I hope you'll fall into something more creative when you get your degree.'

'I appreciate your confidence in me.' She smiled. 'And for recommending me to Miss Mappin...' One of the students was beside them.

'They want you to wind up the debate now, Garth, say something succinct.'

'The story of my life. Sorry.' He was gone.

She went into the hall to hear him, feeling disorientated by their talk. She looked like the other girls in her dress, she had been swept out of one conformity into another, and yet it had been difficult to know which role to adapt when she had been talking to him. So many already, secretary, wife and mother, social worker, now mature student. Which one fitted?

She had fitted with Ben, despite the disparity in their ages. Now Garth Stobo's masculinity had disturbed her, making her wonder if she had done the right thing. She and Ben had been so happy together, a transcendant kind of happiness...she wasn't listening now to the talk on German philosophers, Garth Stobo's plan to get a group together in the summer to follow the Danube from Breg to the Black Sea.

There was an ache in her body, an ache of loss and desolation, a feeling of having thrown away the substance for the shadow. But he threw *you* away, she told herself bitterly. She tried to pay attention. 'Heidegger's oft-repeated claim to be a Black Forest peasant...' Garth Stobo was saying apropos some point she had missed. He looked like a peasant himself, stocky, broad-shouldered, no grace about him.

Chapter Twenty-Three

Towards the end of May, James came for a weekend, this time without Anthony. It was a lovely day, she had the house shining with beeswax polish—it seemed the only thing to use on Aunt Elspeth's mahogany furniture—the garden was blooming with primulas and wallflowers, and they were able to sit outside. No view, but she had become reconciled to that. There was a certain cosiness in the St Albans environs.

'I could do with a pad like this,' he said, lying back in his chair. 'How do you get so many birds around, Annie?'

'I fed them in winter and provided nesting boxes for them. Then there are the trees. The only fly in the ointment is Two.' This was her cat, originally christened Smoky Two, which had proved too cumbersome to say. It was stretched out beside them on the grass, its head turning on its own axis if a bird came within its range of vision.

'I've left the house to you in my Will, and you know you're welcome any time. One of the joys, James—I've never said this to you before—is being near you. I've missed the north a lot, its colour's different, blue-grey compared with rose-green—difficult to explain.' He looked uncomfortable, and she thought how they hated any mention of sentimental dependence. 'Give me my space,' they seemed to say, backing off...

'As a matter of fact, Annie,' he said, stretching out a foot to rub the cat's upturned belly, 'I may not be in London too long. I mean, after I get my Diploma.'

'Are you thinking of going abroad, VSO or something like that?'

'No, no, I'm not that type. I was home a month ago—Anthony was going and I got a lift from him. Went to the Point one day with him for a laugh to see his old aunt. He's hanging in there because of the lolly. Remember that day your chap and us nearly got caught by the tide?'

'He isn't my chap any more, and it was only for a short time.'

'Do you mean you never see him?'

'Nor hear from him. It's over. It wouldn't have worked out.'

'I thought that was why you left Dad?'

'It was what gave me the impetus, but it wasn't to go to him. It was to...make my own life before it was too late.'

'You were never very happy together, you and Dad, were you?'

'No, we weren't. It's an old story. You

probably realized it.'

'Yes, I knew, more or less, but on the other hand he was such a good provider, and I thought maybe most fathers were like that.'

'It isn't an ideal situation for a wife. Her brain atrophies.'

'But you did voluntary work. I thought that would have been enough for you.'

She was irritated. 'Look, James, you're not blaming me for leaving him, are you?' Her mind clicked. 'Heh, he won't give me a divorce. You aren't here by any chance as an emissary, are you?' She would never have spoken as sharply in the old days.

'No, of course not. It's none of my business, really, but...' He withdrew his foot, sat upright, 'I said to you I was home recently. Well, I had dinner with Dad in that Blue Dolphin place. Great grub. He looked sad, and shrunken a little, as if his suit had grown too big for him. He was talking about giving up the business completely. I felt really sorry for him.'

'Did you?' You have never said you felt 'really sorry' for me, she thought. How men stuck together. Was it that they were incapable of seeing a woman's point of view? 'He has plenty of friends. He's well looked after at home. He has his trips away in the best hotels.' He has Margaret. Again she held back. If she told James she knew

347

his father and aunt had been lovers, or still were, she might find herself blurting out how she knew. *That* she was still ashamed to do. She could still blush in bed at the memory of that night at the Depot.

'Yes, I know all that. Annie,' he turned and looked at her, and she saw Alex in him, the fair face, the slightly florid cheeks which, as she had sometimes thought in Alex's case, might indicate high blood pressure. In her own case it was the reverse with her white skin. And James had the same well-groomed air as his father, even in T-shirt and jeans. He probably didn't possess a suit, but he'd like it when he got one. 'He's offered me a partnership in a few years. I would have a BMW, and he would buy me one of those new flats on the river. He took me to see them. They're super bachelor pads. Anthony thinks things are really brightening up back home, better shops, good ethnic restaurants—there have been an influx of Chinese. They can nose out prosperity. And there's a new cinema club, great foreign films, and a Health Club three miles out, with the lot, swimming pool, solarium, sauna, you name it.'

'Are you going to take his offer?' She had heard enough about the bribes.

'I'm thinking about it. Anthony's going back. We've both had London up to here,' he drew the side of his hand across his throat, 'there's a place for him in *his* Dad's firm—well, he's always known it—and he's got this thing going with Debbie Broadbent, you know who I mean. Her people keep the riding stables. *They* would build him a house if he got tied up.'

'It's all happening up there,' she said. She felt alone, suddenly, felt the sensation again of being an alien. She thought she had conquered it. Always the thought of James being so near had been a lifeline.

'You sound disappointed in me.' He had his baby face on now.

'Disappointed? Good gracious, no! I'm all for people pleasing themselves. Finding their own life style. Isn't that what I'm doing here? I'm having a great time, what with my studies and my part-time work and meeting heaps of new people. It's a completely new life.'

'You don't sound like a *mother* any more.'

'But I thought I was Annie,' she said, smiling at him, 'I'm living up to the Annie label. Don't you like it, or did you really want me to stay the way I was, kowtowing to an utterly selfish, chauvinistic man? Did you?'

'Hang on there,' he said, looking frightened, 'I'm just being honest with you, telling you how the wind's blowing. I'm looking to the future. I wouldn't have to *live* with Dad when the time comes, and when he goes, the business would be mine.'

She wanted to shake her head at the cool calculation of it all, but wasn't it *she* who was out of step in her thinking? Everyone had to 'go'. The young realized it. It was only those who were drawing nearer to 'going' who didn't want to face it, she supposed.

'I'm glad you're honest with me, James. Of course you must do what suits you, and I'm sure you would do well at home when the time comes.' She saw the seagulls wheeling over the wide sky, and the tide racing in across the fur-coloured sand. She envied him. 'I can see you making a success of it.'

She leant back so that he wouldn't see her face, 'Have you any news of Margaret or Judith? I haven't heard for ages. Just one brief note from your aunt when the baby was born.'

'I asked Dad, and he told me Judith has gone to live with her mother. Did you know?'

'I told you, I've scarcely heard. But I should have thought that was the *last* thing Margaret would have wanted.'

'You've always had your knife in her.

She's really very kind and great fun.' She closed her eyes against that one. 'I think it's because of the baby,' he replied.

'Can't Judith look after it herself?' After all, that's what she wanted.'

'It isn't that. It isn't doing well. It's under supervision at the hospital. There's something...mysterious there, Annie. Dad was very cagey, as if he knew something.'

'Maybe it's one of those chronic conditions, blood things, infantile eczema, which clear up when they grow older. Poor little thing. Judith won't be happy. She's a good-time girl, likes her fun. She won't be able to leave the little soul. What's she called?'

'Lauren. Yes, you could say that again about Judith. A good-time girl, my cousin. Dad says you can't blame her. She had a terrible time with her husband. "'Miserable little two-timer", he called him.'

'I always thought he was very fond of Judith.'

'Well, he didn't have another woman...' he stopped, red-faced.

'What is it, James?'

'Nothing. But Dad says...oh, never mind. One thing, when the time comes I'll watch what I'm doing. And Judith wasn't blameless either.' She didn't know what he was getting at, but he looked afraid of its implications.

'She's very beautiful. Ben Davies is the father of her baby. Did you know?'

'Yes, Dad told me.' It had been a real man-to-man conversation evidently. 'I expect he got it from Aunt Margaret. No wonder Ben never comes to see you. Too busy. Dad says he's always around, drives Judith to the hospital and so on. I suppose he's got to, really. It's his kid.'

'I suppose he feels responsible.' She sighed, feeling uneasy, but tired of James's gossip. How things had changed, Judith back with her mother, Margaret helping her with a sick baby. Margaret was and always would be unpredictable. That was why you could never write her out of your life, even if sometimes you wanted to. And had she stopped seeing Alex now that she was a grandmother? She thought of the many jokes about men sleeping with grandmothers and that Margaret would know them all. She felt a surge of tenderness for her and bit her lip against the tears.

And now her son was feeling the filial pull. She looked at him fondly, lying back in his chair, his fair face held up to the sun. Dangerous now, doctors said. Everything was changing. When James had gone she settled down to her books. They at least were constant in a changing world.

Chapter Twenty-Four

Rosemary, the other part-timer in the College office, had once again asked Anne to take the evening shift. Her requests were becoming rather inconvenient since buses were infrequent after nine o'clock.

Not for the first time Anne wished she had a car as she walked down the driveway towards the main road. Fortunately it was still light. She wouldn't feel so obliging in winter, but that was ages away yet. Goodness knows where she might be then. One thing she was sure of, her finances would not be any better as long as she was studying, and she was equally sure that unless driven to it she would not give them up.

It was the only completely satisfying thing in a life which at the moment had its fair share of doubts and anxieties. Alex had maintained a stubborn silence although she had written a friendly letter to him. He was obviously still nursing his hurt. Ben had not written, nor had Margaret, except for the one short letter about the birth of Judith's baby.

A car stopped at her side and she saw

Garth Stobo at the wheel. He leant out. 'Want a lift?'

'I think I'll just catch a bus,' she said, stopping nevertheless. She didn't want to appear too eager, but she had still to take kindly to standing at a bus stop with a crowd of chattering young students. It was liable to bring back her feelings of alienation which were beginning to die a natural death.

'Hop in. It's better than standing.' She did, relieved that he had insisted. 'Have you extra classes?' he asked.

'No, I'm working in the office, remember? Thanks to you.' She smiled at him. 'Rosemary, the other part-timer has an ongoing affair which peaks in the evenings. I'm being obliging. Have you?'

'An ongoing affair?'

'No,' she laughed, 'I mean, have you extra classes?'

'Yes, I've been coaching some backward students. I have to rope in a few at a time. Wouldn't dare risk it individually. I might be sued by the parents.'

'No!' She looked at him, interested.

'You have no idea. Those kids are streetwise now, or their parents are. You just have to bend over them to look at their work and they're accusing you of sexual abuse.'

'I can hardly believe it.'

354

'That's because you're new to it all, or perhaps it hasn't reached the north yet.'

'We're waiting to get flushing loos first.'

'Unbearable excitement.' His mouth quirked. 'Why don't you let me take you out for dinner tomorrow night?'

'Well, it would be a change from fish and chips. But would it spoil the pupil-teacher relationship?'

'Enhance it, rather. We could treat it as a tutorial. I'll pick you up at seven-thirty, okay?'

'Thanks. I miss my car.'

'Cars are dangerous things. We've two girls off already, pregnant. I blame the backs of cars.' He grinned at her. 'You're better without one.'

Ben and I, in his car, she thought, in one of those quiet valley roads. I wasn't prudent, but then she hadn't been at risk. Or had there been a greater risk? Nothing was simple any more. She drew in her breath sharply.

'Have I given you pause for thought?' Garth said. She glanced at him. There was a flickering muscle at the side of his mouth. He had a good profile, and, a rare thing in a man, a good nose. So often they were too big for the rest of the face. Alex had trumpeted into his handkerchief like a rogue elephant...

'No, no. I'm wool-gathering.' Trying not

to think. 'I'm probably tired.'

'You're not overdoing it, are you?'

'Goodness, no, I'm a young thing, relatively speaking.'

'You look young enough, and then I remember you have a grown-up son. What age is he?'

'Nearly twenty. He thinks I'm mad.'

'I shouldn't worry about that. I have a daughter who cleaves to her mother and hates me, which is worse. As long as you're all right with yourself, what the hell.'

All this man was doing was making Ben alive in her mind. She still had his book of poems. They could still act like a mantra at her bedside. She had only to open it and she could weep over the pages for her lost love, for its sweetness, for its unique quality, its tenderness.

But lately she had begun to think that she was weaving him into the fabric of her life, like some woollen bedspread. You couldn't make a poem out of a woollen bedspread, could you? 'The rough male kiss of blankets...' That came back to her from somewhere.

Garth called for her the following evening, but she didn't ask him to come in. Nor, she had decided, would she, when he brought her back. He was complicating her life, and her mind had first to be cleared, of anxiety, and of Ben—the same thing. Last night he had been there again, a constant ache which had an underpinning now, a vague unease, too nebulous to be called dread.

'Do you live alone?' she asked Garth.

'No. I ought to have a super bachelor pad to entice women into—and perhaps mature students.' His grin was wicked, 'But I haven't got round to it yet. Meantime I have two rooms in the estimable Mrs Roberts' house who does for single gentlemen with no encumbrances, and does for me very well. I'm lazy enough to appreciate her.'

'I was left my house by my aunt.'

'Lucky you. I expect you have eligible men beating a path to your door. I know many who would give their right arm for a girl with her own house if they could move in.'

'I had thought of it as an attraction.' He was easy to talk to.

'An added attraction, I should say,' he looked sideways at her. When his eyes were on the road again she admired his profile once more, and how his thick grey hair was cut like a cap. There was a Roman quality there, like a head on a coin, imperiousness in the lift of the chin, and yet he wasn't at all imperious. She got the impression that he worked hard at giving a down-to-earth impression. But then appearances were deceptive.

She tried to be bright when they started their meal, but it didn't work. She shouldn't have come. Alex, Ben, that was enough. There was enough sorting out there to do without further involvement. She didn't demur when he refilled her glass at intervals.

'It's as well I'm not driving,' she said, when they were having coffee. She felt slightly hazy.

'Yes, you've had more than me.' He teased her.

'Were you counting?'

'No, watching.' He laughed at her. 'Ah, well, never mind. It becomes you. Your eyes are bright and there's a hidden glow in your cheeks, nothing so banal as a drunken flush.'

'I was trying to drown memories.'

'I'm sorry I'm so uninteresting.'

'Don't make me feel awful.' The coffee came.

'Have a Grand Marnier with it,' Garth said.

'Only if you're having one.' She welcomed the blurring of the edges, the lessening of sensibility.

'Okay. I'll drink loads of coffee afterwards.'

The brandy caressed her, helped her to forget as a gentle hand might have done. She sat opposite Garth listening with one part of her, the other was back in her house at the window overlooking the Bay. Alex. Twenty-one years. And yet they had never really got inside each other. Ben. Immediate impact. All her memories of him, that broken-backed voice, making ordinary words sound strange, his thin springiness, gripped her unbearably like a squeezing fist round her heart, while she smiled at Garth, made suitable replies. And with the longing came the disgust, inseparable now.

Now she was in her car that night, driving past Spiers of the thin, cold face, the water-sleeked hair, stopping at Alex's office, knocking at the heavy door, retreating down the two steps, making her careful way round the back of the building. She bit, like a sore tooth, on the humiliation of the episode, knowing that morbid introspection got you nowhere.

'Self-reproach is a waste of time,' she said. He had been saying that he regretted the loss of his daughter more than his wife.

'It's strange, isn't it,' he looked at her intently, 'when you think of it, there's no blood tie between husband and wife, but there is between father and daughter, mother and son, between brothers, and sisters...'

'Yes, you're right.' Margaret. Don't say anything. 'James can irritate me beyond endurance at times, but basically, I love him. It's the bond. Perhaps the irritation factor is more because the love is greater. He tells me now he's going back home when he finishes his degree to work with his father. I thought, I've lost him, and yet I know I'll never lose him. He's still my son, in here.' She put her hand on her heart. 'But with Alex, my husband, it's different. Whether or not he gives me a divorce, he has nothing to do with me now. There's no blood tie, although I've plenty to regret in my behaviour.'

'An affair?'

She didn't deny it. 'Affairs you can live down, grow past, but regret, no, that's the wrong word, sheer stupidity's better.' The sense of humiliation and shame had got to be got rid of somehow. 'Do you know what aggregate is?' She actually *heard* herself saying that, thinking, I must be stoned out of my mind. (None of James's friends were ever merely drunk. They were always 'stoned out of their minds'.)

'Aggregate?' He frowned momentarily, his face cleared, and he said with a fair mixture of pedantry and pleasure, 'I've got it. It's to do with building. Broken stone and sand used for making concrete. It comes in bags.' He sat back, looking satisfied.

'Top of the class. I fell off one when I was spying on my husband and my sister, through a window. They were...' she swallowed, no, she couldn't say the word, it was a question of limitation of language... 'They were...' she saw his look, comical in its encouragement, and said quickly, 'having sex in what seemed to be quite an uncomfortable position.'

He looked at her for a second, his eyes widening, then throwing back his head laughed uproariously. She could have killed him. She sat watching him while he went on laughing. He said at last, wiping his eyes, 'you can't cope with it, even yet?'

'It's not so much what I *saw*, don't you see, it's me, standing on a sack, watching...besides, it's nothing to laugh at. I fell off and bruised my knees badly.'

'Poor you. I'd got you wrong somehow. I thought you were the last person to worry about being a Peeping Tom.' He was trying to settle his face. 'Maybe that's the real curse of provincialism. You worry about how things *look*.'

'But against that you have neighbourly concern. As it happened I experienced true kindness that night. From my fishmonger

361

and his friend.' She was clowning now. 'In...a...boat.' She knew by the way she spoke that she was tipsy. But the misery was still lurking, not quite gone.

'It's entrancing,' Garth said, 'your story, aggregate and fishmongers in boats. Tea and sympathy. Have a good laugh, go on. You'll never be able to live alone if you don't learn to laugh at yourself.'

'I'm on the brink, I think.' She looked for her handbag, scrabbling. 'And I think I'll have to go home before I say any more. I'll never be able to look you in the eyes again after tonight.'

'Don't feel badly about it. I'll pretend to have a rotten memory. It's a mistake to be too buttoned up. That's what happened between Eileen and me. She said I hardly ever talked to her.'

'Married couples can be like that, taking each other for granted. That's what was wrong with us. Perhaps I should have tried harder.'

She watched him trying to catch the attention of the waiter—Alex never had any difficulty, king of his sand castle. Was that another advantage of living in the sticks?

She also wondered why Garth Stobo's profile was better than his front face. Pity he couldn't go through life walking like an Egyptian carving on a wall...evidently the remnants of the brandy were still floating about in her head. But full face wasn't at all bad when he turned and smiled at her. His eyes were good too. You could become habituated to anyone in time, come to think of it.

In the car, when he stopped at her door, he put his arm round her and squeezed her against his side. 'Any chance of a last coffee?'

'You must be joking. Someone might spy on us.'

'I wasn't thinking of sexual congress. Even in uncomfortable positions.'

'I knew I had talked too much.' She got out and bent to talk to him through the open window. 'Thank you for a lovely evening. And don't smirk when our eyes meet in your class. It would be worse than falling off a sack of aggregate.'

'No, it wouldn't. There would be no bruised knees.' His eyes were laughing at her. 'Thank *you* for a lovely evening.' He lifted his hand and drove away.

When she went in, Two met her, rubbing against her legs. She lifted her, cuddled her, and said, 'On the whole it wasn't bad, do you know that?'

But it hadn't got rid of the apprehension, a heaviness based somewhere behind her ribs.

Chapter Twenty-Five

As if the evening spent with Garth had acted, at second remove, cathartically, Margaret rang her on the following one. Luckily she was not working late at the Polytechnic.

'Hello, Anne.' She sounded quieter than usual.

'Hello.' The old enemy, resentment, stalked. She hadn't exorcized it entirely by telling Garth about the night when she had watched Alex and Margaret making love. She knew it showed in her voice.

'Are you not speaking to me, sister dear?' In spite of the teasing, she still didn't sound like her usual self. There was a lack of insouciance.

She took an instant decision, and a deep breath. 'Well, it's no good pretending, Margaret. I know... I know you and Alex were lovers.' Silence. Count, one, two, three...

'Who told you that?' Very quietly.

'Never mind. I just know. Even allowing for my...fall from grace, it took me a long time to adjust to yours.'

'Is that why you walked out?'

'No, well, partly. Look, why are you phoning me? Is it to gloat? I admit I was a stupid fool, that I couldn't see what was going on under my nose, but...'

'Oh, stuff it! It wasn't important. At least not at the moment. Anne, could I come and see you? Something's happened. I don't want to yammer on about it on the phone.'

'Does it concern me? I told you I'm trying to make something of my life, get my act together...' How handy those phrases were.

'This concerns you. Don't for God's sake tell me all about your psyche. You were always like that. You never just *did* anything. You had to explain it to yourself...'

'It's nice to have my character analysed...'

'Oh, stop being stuffy! Shall I get the train tomorrow and come and see you or not? It's important. Damned important.'

'If it'll do us both any good.'

'I don't know about "good". It's necessary. You've settled in, then?'

'Yes, but I don't know for how long. I don't get any maintenance from Alex.'

'He's trying to starve you out, poor soul. He misses you.'

'He hasn't said so.'

'Alex has never written a letter in his

life. His secretary does them all. Oh, fuck Alex for the time being!'

Margaret could use the word, and not even in its proper context. She felt reluctant admiration. 'I've looked up the trains. I'll be at St Albans around four. I'll go straight to the house. If you're not going to be in, leave the keys under the mat.'

'I'll be there. I never leave keys under the mat. The Neighbourhood Watch Scheme are all against it.'

'Bully for them. Four o'clock, then. See you.' She rang off.

For once her attention drifted in class. Garth was talking about the Romanticists, and once, when she met his eyes, she knew her eager-beaver air of concentration was slipping. His eyes signalled slight disappointment. She had a feeling she was his key student in eye contact.

She was taking off her coat when the door bell rang, and she went running because her footsteps wanted to drag. What dire news was Margaret bringing now? About herself—she always came first—about Alex, Judith, Ben? Whatever it was, it was bound to be momentous, otherwise why would she bother to come at all?

She opened the door and stood facing Margaret. She was wearing a long Burberry, high boots and a Paisley shawl. Her black hair was wind-tossed. She was pale, her eyes looked tired. She had a look of Judith although not as beautiful. There had always been a slight irregularity in her features, difficult to decide where it lay. Judith was the perfected version.

'Aren't you going to welcome your big sister after all this time?' Her cockiness, her brashness, reminded Anne again of that long-ago photograph which Aunt Elspeth had given her. There was the same bold stance, caught for ever on celluloid. If she were shipwrecked, she would go down like that.

'Of course. Come in.' She stood aside. 'I'm in the kitchen. It's cosier there with the Aga.' The day was wet and windy. June had changed places with March.

Margaret knew her way. She strode ahead and plumped down on the one easy chair. 'Bliss! Mind if I pull off those boots? It was so wet when I left but they're too warm, really.' She wrenched them off and wriggled her toes.

'Give me your coat and shawl. I'll hang them up.'

'Thanks. And hurry up with a cup of tea or something stronger if you like.'

'Give me a minute!' The old resentment at being ordered about by an older sister was still there. 'I'm just going to make it.'

She busied herself ostentatiously in the cupboards, getting cups and saucers, opening various tins to put biscuits out on a plate.

'Don't bother arranging them in fancy patterns for God's sake,' Margaret said, watching her. 'You should have given all that up now. How do you like living alone?'

'I like it.'

'Now you'll know how it feels. I've had to do it since Ralph died. No rest for the wicked, bringing up children, the constant worry, constant lack of money. You never knew that.'

'So you keep on telling me.' She infused the tea, stirred it in the pot, then poured herself the first cup to test it. Margaret didn't like milky, weak-as-water tea. 'Good and strong', she would say, if asked.

'Is it good and strong?' Margaret asked.

'It will be.' She poured another cup and placed it beside her sister on the table. When their eyes met, she saw Margaret's were full of tears. 'What's wrong?' Her resentment went.

'I'm worried, that's what's wrong. I can hardly bear to think of the consequences...'

Fear rose in Anne. I'm trying to forget, she wanted to say, your behaviour, my own, Alex having Ben beaten up, Ben, always Ben... Judith's pregnancy. 'Aren't we all, worried?'

'You don't know anything.' Her sister's voice was harsh. 'This will really take the wind out of your sails. A real worry. It's about the baby.'

'The baby?' She had left her out in her catalogue.

'Lauren—although it's difficult to call such a mite anything but "baby". You knew they were living with me?'

'Yes.'

'And that Lauren was ill?'

'Yes, James mentioned something. I'm sorry. It must be worrying.'

'Worrying, she says!' She took a quick sip of tea, helped herself to a biscuit which instead of eating she crumbled between her fingers. 'Worrying! How typical of you, Anne, always on the outside, cool, calm and collected. Things don't touch you, do they? You can't see half the time what's going on under your nose.'

'That's true enough.' Unless I stand on a sack of aggregate. Good word, aggregate. 'What about the baby?' She would say infantile eczema, or nappy rash, make a grand drama out of nothing.

Margaret put down her cup and put her head in her hands. She was weeping. There was no doubt about that. Great, snorting sobs. The tears were running through her fingers.

Anne watched her, feeling her brows contract, her throat thicken, then got up and put her arm round her shoulders. 'You'll make yourself ill, Margaret. Tell me what it is. Can it be cured?' The black head shook, thick, springing black hair, and Anne touched it, stroked it, stroked it lovingly, feeling, this is part of me, my sister, joined to me. 'Tell me,' she said, still stroking, 'come on, tell me about the baby. That's why you came.' The fearful apprehension was now centred somewhere low down in her stomach, it was creeping up, anxious to cover her heart. She must be ready for the blow.

'There's a chance...she's HIV Positive.'

The fear whooshed over her heart like a giant wave. She straightened, staggered a little, then went and sat down. Otherwise she would have fallen. A fearful *dread*, rather, of worse to come. She tried to speak calmly. 'Take your hands away from your face, Margaret,' she said, and then, her voice rising, 'Go on! Take them away! We've got to talk. I have to *see* you when you talk.'

Margaret took her hands away. Even at a time like this the prompt obedience sat strangely on her. It was almost a humility. Her face was haggard, pitiful. 'This is what I've been doing every night when Judy's in bed, crying till I croak like a crow in the morning. I feel I've been downed by a cleaver, the way they do to animals. Getting at me through her, through the baby.'

'How did they find out? About the baby being...?'

'She had been ill, not eating, losing weight ever since she was born, and her doctor referred her to the hospital. The specialist there gave her a series of tests with no definite results. Then he sent for Judith and gave her the same tests...'

'Judith! What has she to do with it?' She wanted to close her ears.

'Everything. He discovered *she* was HIV Positive.'

There was an explosion in Anne's mind. The young man with the old face at the CAB talking about his girlfriend, 'I didn't know what she meant at first...' She must listen to her sister.

'Can you believe it?' Margaret's face was livid, tears were streaming down it, 'My little Judy! Such a beauty. Everybody said so. She got it from that bloody husband of hers, sneaking off with men...did you know *that,* you in your ivory castle, did you? Men!' Jeremy, giving her a rose...

Anne felt sick, shook her head. 'I can't believe this. Don't they test pregnant women automatically now, give them the option?'

'Only some. Judy's doctor is old, past it. It's high time they did. You see, she got this daft idea into her head that she must have a baby because she had missed out with that creep, Jeremy. It became an obsession. But try telling her anything. She goes her own sweet way.'

Well, of course, she had always known about Jeremy's bisexuality, basically, but had buried it. Margaret had always been so touchy about Richard. Let sleeping dogs lie. But they woke up again. Judith, infected by him! Her mind reeled.

To think she could work in the CAB, be supposedly *au fait* with today's social problems and yet not apply her knowledge outside the office, in her own family circle. To be so *blinkered*. No one was immune, given the required circumstances. And now the baby, Lauren. Well, of course she had read pamphlets about the chain effect, had filed them neatly under 'AIDS', compartmentalized them in her brain. 'For Office Use Only'.

Who was next in the chain? Jeremy, Judith, Lauren...Ben! A firecracker burst in her head, filling it with needle-like jabs of pain, and then, as if she had been anaesthetized, she was numb, cold. Even logical. 'What about...Ben?' She heard her voice, calm, barely a tremor.

'I thought you would get round to that

in your tortuous little mind. Your precious Ben. Maybe not so precious. He's going through tests too. Jeremy went to the States, so he's decamped. Don't look like that, for God's sake! It's nothing to do with me...'

She got up and crouched beside Margaret, moaning stupidly, 'You're making this up, aren't you? I know you, Margaret, you're making it up to get back at me because I know about you and Alex.'

'Shut your mouth,' she glanced at Anne, 'shut your *silly* mouth. And get up. I've got enough to worry about without adding *you* to my list.'

She got up and went back to her seat, rigid with shame. 'I'm sorry. Of course, Judith and the baby come first.' She wouldn't say Ben's name again.

Her sister looked at her dispassionately. 'You've never grown up, not really. Behind that cool front you're like a child.' She shrugged, actually smiled, 'Oh, I admit there was a bit of hanky panky between Alex and me but we're two of a kind. That was all there was to it.' Her eyes suddenly filled with tears again. 'Why would I do a thing like that to you, my own sister.'

But she *had*, even if it was only a bit of hanky panky.

It was nothing, she saw now, compared with the terrible things Margaret was telling her...

'I'll make some fresh tea,' Anne said when she couldn't think any more.

'No more tea. Have you nothing stronger in the house?'

'Some sherry.'

'Better than nothing. I'll get some glasses.' She stood up and went straight to the cupboard where they were kept. She had remembered, Anne thought, watching her select two sherry glasses from the carefully arranged set, brandy tumblers down to liqueur glasses. Aunt Elspeth had been proud of them.

'It knocks you out, doesn't it?' Margaret looked at her when Anne had filled the glasses. 'You should see your face. You wouldn't know my Judy. She's never cried once, she's rock-like, unapproachable.'

'I've been living in cloud cuckoo land. You probably think that's a perpetual state for me.' She half-smiled at her sister. 'How great is the danger for the baby, for Lauren?'

'Who knows? Judith won't talk about it, although I've tried with her. Even if it were anything to do with her—which it isn't—I'd never blame her. I've not exactly been an angel myself.' She gave a sidelong, wicked smile.

'She needs outside help.' She summoned some of her CAB experience, a bit late, she thought bitterly, 'You're too close to her. There are addresses. I could get them for you.' This conversation isn't taking place, she thought. Her heart was in an icebox of fear.

'She speaks to Ben. He's in on it too, has to be. God, it's like one of those terrible chain letters they used to have at school. There's no end to it.'

'No end to it.' She and Ben had slept together. She had provided against possible pregnancy, thinking that was the end of it. He had thought the same, or worse still, they hadn't thought at all. The stupidity of it! No excuse, particularly for her who had been involved in social work. She said to drown the sick feeling of guilt, 'Have you told Alex?'

'Yes, it's shaken him. I haven't seen him for, oh, ages. Nothing else seems important now. Judith wouldn't want him around. He'd bring her flowers and chocolates. He doesn't know how to express sympathy except by giving things. But he feels it. You never really understood him, Anne.'

'I expect you're right.' 'Like one of those terrible chain letters,' Margaret had said. She wouldn't wish *that* on him. 'Maybe I'm a poor judge of character. I thought Ben was timid.' She bit her lip. 'Now I see I judged him on the wrong things.' She thought of him scrambling up the bank at Esthwaite, and it seemed merely comical now.

'He'll come to see you when he knows about himself.'

'He's been too busy.'

'The poor chap has a lot on his mind. This is the bit that tears me up, thinking about the consequences, who else...' she didn't look at Anne, '...the, oh, God, what's that word?'

'The ramifications?'

'That's it. It's like water on flat ground, like pee spreading...' She made a queer little noise in her throat, 'goes all over the place, touches things, and people, in its path, avoids others, maybe. It's...'

'Margaret, stop this. I can't take it.'

'You've got to. I had to with Judith. Think it through. Maybe you'll be lucky and the water will avoid you, go round you. You always were lucky. All through our lives you've been the lucky one. You didn't know it when you were with Alex, and I bet Ben will find that he's clear and that will let *you* off the hook. But it won't let *him* off. I've got to know him since all this happened. He's...responsible. He'll *be* there for Judith. She says she isn't depending on him, but I don't believe her...'

The fear was swelling inside her again, a huge balloon of fear. It was going to blot out her brain. She got up. 'I have to get out and walk, Margaret. I can't sit still. Are you coming?'

'All right. Anything's better than this. Then we'll have dinner somewhere together. Can I stay the night?'

'Of course you can.'

'I'll leave first thing in the morning. I've only got two days off work.'

'It's hard for you. All this, and working.'

'I'm glad you recognize it. Judith could go to Ben, he's offered to have them, but she wants to be with me. I'm her mother, and we've always been close.'

'Just as well.'

They put on their coats and walked through the streets of St Albans, up and down, stopping at windows, commenting on fashions, prices. Anyone looking at us would think we were two sisters having a good time together, with no worries, Anne thought. What if we were transparent, or wore feelings inside out like that Pompidou Centre in Paris so the black wedge of grief over our hearts could be seen? People would be sorry for us. But then, wouldn't they be unconcerned since they had their own black wedges?

At eight o'clock they were tired out, and they went into a Chinese restaurant. Margaret said she was starving. Over her spring roll she smiled at Anne, the old,

377

cocking-a-snoot smile in place again. 'I've worked up quite an appetite.'

'Good.' She couldn't say the same of herself. The fear was infiltrating through her digestive tract, causing havoc. The chain, chain letters, like pee spreading, trust Margaret... 'I'm worried sick,' she said. 'My trouble is I have a vivid imagination. I want to talk to Alex, tell him...'

'Go and see him. He's a shadow of his former self, poor sod.' Margaret helped herself to some noodles. She was good with chopsticks. Well, coming from Manchester... 'You don't know it, but nobody could ever take your place with Alex. He's utterly devoted to you, thinks you're far too good for him. When he got wind of your affair with Ben.'

'Did you tell him?'

Margaret looked ashamed, 'I may have dropped a hint. Judith said...but that's where old Alex made a mistake. He got that creep Spiers, you know, at the gate...by God, I gave him as good as I got when I drove in, dumb insolence...'

She interrupted. 'Did you drive from Manchester to meet Alex in the Depot?'

'Well...' she chased a prawn.

'In your white Mini?'

'I haven't got a black one, or a Rolls Royce for that matter. You're a funny kid, Anne.' She thought of how she and Ben had sat up in bed, naked, examining Aunt Elspeth's photographs, and how she had conjectured—it was unimportant now. 'I was telling you about Spiers. Poor Alex was so cut up that he got him to waylay Ben and tell him in no uncertain terms to clear off his patch.'

'I don't believe it. He got Spiers to beat Ben up.'

'He what!'

'Spiers beat Ben up. Alex told him to.'

'You're deranged. Alex would never do a thing like that. He's too careful of his reputation. He only wanted to give Ben a fright.'

'I don't believe it.'

'Will you stop saying that, you clown! It's a lot more likely that Spiers took the law into his own hands. He's a creep. Ask Alex. You can surely believe your own husband.'

'All right, I'll ask him.' Obedience won. Besides, there were too many shocks. She couldn't think.

'You know Alex, Anne. He has a temper, a quick temper, but he's never been violent. Have you ever known him to be really violent?'

'Not really violent.' Or maliciously violent. The terrible thing about the cat had been an accident. She could admit

379

that now, when the suffering had faded. *He* had regretted it. She remembered his misery. Could Margaret be right?

'And you know what you'll have to do tomorrow?' Margaret said, washing down the food with a slurp of wine. She had always used it like mouthwash.

She nodded. Yes, far more important than white Minis under arches, or Ben being beaten up, or not being beaten up as Margaret had assured her...

'First thing.'

'Yes,' Anne replied.

'It will set your mind at ease.'

'I haven't got a doctor yet. I'll have to choose one.'

'Well, you'll be an interesting patient at least.'

They laughed a little, but the joke was too thin and they ate the rest of their meal in silence.

Chapter Twenty-Six

Garth telephoned her the day after Margaret had gone. 'You missed your classes. I wondered if you were ill.'

'No,' she said. 'I'm sorry. I should have let them know. I had my sister staying with me.'

His voice was hesitant, unfamiliar. She had got used to his jokey style. 'Isn't it silly,' he said, 'I can't get you out of my mind.'

'I'm flattered.' She scarcely heard him.

'Don't make pointless remarks.' Direct for a moment. 'I've felt a faint sense of unease about you, as if you needed someone.'

'That was perceptive.'

'You haven't had bad news?'

'I have.' All she wanted was for him to get off the line. 'I'll be back tomorrow. How much have I missed?'

'We did Chapter Two of *Coriolanus.*'

'Thanks. I'll have a look at it. Goodbye.' She hung up.

She went back to her classes the following day because she had to fill in the time somehow before she went

381

home at the weekend. Alex would be in Scotland on business until then. She had caught him on the telephone before he left and he had been pathetically grateful, a different Alex.

'I've missed you, Anne. I'll put this trip off.'

'No, go ahead. I've things to do before I come.'

'Are you all right?'

'Yes. But there's something I want to discuss with you.

'Tell me.'

'It's too much on the telephone. Too complicated. I'll wait till I see you. How are you managing?'

'Oh, fine. The girl you fixed up is okay, Brenda, but the house is like a morgue. It's when I come home at nights...'

'Don't you eat out sometimes?'

'No, that's even worse. Like a pariah, skulking about. The life's gone out of me, Anne. All I do at nights is sit and think, hope...'

Don't lay it on too thick. She didn't say it. 'We'll talk, Alex. There's a lot to clear up.'

She had been to the doctor but he hadn't been of much help.

'I think you're a little, shall we say, premature in your worry, Mrs Garrett.

382

Come back and see me when your, er, partner, knows about himself. I should think it's unlikely you'll be affected.'

He had looked faintly disdainful...those northerners straying down here with their peculiar problems.

In the classroom she made a conscious and difficult effort to become immersed in her work. At first her mind received no message through the printed pages. All she saw was a frail, sickly baby, a stony-faced Judith, a responsible Ben at her side—so different from the carefree young man she had fallen in love with. And in the background Margaret dashing in and out from work but coping with the situation. That was the thing about Margaret. In the end she always coped. She had coped in her own fashion long ago when she had asked Alex for money.

She, on the other hand, had walked away and left her husband. Was it really a search for her own identity or simply a cop out, a refusal to face up to events by at least discussing them? Literature was a cop out. It should come out of events, not be an escape route.

And shouldn't she be in Manchester at this moment instead of taking up valuable space here? But what was the point if she could do nothing to help? Judith and her mother were close, any expression of pity about the baby would be insulting and superfluous, and coming between Ben and Judith would be a mistake. He would let her know if... Margaret had said he would come to see her. Or he could write. Or telephone. She must be the least of his worries.

Garth was waiting for her when she came out of the Polytechnic office at nine o'clock. (Rosemary's affair was still demanding all her time.) She hardly saw him. All she wanted was to get home quickly.

'Hop in,' he said.

She spoke to him through the open window of his car. 'I have to go straight home. I'm sorry.'

'I'll run you there. Hop in, nevertheless.'

'Thanks.' She did as she was told and sat silently beside him while he negotiated the sleeping policemen far too quickly. She wished she had her own car.

'Anyone with half an eye can see you're worried,' he said. 'Would you like to tell me about it?'

'No.'

'No?' He was amiable.

'It's just too complicated.'

'Remember I told you Eileen said I was all buttoned up? Do you know what I did when I came here?'

'Tell me.'

'Went to a Marriage Guidance Counsellor. Don't laugh. Yes, even though my marriage was over. I didn't want Eileen back—she had her own chap—but I felt I wanted to know where I had gone wrong—for the next time.'

'Hope springs eternal.' She was hardly listening. *She* had been a counsellor in the CAB and in spite of that she had been totally irresponsible. She wished she was in her bedroom in Aunt Elspeth's house, alone, the light out...

'You're becoming a cynic. All she said was that only a fool makes the same mistake twice, or words to that effect. She was right. My mistake was I didn't talk.'

'That was mine too.' They had reached her door and she turned to him. 'Thanks. I'll get out.'

'Have you seen your face?'

'I'm not in the habit of scrutinizing it.'

'I was hoping you would ask me in for a cup of coffee.'

She hesitated. 'All right,' she said, 'but only a quick one. I've a million things to do.'

Two ignored Garth as usual, rubbing against Anne's legs, her tail aloft. She picked the cat up. 'Quite right, Two,' she said, 'you should always be wary of strangers.' She buried her face in the smoke-coloured fur, feeling a small comfort.

Garth followed her into the kitchen. 'Cats generally like me. She'll grow used to me in time.'

She put on the kettle, her mind elsewhere, with her impending visit to Alex, with a letter or a telephone call from Ben. She said, 'Alex and I could never talk easily together about important things. And yet now that I'm away from him I see all his good points.'

'So you want to go back to him?'

She shook her head. 'I haven't got to that stage.'

'So what's giving you that haunted, hunted look?' He had found two mugs and placed them on the counter while she spooned coffee and poured boiling water over the grounds.

'Decaf. Is that all right? Something else. Family matters. Shall we go back to the sitting-room or have it here?'

'I like the atmosphere in your room. It's set, like jelly in a mould. Perfect. Mine is very much Mrs Roberts, circa nineteen hundred and fifty something.'

'Mine is very much Aunt Elspeth.'

Once again he followed her, and they sat down on the sofa together in front of the long coffee table piled with her books. The table was an anachronism, but he hadn't spotted it. She lifted a pile of textbooks and put them on the floor. She couldn't even remember what they were about.

'We were talking about Carlyle when you were off,' he said.

'Were you?' She tried to summon up some interest. 'Sometimes I wondered why Jane Welsh spoiled that dog of hers but was so hard on poor old Thomas.' You were hard on poor old Alex.

'The dog was her child. It's always better to have had children even if they aren't all one had hoped for, or vice versa. At least it takes you out of yourself.' He put down his cup and put his arm round her. 'I hate to feel you so miserable, Anne.'

She sat rigidly, thinking it would have been easier going to bed with him than all this talking, probing. She was surprised at herself.

'Family matters can be the end. At the time they seem insurmountable. I remember...' He was talking on and on in his counselling voice.

She wanted to say, 'Shut up, will you. You don't know what you're talking about.' There was a persistent ringing in her ears. She moved her head impatiently.

'The telephone, Anne. Aren't you going to answer it?'

'Yes.' She jumped up, half-fell over the books on the floor in her hurry, reached the hall and took up the receiver. She couldn't get her breath.

'Anne, it's Ben.'

'Ben.' Her auditory memory hadn't been completely accurate. His voice was richer, deeper, quieter. 'Yes, Ben?'

'Margaret visited you?'

'Yes, she did.'

'She told you about...everything?'

'Yes, she did.' Feeling rushed over her, blotting out the fear and resentment. She felt her whole body relaxing. 'I'm so sorry, Ben, for the baby, and Judith, and you.' She forgot about herself. 'It's so terrible. So new. And you, me, we didn't think, even although we were aware...at least I was. I've thought and thought...'

'That's why I didn't write or ring you earlier. I couldn't have said all that was going on in my head, the implications, the guilt. I'm not HIV Positive. I got the results today. Of course there will be regular checks.'

'Still, you're not HIV Positive. So that means...'

'That you're in the clear, although it was a slim chance in the event. But I could never have forgiven myself...'

It sounded clichéd, and she interrupted him. 'But Judith? That's not altered?'

'No. Nor the baby. There are no words for that yet, the feeling you get when you look at her, the innocence of her...Judith has agreed to marry me.'

It was inevitable. 'Maybe it'll turn out all right. They're working like mad on cures. I'm glad about Judith and you. You'll have a beautiful wife.'

'And brave. Now that she's got over the shock she's been practical. She's moving out to my place with Lauren. Margaret will be glad to have her flat to herself again, although she's been marvellous. Judith couldn't have done without her.'

'No, she couldn't.' That was it, then. 'Thanks for letting me know. I don't know what else to say. It hasn't sunk in properly yet. Except to wish you both happiness. And a lot of luck.'

'We'll need it. Would you like me to come and see you?'

'I don't know where I'll be. I'm going home to see Alex this weekend. And after...'

'Ah, yes.' She heard the hesitation. 'Judith's mother told me that it wasn't your husband's idea to have me bashed up. That Spiers had taken it on himself.'

'Can you believe it?' she asked.

'Oh, yes. He was quite capable of it. But...your husband...no, it didn't fit. He was much too amiable.' Hindsight was a wonderful thing.

'I'm going to talk about it when I'm

home. And other things.'

'Will you come to Manchester as well?'

'Not this time, Ben, but, yes, I'll come, as often as you'll let me.' That at least was crystal clear in her mind.

'How do you like St Albans?'

'It's fine, but it isn't home. Oh, Ben,' it came from her heart in a rush of feeling, 'I won't ever forget you.'

'The same goes for me. It was...like another world with you, some place not even on the map. The Land of Delight. Very spe-cial.' The broken-backed word made her wince.

'Very spe-cial.' She repeated it for her memory bank. 'Goodbye.' She hung up, and stood with her head bowed, dry-eyed.

She went back to the sitting-room and sat down beside Garth. 'Sorry.' She blew out her breath and looked at him, biting her lip.

'You look like someone who's been shaken about a bit, but happier. Like someone who's been able to ditch her load.'

'Only some of it.'

'No man is an island?'

'That's about it.'

'Are you going back to your husband?' She looked at him. His eyes were anxious. She saw him properly, a lonely man, perhaps in love with her, perhaps not, but needing the comfort. But then so did Alex, and he had prior claim.

He drew her into his arms. If he had said, 'Shall we go to bed?' she might have said yes, so little did it matter.

But he was being careful. Alex would have had her there in ten seconds.

Chapter Twenty-Seven

She was in the house before him, and she went straight to the view like a homing pigeon, or a drug addict. No pretty brick here, nor pargeted fronts, nor half-beams, just space filled with sea and sky, but fulfilling a need in her.

She was sitting there when he came in and his presence, his big frame, seemed to fill the room. Garth *dwindled* in comparison. Ben was another matter. But when she looked at him his jacket hung loosely and the skin round his eyes was stretched flat with sleeplessness.

'Ah! You got here before me.' He was falsely cheerful, slightly sheepish, smiling. His eyes weren't. They kissed, through habit, and yet like people who didn't know each other very well.

'Yes.' She looked around her own room like a stranger. 'Brenda has kept the place nice.'

'But no flowers.' He was aggrieved. 'She never put flowers in vases, the way you always did.'

'You could have done it yourself Why do men think it is a woman's job?'

'Because women are good at it, I suppose. You look thinner, Anne.'

'Leave your husband and lose weight.' She tried to be jocular. 'So do you.'

'I miss you.' He was more honest. 'I have no appetite for food. Would you like a drink?'

'I hope you haven't been substituting liquid nourishment?'

'I watch that. I have a job to hold down, people depending on me.' He had always been mindful of that.

'James tells me he might be joining you in the firm when he's finished in London.'

'Yes, he seems to like the idea. I'm really chuffed,' he moved his head sideways, 'my own son coming into the firm.' 'Chuffed' was a Sixties word, but then they were Sixties people. He brought her a glass. 'Sherry. Is that all right?'

'Yes. You remembered!' She clowned, wanting to be outrageous, but saw the frightened people behind their posing. 'I could do with this, thanks.' She smiled at him. The smile hovered.

'I've no titbits. You were good at that. And those dips you used to make, fishy, and cheesy. Everybody raved about them.'

A marriage isn't made by titbits nor dips, fishy or cheesy, nor does it founder on the lack of them. 'Margaret says you didn't tell

Spiers to beat Ben Davies up,' she said.

He was pouring his own sherry at the table. He turned, the bottle in his hand, his eyes wide, his mouth half-open. 'Margaret says...beat Davies up! Of *course* I didn't!'

'She says you wouldn't, but he *was* beaten up. He was in hospital overnight.'

He came and sat down opposite her. 'Let's get this straight. Davies...was... beaten...*up*.' His brows were pulled together.

'By Spiers. On your orders presumably.'

He passed his hand over his face. 'This is unbelievable! Incredible! I can hardly take it in.'

'Nevertheless it's true. You could phone the Hospital—they'll have a record—or Ben. He didn't say anything about it because he thought he had it coming to him.'

'Look,' his voice was trembling, 'All I said to Spiers was, "Give him a good fright, tell him off in no uncertain terms", that sort of thing. I've regretted it, God knows, but I was wild with jealousy at the time. I assure you, Anne,' he was trying unsuccessfully to control his voice, 'I never told Spiers to use violence. You never thought I did, did you?'

'Yes, I did. It was the last straw for me.'

'How can I get you to believe me?' He

bent forward and took her hands. She saw his jowls had gone, giving him a good chin line. He had definitely lost weight. It was an improvement.

'You could try sacking Spiers for a start,' she said.

'No problem. I'll do it tomorrow.' He was brusque.

'He'll get back at you.'

He moved his hand, brushing aside the thought like a fly which had landed on him. 'My word is better than his. He'll go, I promise you.'

'You've only yourself to blame, you know that, Alex. You put too much trust in him, in all kinds of ways.'

He nodded morosely. 'Could be. Yes, could be. There was a bit of rapport. But he's got to go. The bugger!' This was more like her Alex. 'The double-dyed scheming bugger! And Davies thought it was to pay him back?'

'For having an affair with me, yes. Not knowing, of course, that you were double-crossing me with Margaret. *Quid pro quo*, he thought.' She took a deep breath. 'I came late one night to the depot and saw you both, you and Margaret...at it...through the window. That was the time I stayed away.' Her smile faltered. 'It would have made a good video.'

She saw the blood go from his face.

His florid cheeks drained of colour like the receding tide on the bay, then, as she watched, it came back again, peony red. It couldn't be good for him. Had he had his blood pressure checked?

'My God, Anne,' he said, 'you know how to put the boot in.'

'We both seem to be pretty good at it.'

'Could you ever forgive me?' He looked like James suddenly. 'It's all over with Margaret...you know about this awful business about Judith and her baby. It's occupying all her time. It makes...playing around seem...well, it rubbishes the whole thing, doesn't it?'

She nodded. 'Rubbishes' was right. All the rest was immaterial. 'Go and get yourself a drink. No, I'll do it.' She must give up those silly notions about sexist division of tasks, flowers, light bulbs, pouring out drinks. She brought it back to him, a schooner. He needed it, even if it was bad for his blood pressure.

'Thanks.' It fitted his big hand which grasped it gratefully.

'What you and I have to do is to sit and talk, Alex. All this weekend. We've never really got down to it, in twenty years. And maybe we'll write as well when I go back.'

'You're going back to St Albans?' She turned away from his eyes. They reminded her of poor Melissa's, her cat, pitiful, not understanding...

'Yes, I have commitments there. I can't just walk out.' Her words to Ben came back to mock her. 'Just a few hurdles to get over and then I'll be free...' When was one ever free? He would know that now. Everyone was a behavioural victim. 'I had enrolled in the local Polytechnic. I've always wanted to study English.' Garth Stobo? He seemed remote.

'We've a good University down the motorway. That friend of yours went, remember? Her picture was in the paper with her gown and mortar board. You could give up all that voluntary stuff.'

She met his eyes, expressing what he had never been able to say. 'And I have a part-time job.'

'That's nothing. You were only doing that for the money.'

'True.'

'You were the best secretary I ever had, Anne.' He was wistful.

'But not the best wife.' She smiled at him. 'You would soon find a better one.'

'Never in a million years.' He shook his head. 'Why have you never believed me? You have always been the only one for me.'

She *could* believe him, in spite of Margaret. That was the strange thing.

It, in a way, proved what he was saying. He had turned to Margaret because of her, just as she had turned to Ben because, of him. Both affairs represented holes in their marriage. Could holes ever be mended?

'I'll think about it,' she said, 'In my *pied-à-terre* at St Albans.' She laughed and he followed her laugh, looking uneasy.

His face suddenly cleared. 'Your sister will need you near now. You've always been close.' That was a bull's eye. That made the *pied-à-terre* seem rather pointless.

It wasn't this limping marriage of theirs which would bring her home. It was her family and her involvement with it, and as her husband, Alex, was part of it. She was involved because she was part of everything which happened to it, now this new blow it had suffered, starting with Jeremy Crump sleeping with a suspect man at the same time as he had slept with Judith, who had slept with Ben who had slept with her who had slept with Alex...and the four-letter word would have been better than that string of euphemisms although she was still unable to use it.

It was a chain, like pee spreading, as Margaret had said, Margaret, her sister, who called a spade a spade. And now the most vulnerable member of the chain was at the receiving end, little Lauren. Just as her cat had been at the receiving end of

Alex's anger. The weakest always went to the wall.

She knew, with disappointment, resignation, and a glimmer of hope, that the blood tie would bring her home.

This Large Print Book for the Partially sighted, who cannot read normal print, is published under the auspices of

THE ULVERSCROFT FOUNDATION